THE DIVA OF DUNDAS FARM

IAN SKAIR INVESTIGATES

HILARY PUGH

Copyright © 2022 by Hilary Pugh

All rights reserved.

No part of this book may be reproduced in any form or by any electronic or mechanical means, including information storage and retrieval systems, without written permission from the author, except for the use of brief quotations in a book review.

❦ Created with Vellum

1

She heard him even before he opened the door. Too small to jump the fence, Lottie was hurling herself against it, yapping wildly. He'd never been away for this long before. In the three years she had been with him, Ian had only left Lottie for an occasional night away. But this time he'd been gone for a week. He'd been away for a holiday in the sun, leaving Lottie with his neighbour. Lottie probably wondered if she'd ever see him again. He'd worried that she wouldn't forgive him, that she'd sulk and take no notice of him when he returned, that she'd been so spoilt and cosseted by Lainie, been for such long and exciting walks with Molly and Ryan, that she'd barely notice he'd gone. She might have decided that she'd much rather continue with this life than return to her usual dull routine with him. But dogs weren't like that, were they? They forgave and forgot. Their love was unconditional and enduring. At least, that was what Ian hoped. And as Lainie gathered up the wriggling bundle of over-excited fur and lifted her over the fence, Ian knew he was right. Lottie leapt from Lainie's arms and hurtled towards him, licking his face and drooling with excitement as Ian gathered her into his own arms.

'The suntan suits you,' said Lainie as she passed Lottie's lead and blanket to him.

He thought so too. A week in the sun had made a big difference. He'd not noticed while he was there, but looking at himself in his rear-view mirror in the pale Edinburgh sunlight as he reclaimed his car from the long-stay airport car park, he could see the change. A week in the south of France, lounging by a pool sipping some of the best wine he'd ever tasted, was a lifestyle he could get used to. Or he could if he hadn't missed Lottie more than he'd ever thought possible, and if he hadn't felt anxious about leaving Molly in charge for a week. He'd jumped at the chance of a cheap flight down to Carcassonne before the school holidays started and prices soared. Added to that, he'd been the guest of Anna's family. Anna, who was an excitable nineteen-year-old and central to his case at Drumlychtoun three years ago, was now training in estate management. Six months employed by her stepfather on his vineyard, while studying at college for two days a week. And in the autumn she would be returning to Scotland for another six months working with her great-uncle on the Drumlychtoun estate.

Ian fished into a small wheelie suitcase and pulled out a box of exquisitely wrapped chocolates, which he'd bought at a shop in Montpellier. He'd considered a box of the local nougat but couldn't be sure of the state of Lainie's teeth, so had played it safe and settled on soft-centred chocolates. 'A thank you for looking after Lottie,' he said, passing the box to Lainie and trying to keep it above the level of Lottie's nose.

'Och, you shouldn't have. It's always a pleasure to look after Lottie,' said Lainie, who was clearly delighted with her gift, before sadly waving Lottie goodbye and returning to what she had been doing. Probably either knitting or washing. Or possibly to bake a cake.

Ian closed his bag and carried it inside, Lottie following anxiously. Did she think he was about to go away and leave her again? He felt a moment's satisfaction that Lottie had never shown any hint of missing Stephanie. Lottie hadn't given her previous owner so much as a backward glance as Ian drove away with her. But then Stephanie had left him without so much as a backward glance when she deserted him all those years ago. Seemed fair enough.

As he'd expected, the office was immaculate, with not so much as a paperclip out of place. Molly was always well organised and for the last week she'd not had his untidy ways to put up with. She'd left a note on his desk, held down with a jet paperweight she'd brought back for him from her own break a few weeks ago, when she'd taken Ryan to Whitby for a bucket and spade holiday. He picked up the note and read it.

Welcome home! Jeanie popped in with a shepherd's pie, which I've put in the fridge with a few cans of Seven Kings. Work files are all up to date. No problems except for one rather strange phone call – no number, but said he'd call back tomorrow. See you in the morning. Molly.

Ian looked at his watch. It had been a long day and he could think of nothing better than sitting in the garden with Jeanie's shepherd's pie and a glass of beer. Work could wait until the morning. He turned on the oven and went to find a jumper. This was Scotland, not the south of France.

It was always good to sleep in one's own bed again after being away, and sleeping was a whole lot easier in the cool of a Scottish night when there were no noisy cicadas keeping you awake and no mosquitos using you as a larder. Ian slept well and was awoken early by Lottie, who was anxious to make sure he'd not forgotten any of the morning routine, which involved a walk down to the village shop to buy breakfast. Between them, Molly and Jeanie had stocked his fridge with milk, butter and eggs, but what he wanted right now was a bag of freshly baked pastries. He'd been spoiled in France with the early morning delivery of warm baguettes served with unsalted butter and strong coffee. But the village shop here in Greyport did a good job of providing him with breakfast, and Lottie was always happy to trot along at his side while he walked down the hill to buy it.

Molly was parking her car as Ian and Lottie arrived back, and they walked up the path together. He paused at the door to pick up some post, most of which went straight into the recycling bin, and then let them both into the office. 'So,' he said, turning on the coffee machine and sitting down at his desk. 'Everything's gone smoothly while I've been away?'

'It's all in the files,' she said. 'I finished the background checks for the school, sent off the report on the office pilfering and put a file together for the wrongful parking fine case.'

Run of the mill stuff. Molly knew her way around all of that and he'd gone away feeling sure he wasn't leaving her with anything she couldn't manage. She was sensible enough to know what she wouldn't be able to handle and to make notes for his return. But nothing like that had happened. Except the mysterious phone call. Which reminded him to turn off the redirect on his phone that had sent all calls to Molly while he was away. No sooner had he done it and put the phone down on his desk when it rang with a number he didn't recognise. He clicked to take the call.

'Am I speakin' to Mr Ian Skair?'

He couldn't quite place the accent. It wasn't Scottish and he'd watched enough TV to guess that it was Estuary English. This was someone from the south. Not London exactly and not posh Home Counties. More likely Essex or somewhere south of the river like Penge or Surbiton. 'This is Ian Skair,' he said. 'How can I help you?'

'I'm hoping to use your services. Need you to do a bit of detecting and to keep an eye on someone.'

It sounded like a typical case of marital suspicion. 'Can I take your name?' Ian asked, reaching for a notepad and pencil. He wrote it down and Molly gasped. He couldn't imagine why. The name meant nothing to him. He tapped to put the phone on speaker. 'You've seen our website?' he asked. 'You are aware of our fees and expenses?'

'Yeah, yeah, I know all that. But I'd need you full time for two weeks.'

'I don't really…'

'Hear me out. You'll enjoy this. Trust me. There's thousands would give an arm and a leg for what I'm offering.'

Molly was hopping up and down at his side, waving her arms around and mouthing something he couldn't make out at him. 'Can you tell me a bit more about what you need?'

'Look,' he said. 'Come over to my place and we'll talk about it.'

Molly started nodding furiously at him. It obviously meant a lot to her. 'I can send Molly Burrows, my assistant,' he said.

'Nah, this is a job for the boss.' Molly scowled at Ian. 'But bring her with you. The more the merrier.'

'Where are you?' Ian asked. 'Will I be seeing you at home or at work?'

'Bit of both, I suppose.'

'You're working from home?' Ian suggested.

'Yeah, in a way. It's not far from you. I'll text you the address. Tomorrow okay? Mid-morning?'

Ian agreed. Molly would probably never forgive him if he said no, and as far as he knew, not having had time to look in the diary, there was not much on right now.

He ended the call. Molly was looking at him wide-eyed. 'That was really him?' she gasped.

'Really who?'

'Gavin Stamper.'

'Well, yes, that's who he said he was.'

'You don't know who he is, do you?' she said, with a look that suggested he lived most of his life in a cave.

'Should I?'

Molly sighed. 'I'd forgotten how old you are,' she said. 'He's only the lead singer from one of the most popular boy bands of all time.'

At that moment Ian did indeed feel very old. 'I'm not much into boy bands,' he said. 'Tell me more.'

'They were absolutely my all-time idols fifteen years ago. I had posters of them all over my bedroom walls.'

Fifteen years ago Molly would have been twelve. It passed through Ian's mind that Nigel Burrows, Molly's father, might not have appreciated Blu Tack all over the walls and probably had old-fashioned views on teenage rock idols and their effect on young girls. Not to mention loud music blaring through his house. But that was all in the past, and boy bands, he supposed, grew up. 'They're not still famous then?'

'I suppose not. I'm not sure what teenage girls listen to these days.'

Ian laughed. He was not the only one feeling his age. 'Then I guess you're not that keen to go and visit him tomorrow?'

'You've got to be joking. You're not thinking of leaving me behind, are you?'

'And deprive you of the chance to drool over your teenage crush? I wouldn't dare.'

'What do you suppose he wants us to do?'

'At first, I thought it sounded like a typical bit of marital infidelity, but I don't think he'd want live-in surveillance for that. Google him and find out what he's up to now.'

They checked him out together. The band, Gav and the Guys, had parted company in 2011 and scattered in different directions. Two were now working in the music industry in America, one had gone into music management, and Gavin Stamper had bought himself an estate in Scotland and taken up farming. To be precise, alpaca farming. 'Quite a career move,' said Ian, tapping on the address Gavin had given him. Dundas Farm, he discovered, was thirty miles northwest of Dundee. He checked its website and found pictures of alpacas, beguiling creatures with appealing eyes and curly hairdos. He clicked on a list of produce sold by Dundas Farm, hoping he wasn't about to be treated to a range of alpaca steaks and sausages. He didn't think he could eat something that gazed at him with such soulful eyes. What a hypocrite he was. He happily tucked into lamb kebabs without giving a thought to the poor little lambs he saw frolicking in the fields every spring. But he needn't have worried. Gavin Stamper's alpacas led long and happy lives. They enjoyed the green and sunny pastures of Perthshire with strategically placed shelters to protect them from the cold winds in winter. Their main job was to provide wool for a selection of luxury knitted gloves, socks, scarves and rugs that were sold online and in a small gift shop on the farm itself, where visitors could pay thirty-five pounds to take one of them for a walk. Dundas Farm also provided a range of tastefully restored barns and outhouses for events from weddings to concerts and corporate celebrations. The next major event was something called Camp Opera. An unfortunate name, Ian couldn't help feeling.

At the end of the day Molly left in a state of excitement. She was going to wash her hair and she needed to sort through her wardrobe, she told him. He planned an evening in the pub catching up with Duncan and Jeanie.

2

'There it is,' said Molly. Half an hour's drive from Perth they had crossed a stone bridge over a stream and were now driving up a quiet road, past a few white stone houses towards lush green hills. Molly pointed to the sign that said *Dundas Farm Alpaca Centre* with a picture of one of the residents peering over the top of a line of words appealing to visitors to *take our sociable woolly friends for a walk for £35*. Ian turned the car off the road into a wide drive and pulled up at another board with a map and a series of arrows pointing to alpaca walking reception, gift shop, café, conference centre and car park. Nothing about a house or an office where he might expect to meet Gavin Stamper.

'It's a huge car park,' said Molly. 'We can park here and ask at reception for directions.'

It must have been a busy day for alpaca walking, barn conferencing or whatever else was going on there. The car park was nearly full, but Ian found a space close to a cedar shed with glass doors and a wooden patio. A sign announced *book your alpaca walk here 10am – 4pm*. He put Lottie on her lead, and he and Molly strolled up to the patio and opened a door leading to an office where a man was sitting in front of a desktop computer playing solitaire. He was wearing a badge with a picture of an alpaca and the name 'McLean' printed in gold letters. 'Morning,' he said. 'You've come for the walk? You'll need to keep the wee dog on a lead.'

Ian shook his head. 'No,' he said, assuming McLean to be the man's name, not the alpaca's, but hesitant to use it in case he was wrong. 'We're here to see Mr Stamper.'

'Oh, aye,' said McLean, staring at both of them. 'Fans, are you? He'll not be seeing you without an appointment.'

'Mr Stamper is expecting us,' said Ian, wondering if he was going to be asked to prove it and if he was, how he was going to do it.

'I'll call through,' said McLean, yawning, reaching for a phone and pressing a button. 'People to see you,' he said abruptly, the phone clearly having been answered. After a moment he muttered something and ended the call. 'You've to write your names,' he said, pushing a ledger towards them. 'Car registration and mobile number.'

Ian did as he was told.

McLean dragged himself out of his chair and walked stiffly down the steps. He pointed to the far end of the car park, where Ian could see two large barns. 'Take the path between the barns and you'll see a tunnel ahead of you. It'll take you to the house and Mr Stamper will meet you there in about twenty minutes, when he's done with his voice coach.'

Molly looked at her watch. 'Is there time to take a wee look in the shop?' she said, pointing out another, larger cedar shed, close to the entrance to the barns.

It wasn't an idea that thrilled Ian, but he knew Molly

loved shopping and they did have time to spare. 'Okay, just a quick look. I'll wait outside with Lottie.'

Molly disappeared inside the shop and Ian waited by a wire security fence, beyond which were alpacas as far as the eye could see. One of them wandered up to the fence and looked at them with an inquisitive expression. Or perhaps that was how they always looked. Lottie seemed unsure of it and edged closer to Ian's legs, growling softly. Ian picked her up and held her up to the fence for a closer look. The alpaca stared at Lottie, then shook its head and spat at her. Not a promising start if they were going to be working here. Perhaps she would need to be left with Lainie again. Ian hoped not. Alpacas apart, it looked like a good place for dogs. Plenty of space to run around and interesting smells to explore. 'Don't be a wimp,' he hissed at her. 'It's not going to hurt you.'

Molly returned empty-handed and looking disappointed. 'There's some lovely stuff,' she said. 'Beautiful scarves, but massively expensive.'

'Perhaps it will be a lucrative case,' said Ian. 'And you'll be able to buy something to remind you of it.'

'It would need to be more than lucrative,' she said. 'An alpaca floor rug costs more than a thousand pounds.'

Ian looked at the alpacas with more respect than he'd shown them earlier. 'We're in the wrong job,' he said. 'I suppose they're chasing the rich tourist market. Or the international bankers that come up here for the shooting season.' He looked at his watch. 'We'd better get on,' he said, heading towards the barns.

'Did he say we had to go through a tunnel?' she asked. 'Does he live underground or something?'

'Probably just a tunnel under a road,' said Ian, although

he couldn't see either a road or a house, and an ex-rock star would live in the kind of house one noticed.

They skirted round the barns. There was no one in them and the doors were locked, but they took a moment to peer through the windows. 'This one's like a theatre,' said Molly. 'There's a stage and rows of seats.' She ran over to the other smaller one and read a sign on the door: *Apologies – the bistro is closed. Visit the café for tea, coffee and light snacks.* 'I wonder when it opens,' she said. 'It looks very nice.'

Ian read the menu that was pinned to the door and agreed that it looked like a good place to eat. If they took the case, they would probably get to know it well. 'I suppose it opens when they have weddings and conferences here. Alpaca walkers probably bring picnics or eat at the café.'

They followed the path between the two barns and found themselves in a paved garden with seats, and plants in earthenware pots. At the far end of the garden was a fence and then the ground rose steeply towards a grassy hill.

'There's the tunnel,' said Molly, pointing towards a cutting in the hillside and heading towards it, laughing. 'I told you he lived underground.'

The tunnel began with a glassed-in walkway, with steep, grassed banks on either side. Lights came on overhead as the path took them downwards into the side of the hill. After a short walk, the tunnel opened out into an atrium with a glass roof and a fountain at the centre. There were doors all around them, and from behind one of them they could hear singing and shouting.

'I know that song,' said Molly. 'It's been an advert for something, hasn't it?'

'It's the toreador song from *Carmen*,' said Ian. He couldn't remember if it had ever been used in an advert, but it seemed likely. It had definitely been a popular ringtone at one time.

The shouting stopped abruptly, the door opened and a man swept out clutching a fistful of sheet music, an overcoat slung over one shoulder and an expression of fury on his face. He slammed the door behind him, ignored them both and headed for the tunnel. Ian had done some Internet research and he was fairly sure that it wasn't Gavin Stamper. Must be the voice coach, and it didn't look like the session had gone well.

The door opened again, and this time Ian was sure it *was* Stamper. The photos Ian had found were more than fifteen years old, but apart from a receding hairline and slight paunch, this was their man. The ponytail, leather jacket and biker boots suggested he hadn't altered his image in the last fifteen years.

'Welcome,' he said, reaching for Ian's hand and then placing a kiss on Molly's cheek, which promptly turned a bright shade of beetroot. Then he noticed Lottie and reached down to let her sniff his hand. Lottie wagged her tail and licked him. She had just won Ian a client. If Lottie liked Stamper, then Ian would work for him. No question.

Stamper led them back through the door into a large room with a grand piano, and opera posters on the walls. 'Sit down,' he said, indicating two leather chesterfields.

'This is an amazing room,' said Molly. 'Are we under the hill?'

'We are,' said Stamper. 'This is my music room. I had it designed for the best possible acoustics.' He pointed to the wood-panelled walls. 'Same wood they used when they rebuilt Glyndebourne,' he added. 'Wooden wall panels allow soundwaves to reverberate with a better tone than you would get through concrete or steel. Plus, it's all sustainably grown and designed to blend in with the natural surroundings.'

'Are all the rooms underground?' Molly asked.

'They are, but this is the only room that doesn't have windows or skylights. We designed the house to be invisible from the road. Looking down from the air you'd see we have picture windows that follow the shape of the hill, with stone terraces outside built from local materials. Even from the farm side all you can see is the glass dome over the atrium.'

'Is the only way in through the tunnel?' she asked. 'How do you get stuff delivered?'

Stamper laughed. 'A good question,' he said. 'An eye for the practicalities. But you are right. The only way in and out is through the tunnel, but delivery vans can drive up to the tunnel entrance.'

'I suppose security is something you had to think about when the house was designed,' said Ian. 'Being as famous as you are.'

'As famous as I *was,* you mean,' he said with a grin. 'It was more that I liked the idea of being able to get away from everything. And of course, I can sing to my heart's content and not worry about disturbing any neighbours.'

'I'm sorry we interrupted your singing session,' said Ian, thinking they were not there to talk about the house and should get down to the reason they *were* there.

'No problem, we were just finishing.'

'It doesn't sound like it was going very well,' said Molly. 'There was a lot of shouting.'

'What?' said Stamper. 'No, it was fine. The opera camp starts in a week or two and Quentin Lyle, the guy you bumped into just now, is taking over as our musical director. He's been my voice coach for years. He always shouts at me like that. He shouts at everyone. It's the only way he gets results, particularly with me. I'm basically a lazy toad. Need to practise more.'

'You're singing opera now?' Ian asked.

'It's been a lifetime ambition. Well, since I retired from the band. It's partly why I want you here.'

That sounded interesting, although he couldn't imagine what use he and Molly would be. Ian had never considered opera singing himself, any kind of singing really. 'Tell me more,' he said.

Stamper led them back past the piano then through another door into an office where two young women were working at computers. Stamper ignored them and pointed to a poster on the wall. *CARMEN. Dundas Farm Opera Camp, 2022 season starring Lucia Pedro Morales,* Ian read. Below that was a picture of a woman with dark hair wearing a red dress, and a man in full toreador outfit complete with white breeches and a red cloak.

Molly stared at the figure in the picture. 'It's you,' she said.

'That's right, darlin'. Dashing, ain't I?'

'Very,' said Ian. 'But I can't see why it should involve us.'

'It's me leading lady,' said Stamper, tapping the red dress. 'Fantastic voice, but a right diva. Thinks someone's out to kill her. And I'm telling you, if I can't get her sorted, it'll be me that's first in the queue.'

Ian laughed. 'Perhaps you'd like to start at the beginning. Tell me about the opera camp.'

'Long term ambition of mine. Once I'd settled in here and built the house, got going with the alpacas and had the business up and running, I decided to start up the opera seasons. Gives me an opportunity to sing some leading roles and turn my hand to production.'

'Like Glyndebourne?' Molly asked.

'Nothing so posh,' said Stamper. 'We started three years ago with *The Barber of Seville*. Hired pros for the leads, me and some friends for the smaller roles, local choirs in the chorus and students from the Scottish Academy to play in the orchestra. We rehearse for a week and then put on five performances in the barn. You saw the barn on your way in?'

Ian nodded. 'You put it all together in a week?'

'Just the final staging. The chorus and orchestra all rehearse off site during the summer. Then they come up here and camp for the two weeks in one of our fields. It's good fun. A lot of them bring their families with them. Reminds me a bit of our good old days at Glastonbury.' He sighed wistfully. 'Anyway, we had to cancel the second year because of lockdown. Last summer we did *HMS Pinafore* because it didn't need a big cast or orchestra and I couldn't find any big-name singers at short notice. I enjoyed singing Corcoran though.'

'Corcoran, the ship's captain?' said Ian, remembering a production he'd seen in Edinburgh. One his then not-quite-girlfriend had been working on as rehearsal pianist. 'And this year you're going for grand opera?'

'That's right. I've got a tenor called George Strike for José. He sang in *Barber* and *Pinafore* and now he's making a name for himself with Opera Scotland. Nice chap, quiet, not the sort to make a fuss. He'll be staying with me here in the house. We can't have our stars under canvas. Then I've a pretty little thing singing Micaëla, name of Cara Curtis. Studied at the Edinburgh Opera Centre. She was Josephine in *Pinafore*. She's got family living nearby and will stay there. I'll be doing Escamillo and, like I said, I've got Lucia for Carmen. Quite a coup actually, but I've known her for years. Said she'd do it just to get back into practice again after lockdown. She'd not accepted any bookings until the autumn, worried the pandemic might all kick off again.'

'You say she thinks someone wants to kill her?'

'Yeah, that was a bit unfortunate. A letter was delivered here last week with her name on it, and I forwarded it to her in London. I should have opened it and read it first, then torn it up. She freaked out when she got it. Sent it back to me in a rage and nearly backed out.'

'Have you still got it?' Ian asked. 'Can I see it?'

Stamper unlocked a drawer in his desk and handed it to him. It was an oddly old-fashioned-looking letter modelled on crime stories of the past, where letters were cut from a newspaper and glued together as a text.

WATCH OUT! A REPEAT OF LAST YEAR. ANOTHER YEAR ANOTHER DEATH.

Ian took a photo of the letter and handed it back to Stamper. 'Someone died last year?'

'Yeah, unfortunate but nothing to do with the opera. Natural causes, they said.'

'One of the cast?'

Stamper shook his head. 'A stagehand, Andy Meade. He'd been working for me on the farm and fancied being part of the opera. But it turns out he had a heart condition. Dropped dead just after the final performance.'

'And your singer friend thinks the same will happen to her. Why?'

'Who knows? Guess she's made a few enemies.'

'And how do you think Molly and I can help? We're not bodyguards.'

'Sure, I know that. I've got a security team, but I need someone who can get to the bottom of it. Find out if there really is a threat.'

'You'd like me to find out who sent this letter?' he asked.

'Yes, and I'd like you to be here to keep an eye on things. But first I need your advice about Lucia. I don't think she should stay in the house. Apart from anything else, it wouldn't look good.'

'Worried about your reputation?' Ian asked with a grin. 'Or hers?'

'More worried I'd stab her across the breakfast table to be honest. I don't suppose you know anywhere she could stay? Somewhere a bit out of the way. Money no object, of course. Somewhere she'd feel a bit pampered and special.'

This was more travel agent work than a job for an investigator. Arranging accommodation for opera stars wasn't what he'd done all that training for. He was about to object when he had an idea. He took out his phone and tapped open the Maps app. 'It's not really what I do,' he said. 'But I might have an idea. You could provide a car for her?'

'She can have a bloody limo if it keeps her away from here.'

'Then I think I might know just the place.' Before lockdown, he'd worked on a case that involved visiting a quirky boutique hotel in the Trossachs, run by an eccentric character called Mickey Rix. Probably an ideal type to keep stroppy divas under control. He opened a website and handed it to Stamper. 'It's about thirty miles from here,' he said, taking the phone back.

'Not a problem. Less than an hour away. Give her a chance to do some in-car voice exercises.'

Molly peered over his shoulder. 'Won't somewhere like that be fully booked?' she asked.

'Quite likely, but I could find out. He might have a cancellation.'

'I'll pay over the odds,' said Stamper.

'I could go and see him,' said Ian, fancying a drive out to

the Trossachs and perhaps dropping in on a friend in Bearsden on his way back. The case was taking shape. 'We'd need to discuss terms and set out exactly what you would like us to do here. And I'd need to talk to your security team. I assume we'd be working together.'

Stamper nodded. 'Think it over and drop me an email. I can arrange a meeting with my security guys, nice reliable lads. I'm sure you'd get on. And of course, you would be in charge.' He walked with them back to the tunnel entrance, where they shook hands. 'Hope to see you again soon,' he said.

'Are we taking the case?' Molly asked as they drove away from Dundas Farm.

Of course they were taking the case, but he'd keep Molly in suspense for a little longer. She was tripping over herself to work for someone she'd idolised since the age of twelve. She was like Lottie when he put on his walking boots or picked up her lead. 'What do you think?' he asked, unable to suppress a smile.

'From that grin on your face I'm guessing we are.'

'Two weeks in an all-expenses-paid place like that? It's a no brainer, isn't it?'

'As long as it's not you having all the fun at Dundas and me stuck in the office with the employment checks.'

He pulled the car off the road into a layby and turned to face her. 'Is that how you feel things are?' he asked. 'I do all the fun stuff?' He'd never meant it to be like that. Certainly not since Molly had finished her course and was now a licenced PI.

'No. I didn't mean it like that. I've done lots of interesting stuff. It's just that it's had to be very local because of being there for Ryan after school. Dundas is miles away from Greyport. I don't see how I could be there very much.'

He could see her point. He was free to work all over the place. Molly was tied to Greyport. 'We'll have to plan it carefully,' he said. 'We both need to be there. If we're dealing with students, you're going to be much better at getting them to open up and talk to you. How's your dad fixed for childminding for a week or two?'

'Ryan's term finishes soon and I'm not sure if I can ask Dad to look after him for two weeks. Even if I commute, it will still be a long day for him.'

Ian started the car again and headed for Greyport. Molly was right. It was a long commute. Bad enough for him and Lottie, but with childcare to sort out, well...

Molly was staring out of the window as they drove through Perth. Then as they crossed the bridge, she said, 'I think there could be a way round it.'

That was what he liked about working with Molly. She was good at problem solving. Single mothers had to be, he supposed. Juggling childcare with work wasn't easy. 'What are you thinking?' he asked.

'What if we join the campers? Gav said there'd be families and children there.'

'Gav now, is it?'

Molly blushed. 'He said to call him that when he was telling me about the house.'

Ian had noticed that they'd got on well once Molly had got over her blushes and nervousness about talking to someone whose portraits she'd had pinned to the wall of her teenage bedroom. 'He's got some great things planned for all the children. Their mums and dads will be rehearsing so he's organised a company that does kids' holiday clubs to come and teach them stuff like circus skills. Ryan would love all of that. And it would leave me free to work.'

'Good thinking, Molly. I'll suggest it to Gavin when I email him.' It was a great idea, at least for Molly. He wasn't so sure about himself grubbing around in a tent. Perhaps he'd be the one having to commute. Or perhaps there was a local pub he and Lottie could stay in. But there was time to sort all that out. They'd get back to the office and make a plan. He looked at his watch. The day had gone quickly, and by the time they got back Molly would have to leave to collect Ryan, Lottie would expect a walk and he'd need to get something to eat. 'We can't really plan until I've sorted out somewhere for the diva to stay. I'll drive out to Inverbank first thing tomorrow and talk to Mickey. Better if it's face to face rather than a phone call.'

'And me?'

'Find out all you can about Andy Meade, the guy who died. When I get back, I'll do some research on Lucia Pedro Morales and we'll make a plan. Decide what's best done in the office and what can wait until it all kicks off at Dundas.'

3

Ian set out early the next morning. It was more than an hour's drive from Greyport to Inverbank and he wanted to be back by midday. There was a lot to plan before he contacted Stamper again and it wasn't fair to leave Molly with all the hard work, even if she did enjoy Internet searches and delving into people's lives. He'd set his alarm for five-thirty and was on the road by half past six, hoping that Mickey might invite him in for breakfast.

He had forgotten how much he enjoyed the drive to Inverbank. It was the perfect time for a drive like this, with the sun still low in the sky. At least it was in the summer. He wouldn't want to do it in the snow. He knew Mickey had guests up here all year round and that occasionally they were snowed in. By half past seven the gentle hills around Perth and Dundas had given way to more impressive scenery with densely wooded slopes, and roads cut into the hillside, climbing steeply on one side, dramatic drops on the other. For several miles his car climbed, and the narrow road twisted and turned often with the additional hazard of traffic coming from the opposite direction. Farm vehicles were the worst. Cars could pull into gateways or squeeze past each other, branches of hedges scraping against windows. But tractors and trailers had right of way, which often meant he had to reverse for several hundred yards before finding somewhere wide enough to pull over and let them pass. It didn't do to be in a hurry when driving anywhere near Inverbank, but most drivers around there had all the time in the world. The pace of life was slower; tourists visited the area for that very reason. They could take their time and pause to enjoy the scenery.

It must have been a couple of years since Ian had last been to Inverbank. All those months in lockdown had passed in a blur, and it had been hard to keep track of dates. He wondered how Mickey had fared, but knowing Mickey, Ian suspected he had been just fine. Probably doing better than ever as people looked for holidays that didn't involve jetting off to exotic places. Mickey provided the exotic right here in an underpopulated part of Scotland.

He drove down the steep valley and crossed the bridge, which took him past Mickey's quirky rococo sign with 'Inverbank' inscribed in gold lettering and a picture of an extremely beautiful young man bedecked with flowers. From here, it looked as if nothing had altered, but as he turned into the white gravel drive, Ian could see that the place *had* changed. Not the house itself. That was every bit as colourful and flowery as he remembered it. But now the drive extended well past the house towards an area newly planted with small trees. He could see the roofs of wooden chalets and the tops of what he thought could be yurts. Mickey must be expanding, and Ian wasn't surprised. Mickey knew what he was doing. He'd never been short of customers, even when he first started the hotel. The only problem for Ian was that he was now too popular and probably wouldn't have room for another guest, even with the temptation of double his usual rate.

Ian pulled the car up outside the front door and climbed out with Lottie on her lead, ready to greet Mickey. The door opened but it wasn't Mickey who met him. It was a woman with red hair. One of his favourite people. Elsa Curran, who he hadn't seen for six months and who ran a B&B with her sister in Bearsden, not far from Glasgow. She'd been the reason for his first visit here during his hunt for a man accused, but as it happened not guilty, of the murder of a hotel magnate. But he and Elsa went back even further than that. It had been her discovery, during a loft conversion at her B&B, of a shoebox full of letters and photographs that had been important in an even earlier case, that had brought them together. Ian knew she and Mickey were colleagues and friends but was surprised to find her here looking as if this was now home.

'Ian,' she said, jumping down the steps and giving him a hug. 'How lovely to see you. I was waiting for our bread delivery. We weren't expecting you.'

She was wearing a tartan apron with a picture of a highland cow and the word McCoo scrawled above its head. She looked well and happy, he thought. 'Nice apron,' he said. 'And I wasn't expecting to see you, either. What are you doing here so early in the morning?'

'I've been serving the full Scottish fry-up to some guests who wanted an early start. Come in and have a coffee. There'll be breakfast left as well if you're hungry. I'll explain everything.'

She led him inside and into the kitchen, where Mickey was finishing a plate of scrambled eggs and a woman Ian remembered as Flora was loading a dishwasher.

'Ian,' said Mickey, pushing his plate away. 'And Lottie. How nice.'

'Any breakfast left?' Elsa asked Flora. 'Ian's always hungry.'

'Aye, there's a few sausages and a couple of fried eggs. And there's just enough bread left to make a few slices of toast.'

'That would be lovely,' said Ian, his mouth watering. He looked down at Lottie, whose mouth would also be watering. One of the sausages could well be coming her way.

'Pull up a chair,' said Mickey. 'And tell us what you're doing here. Not that it isn't lovely to see you.'

Ian sat down and Flora passed him a plate of food. He tucked in with Lottie drooling at his side. He cut a sausage in half and shared it with her. 'I've come to ask a favour,' he said. 'But tell me what's going on here. I didn't expect to see Elsa. And it looks like you're expanding.'

'We are,' said Mickey, looking pleased with himself. 'That's why Elsa's here. I couldn't do it all on my own. She's my manager now.'

Ian looked at Elsa in surprise. 'You've left Bearsden and your sister? What happened to your B&B?'

She shrugged. 'My sister's still there but I got a bit bored with it and we argued a lot, so I started looking around for something else.'

Ian remembered that Elsa was the one who always got landed with the cleaning while her sister – he couldn't remember her name – was out and about, doing... well, he wasn't too sure what she was doing.

'Elsa asked me if I knew anyone looking for a manager,' said Mickey. 'I'd been planning to expand for a while, so... well, here we are.'

'That's right. When Mickey told me about his plans and offered me a job here,' Elsa continued, 'I jumped at it.'

'Everyone's staycationing now,' said Mickey. 'We've moved into glamping. Self-catering chalets and luxury yurts. We're expecting our first guests in a couple of days.'

'Are you living here?' Ian asked Elsa. She couldn't be driving over from Glasgow every day. Not in time to serve breakfast.

'I'm staying in one of the chalets, but if it all works out I'll buy a wee place in the village.'

And if it doesn't? Ian wondered but didn't ask.

'So what's this favour?' asked Mickey, pouring coffee for all of them.

'A bit of a long shot, but I'm hoping you might have room for an opera singer.' He told them about Gavin Stamper's opera season and about his temperamental leading lady who would need somewhere to stay for two weeks from a week on Sunday. 'He'll pay double what you normally charge, and she'll only be here overnight and for breakfast.' Did opera singers eat breakfast? Ian wondered. He couldn't think of any reason why they wouldn't, but who knew?

'So what's the problem?' Mickey asked. 'Gavin Stamper has that enormous place in the side of a hill. Why can't she stay there?'

He had a point and Ian had rather hoped he wouldn't ask that. He played for time, taking a gulp of coffee and cutting another piece of sausage for Lottie. But he decided he'd better come right out with it. 'Two reasons,' he said. 'She's, er… difficult. Stamper thinks she'd annoy him.'

'Great,' said Mickey. 'But he's happy for us to be annoyed?'

'It's just with other musicians,' Ian offered hopefully, although he'd really no idea. But it seemed like a reasonable theory. Musicians were probably a competitive lot with each other. No reason to suppose they were like that with the rest of the population. 'She's probably a pussy cat with everyone else. And like I said, she'll only be here at night. And we're arranging a driver for her. She'll be taken away first thing every morning and brought back late each evening.'

'She's famous, is she?' asked Mickey, looking as if he might be coming round to the idea.

Famous guests would probably do a lot for his publicity. He would be able to put up little plaques in the rooms with things like *So-and-so slept here* the way they did with Elizabeth the First. 'I believe she is but I'm not really up in opera.' He'd need to do something about that if he was going to spend two weeks surrounded by opera singers.

'Why are you involved?' Elsa asked. 'Is she having an affair with someone, or stealing from the petty cash?'

She had a good grasp of his usual clientele, Ian thought, smiling at her.

'You said there were two reasons,' Mickey interrupted before Ian could answer. 'What's the other one?'

Ian scraped his plate with a piece of toast, which he ate slowly. 'She thinks someone wants to kill her. But she'll have a bodyguard,' he added, noticing Elsa's expression of alarm. He still needed to discuss security arrangements with Stamper, who was presumably knowledgeable about such things, having been famous himself. Whoever was employed as her driver could, for a bigger fee, also be co-opted to guard her. 'Anyway, Stamper thinks she's probably making that up to get attention. There doesn't appear to be any real reason why anyone would want to kill her but, you know, temperamental diva and all that. Stamper needs to keep her happy. He can't afford to lose his star just before the production.'

'Hmm,' said Mickey. 'I suppose she could have a yurt. They're not fully booked yet, are they, Elsa?'

'No, but they wouldn't be all that secure. They're fitted with safes and lockable doors but basically, they're just tents. A murderer with a knife could easily get in.'

She's enjoying this, Ian thought. He'd never realised she had such a vivid imagination.

'I've an idea though,' she said as she cleared away plates and started to stack them into the dishwasher. She fed the machine with a tablet of detergent and turned it on. Then she took off her apron and hung it on a hook near the door.

'Going to enlighten us?' asked Mickey. 'Or are you trying to delay Ian a bit longer by keeping us in suspense?'

I wish, Ian thought.

'I need to check the diary,' she said, opening an iPad and flicking through dates on the calendar. 'Yes, I thought so. The Robinsons are booked in for those two weeks. They're regulars, aren't they?' She looked up at Mickey who nodded in confirmation. 'They've booked the Rose Room. But when I talked to them on the phone, they did say they thought the yurts sounded glamorous. Can't remember why they settled for the Rose Room rather than a yurt, but they took a while to decide. What if we offered them the yurt for nothing? You said Stamper was willing to pay double so we wouldn't be out of pocket.'

'And do we get to see the opera for free?' Mickey asked. 'I love a few singing gypsies, not to mention a toreador.'

'I'm sure that could be arranged,' said Ian, thinking that this was all working out better than he'd hoped.

'All sorted then,' said Mickey. He drained his cup of coffee and stood up. 'I need to get on. Elsa, can you sort the details with Ian? I've got yurt décor to see to.'

'Would you like to see the room?' Elsa asked.

He would. He'd happily do anything that gave him a bit more time with Elsa, he realised, following her out of the kitchen and up the stairs.

The Rose Room was perfect. Typical of Mickey, of course. His décor was always quirky and over the top, but for reasons Ian couldn't work out, it was never flashy. He hadn't met Lucia Pedro Morales, but her picture suggested she'd be perfectly at home surrounded by hand-painted, rose-covered wallpaper, deep red chintz chair covers and a flamboyantly carved dressing table laden with complimentary perfumes and lotions. And just supposing her fears were real and there actually was someone out to kill her, the room was at the front of the hotel with windows overlooking the main drive. Security inside the hotel looked excellent, he'd noted, with keypads on the doors to the stairs and programmed cards for the rooms. Anyone trying to climb through the windows would be seen from the drive, which was covered by CCTV cameras and viewed twenty-four hours a day at reception.

'You think it will do?' asked Elsa.

'Definitely,' he said. 'Thank you so much for doing this.' It had been a highly successful morning. He'd not expected Mickey to have a room available and he'd certainly not expected to see Elsa here. That was a real bonus. Perhaps he'd take on Lucia's security himself. Being here, even if only to sit in his car, had just become a rather attractive proposition.

'Would you like to see what we've done with the glamping?' Elsa asked.

'I'd love to.' Glamping was not something that had appealed to him before, but he had time to spare. Molly had plenty to get on with so there was no need to rush back. 'If you're sure I'm not keeping you from working,' he said.

'Not at all,' she said, smiling. 'We haven't spent any time together for ages. Bloody lockdown, I suppose.'

He was happy to wander around yurts with her. They looked surprisingly glamorous and comfortable.

'Mickey's gone for sheik chic,' she said with a laugh.

'I can see that,' said Ian, looking at the brocade cushions, silk wall hangings and beds draped with covers in exotic colours. 'Been visiting souks, has he?'

'Sneaked off to Morocco as soon as travel was allowed,' said Elsa. 'And he has a friend in the sari trade who's responsible for the drapes.'

'Does he entertain the guests with belly dancers?'

'Now, that's something I don't think he's thought of. Perhaps I should suggest it.' She took his hand and walked with him to his car.

He was sorry to leave, but he knew he shouldn't keep her from her work any longer and Molly would have a few stern words if he was late.

'Come again soon,' said Elsa, blowing him a kiss as he headed off down the drive.

Looked like he definitely would be coming again soon, he thought with satisfaction as he turned onto the road and headed for home. The morning had gone extremely well. Stamper was going to be pleased, and Molly would like the idea of running things at Dundas while he concentrated on security up here. It was a good start, and he hoped the rest of the case would be as successful.

4

It was a pleasant drive back to Greyport. There was very little traffic and it was a nice sunny day, warm enough to open a window and let Lottie sniff the air. Ian picked up some sandwiches from the village shop and arrived back at the office at midday.

'How did it go?' Molly asked, studying his choice of sandwiches and choosing a prawn mayo one, leaving him with beef and mustard.

'All sorted,' he said, biting into his sandwich and enjoying the taste of the mustard. 'I've booked one of their best rooms. It's got hand-painted wallpaper and antique furniture. Security looks good as well.'

'It was that easy?' Molly looked at him in surprise. 'I thought you said they'd be fully booked.'

'Turns out they're expanding and still have vacancies on their glamping site.'

'But you said you'd booked a room. I don't think Gav would have wanted her to sleep in a tent or she could have stayed at Dundas.'

'They have yurts, not tents.'

'What's the difference?'

'Yurts are very upmarket and exotic, but you're right. That wouldn't suit the diva. They're going to move a couple of their regulars into a free yurt and give Lucia their Rose Room at double the normal rate. It's a very glamorous room. Probably a diva's dream,' he said, brushing some crumbs from the front of his shirt and watching Lottie catch them as they fell. *Mean pickings*, he thought, breaking off a piece of beef for her. 'How did you get on with your search for Andy Meade?'

Molly clicked open a file on her laptop. 'I found some local news reports about last year's opera camp. Andy's death was barely reported.'

'Barely?'

'There was a photo of the stage crew and a mention of how he'd be missed.'

'Nothing about how he died?'

'I checked the death record. It was an embolism.'

'Not sure I'm any the wiser.'

'It's like a blood clot. Doesn't cause much trouble unless it moves into the bloodstream, and if it does it can set off a heart attack, usually instant death.'

'Scary.' But quick, he supposed. There might be worse ways of dying. But in the light of the letter, perhaps there had been. Could Andy Meade have been murdered?

'The thing is, Andy had been seeing a local doctor about it and was on medication that needed regular check-ups. The doctor signed the death certificate and because he'd seen Andy within the last month there was no need to enquire any further.'

'So it's possible he died of something else? Been a victim of murder?'

'Yes, but if he was murdered it would have been by

something untraceable. If there'd been bullet holes or stab wounds it couldn't have been recorded as a natural death. There would have to have been an enquiry.'

'Poisoning?' Ian suggested. 'It would be traceable at a post-mortem, but if the doctor assumed it was a natural death no questions would have been asked. He'd have just signed the certificate.'

'Poisoning is possible, I suppose. I've been doing some research into ways of killing people without leaving any evidence.'

'What have you got so far?'

'The obvious would be an overdose of whatever drug he was on. Then if there had been a post-mortem, finding traces of it wouldn't raise any questions. Like you said, it could have been some other kind of poison but that would be taking a chance on the doctor signing off the death without asking any questions.'

One or two things were running through Ian's brain. He remembered something about pressure points that could kill, and he'd read about a death caused by injecting air. That could certainly mimic an embolism. But either of those would be difficult to administer. The victim would have noticed someone coming up to him with a hypodermic needle, wouldn't he? The same with pressure points. Unless he was in a wrestling ring, or asleep. 'Where was he when he died?' he asked.

Molly checked her notes. 'It was right after the final performance. He was backstage packing up the props hamper, ready to return it to the hire people.'

'Many people around?'

'Lots. There was going to be an on-stage party once everyone had changed out of their costumes. There'd have been people from the audience, members of the orchestra, other backstage crew and front of house staff all hanging about waiting.'

'We should talk to some of them. Presumably a lot of them will be there again this year. We need to know who found him and whether anyone saw anything fishy just before it happened.'

'There will be a rehearsal week at Dundas. We can chat to people then.'

Ian nodded. 'Good idea. Did you find out anything about Andy, apart from the embolism? Was there any motive for killing him?'

'No obvious one or they'd have treated his death as suspicious. I've started doing a background check on him. Gav has sent me his employee file. Before he worked at Dundas, Meade was employed at the Murray Leaf Wildlife Park for two years to clean the animal pens and do some heavy work in the garden. He left because he got into a fight with one of the keepers.'

'Interesting. I don't suppose you know what the fight was about?'

'No. Gav didn't employ him personally. He has people to do that.'

'Of course he does,' said Ian. He'd have people to do everything from updating his social media to sorting his laundry. It would be interesting to know more about the Meade guy before he worked at Dundas. 'Do you think young Ryan would like a visit to the wildlife park on Saturday if it's not too far away? We could ask around a bit. See if anyone remembers him.'

'I think he'd love it.' She searched for the Murray Leaf website and clicked on Google Maps. 'It says it's a forty minute drive from here, although right now there's heavy traffic. It would be less on Saturday. But we should go early.

That's when pens get cleaned out and the animals are fed, so there would be plenty of people we could talk to who work there and might have known him.'

'It sounds like you know a lot about zoos,' he said with a laugh. 'Regular visitor, are you?'

'Of course, I've a seven-year-old animal-mad son with an ambition to be a zookeeper when he grows up. There's not a lot he won't be able to tell you about how they run wildlife parks.'

'A working day out on Saturday, then. Keep a tally of your hours so I can pay you overtime.'

'Overtime and a day out with Ryan,' said Molly. 'I've landed myself in the perfect job.'

It seemed she was pacified after her outburst about him doing all the fun stuff. It was always good to know the staff were happy. Perhaps he wasn't such a rubbish employer after all. But they had been working together for nearly ten months now and, on the whole, they'd got on very well. He'd supported her training and paid towards her licence, so he needed to be a bit more confident about his role as boss.

'Keep checking Andy,' he said. 'Try social media and the local newspaper archives and see if he's got any kind of history we need to know about.' The more they knew about him, the easier it would be to work out whether or not the diva's worries were justified, and also who might be threatening her.

'I'm on it,' said Molly. 'What about you? Are you staying in the office this afternoon?'

'I'm going to get some background on Lucia Pedro Morales. I've a few starters from Gavin but I'd like to know why she thinks someone wants to kill her. I'll dig around a bit and see if anyone has a grudge against her. And we should plan our two weeks at Dundas. I think we should both give it all we've got. We can't be in and out of the office trying to run other cases. Is there anything in the diary we can't either wind up or put off for a couple of weeks?'

Molly opened up the calendar. 'If we put in a few extra hours we can tie up everything we're doing right now by the end of next week. I'll need to do some of the paperwork at home and you'll be working into the evenings. Is that okay?'

She was taking over his free time. Not that he minded. He was relying on her more and more to keep things organised and this was a big case and highly lucrative. And good for publicity. Or it would be if there really were grounds to think the diva was under threat. Not the best way to be thinking, and he really didn't wish the woman any harm. But any sniff of a murder would put them in the limelight as far as their reputation as investigators went. He only had to think about the inrush of cases after the Lansman murder.

'Of the new cases,' Molly continued, 'there's nothing that can't wait. The new clients already know we have a waiting list. I'll contact them all and give them some possible starting dates.'

'Good,' said Ian, picking up a pen and drawing columns on the whiteboard.

He headed one *Ian* and the other *Molly*.

In his own column he wrote:

Find out who sent the letter
Research Lucia Pedro Morales
Visit wildlife park
Kit out car for sleeping at Inverbank
Carry out searches of barns – theatre and restaurant
Check out Stamper's security arrangements

On Molly's list he wrote:

Research Andy Meade

Chat to people at wildlife park
Hire tent and camping equipment
Ask Stamper for a list of all participants
Check background of stage crew

He stood back and read it. 'We can add more as we need to.'

'We'll know more if you can find out who sent that letter.'

She was right. He should make that a priority. He'd call on Duncan and ask if his forensic people could help.

She read his list. 'You're planning to sleep at Inverbank? Why?'

'Extra security. I can camp in the car close to the Rose Room window.'

'But Gav's hiring a driver and security people to do that.'

'A bit extra won't hurt,' he said. 'And it means you're in charge at Dundas in the evenings and overnight. Gavin's giving us an office to work from, so your job will be to keep everything up to date there and to get to know people. You're good at that.'

'Mix with the campers?'

'Yes, you can pick up all the gossip. And we'll run the office much as we do here.'

'Do you think people will be suspicious about us and think we're spying on them?'

'I suppose we are, in a way. We should make it clear we're there for security. It's a big operation. People will want to feel safe, so we make sure they know that's what we're there for.'

'It's really exciting,' said Molly.

Ian agreed. It was an exciting case. He just hoped it wouldn't turn out to be dangerously exciting.

5

Duncan couldn't do very much with a photocopy of the anonymous letter. His forensic team would need the real thing, and that was still at Dundas Farm in Stamper's office. Molly could drive up there in the morning, collect the letter, and obtain lists of everyone involved in the opera and details of Stamper's security team. He'd spend today putting a contract together and Molly could collect Stamper's signature while she was there. She'd come back with it all well organised and she'd be glad to be out of the office for a while, particularly when neither of them was going to be leaving it much over the next week. And he suspected she'd be more than pleased to spend some time with Stamper. They'd got on well once Molly got over her blushes and realised there was a real person underneath her idolised teenage version of him. He'd be easy to work with, Ian thought. An affable, laid-back type, ready to laugh at himself and not take things too seriously. Of course, he'd no idea at this stage what the rest of the opera crowd would be like. For all Ian knew of them they could be as temperamental and difficult as the diva herself. But people came back to the camp year after year so presumably there was some feeling of camaraderie among them. What went on behind closed tent flaps, he could only guess. They might all be seething with jealousy and resentment. One of them could even be a murderer. But at least the man at the helm seemed to know what he was doing.

Tomorrow was Jeanie's line dance night in the village hall and the evening he and Duncan met for a drink in the Pigeon. Molly would be back in plenty of time with the letter for him to hand over to Duncan. He'd also ask him to check the files on Andy Meade. The rest of the evening he'd relax and try not to let the possibility of murderers lurking among the alpacas bother him too much.

Having sorted that out, it was time to find out more about the diva. It shouldn't be difficult. If she was famous, she'd be all over the Internet. He typed her name into Google. She was famous all right. He found several pages of images of her, Wikipedia entries, fan pages, opera websites and links to newspaper reviews.

He began with a biography. Lucia Pedro Morales was born in Guatemala but moved to London with her family when she was eighteen months old. She grew up in Tottenham, where her father worked for what at the time was called London Transport — now oddly known as Transport for London — as a bus garage supervisor. Why change a nice simple name like London Transport to something not very different but, in his opinion, more cumbersome? But he was getting sidetracked. The name of her father's employers was irrelevant. Lucia's talent must have been inherited from her mother, who had been a cabaret singer. Quite a successful one, working in and around Soho until she succumbed to lung cancer when Lucia was fifteen. It must be hard losing one's mother at fifteen. Ian wondered if it was why she was, according to Stamper, difficult to get on with. It seemed that Lucia herself had been ambitious from an early age. She had won a scholarship to the London College of Music junior department, also when she was fifteen, and three years later another scholarship had taken her to the Royal Academy of Music. She was clearly a very driven teenager – the result of bereavement? he wondered; wanting to follow her mother's legacy as a singer? That was followed by a year at the London Opera Centre and regular appearances on London opera stages as well as in Milan, Paris and Rome. So yes, she was the real deal opera-wise. Not that Ian was any kind of expert. But with that background there was no doubt that she was all she said she was, and he could find no evidence of any animosity towards her from colleagues. She'd got where she was through talent and hard work.

Then he found a newspaper article and alarm bells began to ring. Shortly before the first lockdown Lucia had fallen down the stairs backstage at the theatre where she was performing Aida, and spent three months in hospital with a badly broken leg. Ian's leg started to throb at the memory of his own stay in hospital with an injury. He wondered if anyone had looked into why she fell. Was the lighting bad backstage? Had she been drinking? Or, and this was where he began to feel prickles down his spine, had she been pushed? There was nothing in the article to suggest foul play. Merely a few sentences saying she would not be appearing on stage again for a while. She was released from hospital while the country was still in lockdown and work for musicians dried up. Ian felt sorry for her. A run of bad luck that had brought her career to a full stop. He checked Spotify for recordings she had made and found what he assumed were enough for her to live on while she got her career back on track again. She'd had a few live bookings in the last year, all UK based because of travel restrictions, but Stamper's opera was the only stage production on the horizon. No wonder she had accepted his offer to spend two weeks in Scotland working with students and amateurs.

He'd found the facts about the diva. Now he turned to social media to check out opinions. There were Facebook opera pages that were generally kind about her, posting reviews from audiences who had seen her onstage and listened to recordings. Mostly, he felt, people who belonged to an opera-loving demographic whose posts were well-informed and literate. Twitter, on the other hand, was cruel in the extreme and he hoped that, for her own sake, the diva didn't read them. Twitter was a hotbed of fake news to which Lucia Pedro Morales did not subscribe. *Just as well*, Ian thought. According to many tweets she was too old, too fat, sang like a bullfrog and, worst of all, was foreign. Some were threatening and Ian wondered if, and how, he should take these seriously. He'd keep an eye on them but beyond that there wasn't much he could do. It was all too anonymous.

Next, he clicked through the images of her. If he'd been asked to conjure up an image of an opera singer in her mid-forties and at the peak of her career, Lucia Pedro Morales would come close to what had been in his head. A typical South American beauty with glossy dark hair and flashing black eyes. Not petite, certainly, but hardly the frumpy, overweight hag that Twitter portrayed. She'd sung Carmen many times before and Ian found a photo of her in the role, which he printed and pinned to the whiteboard. She was wearing a tight-fitting black dress with red flowers in her hair. She held a single red rose against her cheek and was gazing into the camera with what he could only describe as a suggestive expression.

He wondered what her connection to Stamper was. He appeared to know her well. But Lucia had grown up in Tottenham, Stamper in Essex. In any case, there was a ten-year difference in their ages, so they couldn't have met at whatever kind of music events teenagers went to. Lucia was highly trained. Stamper, on his own admission, couldn't read music and until he engaged the services of a voice coach four years ago, had never had a singing lesson. But they were both famous, if at the extreme ends of the music profession. They could have met at parties or been involved in high-end charity events. He made a mental note to ask Stamper for more information about her. An insider's view was going to be a lot more accurate than what he'd found in newspapers and on social media. He remembered Stamper hinting that she could have upset people.

He typed up his notes and decided it was time he learnt a bit more about the opera that was about to take over his life. *Carmen*, now one of the best-loved operas in the repertoire, had launched in Paris in 1875 to an indifferent audience who didn't like the depictions of proletarian life, immorality, and lawlessness. *Why not?* Ian wondered. He thought that would be one of its attractions. What he knew of Paris in the late nineteenth century didn't suggest a particularly buttoned-up population. He doubted there was much there to shock an audience in twenty-first century Scotland, except perhaps the smoking. Funny how what was and wasn't acceptable changed over time. These days, the average audience would think nothing of a bit of immorality and lawlessness but would throw their hands up in horror at people smoking in public. The cigarette factory setting made Ian wonder about Stamper's fire insurance when putting on a production in a barn. There was a lot of wood around, not to mention straw bales. A cigarette casually tossed into a straw bale would be a disaster. Not Ian's problem, of course, and they wouldn't be allowed to smoke there anyway. But he'd be interested to see how Stamper got around the problem of producing an opera set in a cigarette factory without anyone actually smoking.

The cigarette factory was pretty much all he knew about the opera, and he decided he should learn more, since he was going to be absorbed in it for two weeks. He searched for a performance he could stream and watch with his evening glass of beer. He discovered that *Carmen* had been updated, turned into a ballet, rewritten as a story set in Harlem – for all he knew it could have been set as a modern crime drama for Netflix. But from the poster he'd seen in Stamper's office, this was a traditional performance and, oddly, it was hard to find one of those. He settled eventually for a Paris National Opera live recording, for which he had to stump up a fee of ten pounds. He paid it willingly. It would be a drop in the ocean on Stamper's expenses invoice.

By the end of the performance, he was an opera convert. Much of the music was familiar and he'd heard recordings, but nothing could beat seeing it in action on his big computer screen. It had everything; beautiful gypsies, smugglers, a matinee idol bullfighter – he absolutely understood why Stamper was so keen to take the role – and a sweet, unsuspecting and eventually broken-hearted soldier turned murderer.

He took Lottie for a trot round the garden then went to bed with the music still swirling around in his head. He'd enjoyed the evening sitting in a comfortable chair with a can of beer and one of Jeanie's pies, only Lottie for company. He'd search out more opera. He might give *Aida* a go next. He'd educate himself a bit, he thought. There was a world of stuff out there that he'd never got around to.

6

It was good to keep at least a toe in the police camp. It led to short contract work, which was good for his bank balance, and often gave Ian a shortcut to information and records that were useful in many of his enquiries. No PI should be without a friend in the local police. It had also provided him with his car. His beloved Touareg, ex-police car and sold to him for a snip because some of his colleagues thought he'd had a raw deal from the force after being shot in the leg. At that time the car had been way above his pay grade. Now he could have afforded it outright, but back then he was grateful because it showed people had cared what happened to him and because he was badly in need of a decent way of getting around. He could never have contemplated sleeping in his old car, an ancient rust bucket that dated back to the days when cars actually did rust. And this one had. It was more rusty holes than actual bodywork. The car he had now was not only a pleasure to drive, but had on more than one occasion provided him with a bed for the night. The first time he'd slept in it had been after a booze-ridden celebration with a police inspector – now a chief inspector – following the end of a successful murder enquiry. That had been a chilly night and all he had was a blanket. After that, he'd kitted it out with a sleeping bag, a couple of pillows and a warmer blanket in stripes of many colours (knitted by Lainie using yarn from an enormous bag of remnants that she'd bought on eBay for a knockdown price). With the seats laid flat, he had enough room to stretch out diagonally. Since then, he knew he always had an impromptu bed for the night.

But tonight's meeting with Inspector Clyde, a former colleague from their days in Leith and one of Ian's oldest friends, was pleasure rather than business. From his house to the Pigeon was a ten-minute walk, which meant he and Lottie got some exercise, and he didn't need to worry about drinking a few pints. It was convenient for Duncan as well. His wife Jeanie danced the evening away in the village hall and then drove him home at closing time. Usually after Jeanie had given Ian a serious ticking off for not marrying Caroline. If he'd felt like marrying again he might have chosen Caroline, who was feisty and skilled at getting them out of tricky and sometimes violent situations. But he didn't feel like marrying again and neither did Caroline. They had discussed it and decided that close friendship was a way better idea than marriage, both of them having extricated themselves from badly chosen spouses. Although, in his case, it wasn't really a decision *he* had made. He'd been deserted for a man who was richer than he was, or was ever likely to be. But however hard they tried to persuade Jeanie otherwise, she wasn't convinced and still seemed hell-bent on getting them to the altar.

He hadn't seen Caroline for a while, he realised. But it was the end of the school year, a busy time for teachers. What did surprise him was that he hadn't really missed seeing her, or even noticed that he hadn't. They were both too busy, he supposed. But good friendships were like that, weren't they? No pressure to spend time together, but thoroughly enjoyable when they did. Caroline and Molly belonged to some women's group in Dundee who went out for meals together, so it was likely that Molly was seeing more of Caroline than he was. He was extremely fond of Caroline. They had some good times together; sometimes exciting, sometimes, well, just pleasurable. And in spite of Jeanie's constantly trying to persuade both of them otherwise, what they had was a good friendship, nothing more than that. He knew Caroline felt the same. But good friends were too precious to waste. He'd call her and arrange an evening out soon. Well, possibly not until after the opera camp, but definitely soon.

The pub was packed. It was a mild summer evening and people were spilling outside, some into the garden at the back, others to sit on the harbour wall and watch the boats in the estuary. He and Duncan decided to sit inside with the locals. They chatted for a while about Duncan and Jeanie's upcoming holiday in Cornwall and Ian's own recent trip to the South of France.

'How's the wee girl?' Duncan asked.

'Anna?' He was surprised Duncan remembered her, although the mugging of a pretty student, even a mild mugging that had been diverted by a group of undergraduates, was something he would remember. 'She's fine. She'll be back in Scotland in the autumn and working on the Drumlychtoun Estate.' That was something he was looking forward to. Reunion celebrations at the castle, probably involving hog roasts and dancing, and no doubt excellent local whisky and wine from Anna's family's estate in the South of France.

The Diva of Dundas Farm

'She'll be working for the laird?'

Ian nodded. 'AKA Great Uncle Xander.'

'Grooming her to take over, I suppose. And all thanks to you.'

'Not really. They'd have found each other eventually.'

'You're too modest, laddie.'

Was he? Ian had enjoyed that case. He'd made lasting friendships and it hadn't done his reputation any harm. Not as high profile as the Lansman murder perhaps, or even unravelling the Murriemuir mystery, which had caught the attention of local newspapers and brought in a nice batch of new clients.

Duncan drained his pint and ordered them both another. 'What have you got on at the moment?' he asked, returning to their table. 'Anything interesting?'

'Molly and I will be at the Dundas Farm opera for two weeks, keeping an eye on a high-profile singer with paranoia.'

'Didn't know you were an opera fan.'

'I'm a recent recruit. I watched *Carmen* last night and loved it. But I'll be there to work. Actually,' he said, pulling an envelope from his pocket. 'I wondered if you could give me an opinion on this.'

Duncan opened the envelope and took out the letter, unfolding it carefully. He read it and laughed. 'Bit of a cliché, isn't it? Letters cut out of magazines and stuck to Basildon Bond notepaper went out with Miss Marple, didn't they?'

'It's enough to frighten our leading lady, though.'

'Does she have reason to be frightened?'

'That's what I need to find out.'

'So what was the unfortunate incident last year? Who died? And how?'

'One of the stagehands collapsed and died after the final performance. A guy called Andy Meade.'

'A suspicious death? I don't remember anything about it.'

'He had a well-documented embolism that could have carried him off at any time.'

'No need for an enquiry then. Very convenient if you happen to want to murder someone that everyone knows could peg out at any moment.'

'It's a bit of a coincidence along with that letter. Do you think we're right to be suspicious?'

'Possibly. Not enough to open a police enquiry, and I can't see how it could ever be proven now. But you should certainly consider that it might be linked to this new threat. And I'm sure you are the right person to take it on.'

'Thanks for the endorsement. Could you check if Andy Meade had any kind of police record? And can you get someone to look at the letter for me?'

'I'll get forensics onto it tomorrow. And I'd recommend you look into security for this lady. Although she's not mentioned in the letter it *was* sent to her so she's the likely target.'

'They're on to that already. Have you heard of a bloke called Gavin Stamper?'

'I don't think so,' said Duncan. 'Should I?'

'Molly was shocked that I hadn't heard of him. He was lead singer in a very famous boy band about fifteen years ago.'

'There you go then. I've never been into boy bands.'

'Me neither. Trouble is, Duncan, we've never been teenage girls.'

'True. And something I'm quite glad about. Career-wise as much as anything. I could have turned out like Kezia Wallace.'

It was quite hard to imagine Kezia as a teenage girl, although she must have been one. A bit old to have been a Stamper groupie, though. 'What's it like working for her?' Ian asked.

'Not as bad as I expected. She's very supportive but keeps out of our way most of the time. Not that we've had any serious cases recently. But if this lady of yours gets herself murdered you can be sure she'll be there blasting everything she's got at it.'

For that reason alone, Ian sincerely hoped that Lucia's fears were unfounded. Kezia Wallace had a way of hurtling into his life when he least expected or wanted her to. Her opinion of PIs was low. She treated him as an amateur, constantly getting in the way of real police work. On the other hand, he'd be the first to admit she was good at her job.

They'd just downed their third pints when Jeanie arrived. Dancing was thirsty work so Duncan went to the bar to buy her a St Clements. She sat down next to Ian.

'Nice to see you, Jeanie,' he said. 'Thanks for the pies.'

'You can thank Molly for that,' she said. 'If it had been down to me I'd have left you to starve, holiday or not. I'm not pleased with you, young man,' she said. 'Not pleased at all.'

Ian had an uneasy feeling he knew what was coming. He smiled at Jeanie with what he hoped might be a look of sweet innocence. 'What did I do?' he asked.

'It's what you didn't do,' she said as Duncan returned with her drink.

'Okay, what didn't I do?'

'You went off to the South of France and didn't take Caroline with you. Didn't it occur to you that Carcassonne is one of the most romantic places in the world? All those medieval buildings and vineyards, perfect weather, glorious scenery.'

'It was term time,' he said. 'She was in the middle of exams.'

'You couldn't put it off for a week? She works like a slave with those wretched brats. The least she deserves is a holiday in the sun.'

'And I'd be the last person to stand in her way. As soon as term ends, she can go on as many holidays in the sun as she wants.'

'But not with you.'

'That might be seen as an advantage,' Duncan chipped in.

'Duncan Clyde, you can shut up.'

'Just saying...'

'Well don't. Here are these two lovely people absolutely made for each other. The south of France is the perfect place for a honeymoon.'

'I'm sure it is,' said Ian. 'Just not mine.'

'Give him a bit of peace,' said Duncan. 'He's about to spend two weeks at an opera camp.'

'Whatever for? You're not an opera fan, are you? And camping? You must be out of your mind.'

'It's work,' said Ian. 'And Molly will be the one in a tent.'

'Molly's young,' said Jeanie. 'She'll enjoy it. You are old enough to know better. Why not book yourself into a nice hotel and take Caroline along to help you?'

'Ian's going to make sure the star of the show doesn't get bumped off,' said Duncan.

'Why? Is her singing that bad?'

'I can't discuss a case,' said Ian. 'And I can't expect Caroline to be an unpaid assistant. Anyway, you said she needed a holiday in the sun and I couldn't guarantee that. Not in Perthshire.'

'Anyway, he's got Molly now,' said Duncan.

Jeanie sighed loudly. 'I despair, I really do.'

'Nice try,' said Ian with a laugh. 'You'll never give up, will you?'

'Not while I know what's good for both of you,' said Jeanie.

'Leave them alone, love,' said Duncan. 'They're old enough to make up their own minds.'

'Just don't start telling me you regret it when you're seventy and lonely,' said Jeanie, draining her glass and thumping it down on the table.

'He'll have to go and live on one of those wrinkly retirement ghettos they're building down the coast,' said Duncan. 'Come on, love. Time to go home and stop teasing Ian.'

Jeanie picked up her bag and buttoned her jacket. 'It's fun teasing Ian,' she said. 'And you don't mind, do you, love?' she asked, kissing his cheek.

He supposed he didn't. He just wished she'd find something else to tease him about.

7

Seven in the morning was an unreasonable time to get up, particularly on a Saturday. But Molly had insisted they needed to leave early, so Ian dragged himself out of bed and took a surprised Lottie for a short walk. She wouldn't be allowed into the wildlife park, but he'd checked the website and discovered that they provided kennels at the entrance. Lottie had never been left in a kennel, or at least not since she had lived with him. Stephanie might have kennelled her regularly. He hadn't asked her, but he wouldn't be surprised if she had. She liked exotic holidays and had probably made up for his lack of providing them once husband number two was on the scene.

Would Lottie mind being left in a kennel, or would it be better to leave her with Lainie for the day? He knew she liked being with Lainie and that Lainie loved having Lottie. And however friendly the kennel people were, it was bound to be lacking in home comforts. So Lainie it was. But when he called in to ask what she thought, he found the decision had been made for him. Lainie was planning to go curling.

Curling? Wasn't that what they did on ice at the Winter Olympics? He'd watched it a few times. A strange sport that he'd never quite understood, involving people flinging heavy stones across the rink while other people scrubbed at the ice with brooms. Try as he might, he couldn't see Lainie doing that, either as the stone flinger or the sweeper. Although, being a domestic type, he supposed it was more likely that she would do the sweeping. Should he be worried about Lainie? She sounded sensible enough most of the time. She was well into her eighties, healthy and living alone. But was she getting confused and losing her grip on reality? And if she was, what the hell was he going to do about it? Lainie, as far as he knew, had no relatives. She'd never been married and had never mentioned anyone she was close to other than a few friends around the village and at her knit and natter group. Perhaps this was the first sign that she was losing it. What other batty ideas might she come up with? But he needn't have worried. He'd misunderstood. Lainie roared with laughter when Ian suggested that taking up ice skating could be risky if she'd not done it before. Adding as tactfully as he could that it was a sport most people embarked on in their youth.

'Bless you,' she said. 'It's my over-sixties morning. Usually we meet in the village hall on a Tuesday, but this week we have a curling match with another group in Forfar. We've hired a minibus to pick us up outside the post office. And it's not on ice. We'll be in the sports hall of a school.'

'How does that work?' Ian asked. 'You hurl stones across the floor?'

'We have wooden weights on wheels and a pusher thing so we don't even need to bend down. It's fun. And very competitive. The winners get a free cream tea.'

That was a relief. Fond as he was of Lainie, he had no

idea what would happen to her if she could no longer manage on her own. Should he talk to her about it? And spoil her day out? Not right now, he decided. 'Do you still have people with brushes?' he asked.

'No, that's only the ice version. The sweeping melts the surface of the ice so the stones glide more easily.'

That was all right then. He was relieved, even if it did mean Lottie would be confined to a kennel for most of the day. He'd make it up to her on Sunday. Take her to Tentsmuir perhaps and let her scamper along the beach.

Molly arrived at seven-thirty with a very lively Ryan. 'He's been up for hours,' she said. 'He's so excited.'

'Lucky you,' said Ian, quite glad that he didn't live with a seven-year-old. 'Your dad didn't fancy joining us?' Molly's father, Nigel, was an up-for-it type. Particularly where Ryan was concerned. He threw himself into grandfather duties with dogged determination and a degree of thoroughness that most parents only dreamt of. Helpful for Molly, of course, since he was retired and always ready for school pick-ups if she had to work late. But all that enthusiasm could irritate in a way that was hard for Molly, who must sometimes long to just chill out with Ryan with a bag of chips and children's Netflix. Ian had expected Nigel to tag along today, but it seemed he'd had a better offer.

'Would you believe he's got a date?' Molly said, in a way that suggested Nigel was about forty years too late for anything of that sort.

Even for Ian, who in age probably came somewhere at the midpoint between Molly and her father, it wasn't an easy thing to imagine. 'Who with?' he asked, trying to recall ladies in the village of suitable age and respectability. A local councillor, perhaps, or one of the meals on wheels women.

'Joy from the Pigeon,' said Molly.

'Really? Joy the barmaid?' That was a surprise but, well, why not? Nigel was a regular at the Pigeon. He must have got to know Joy pretty well over the years. And he was a well turned-out man in his sixties with his own house and no apparent shortage of money. Quite a catch. And Joy, now he gave it some thought, was an attractive woman. Good luck to him, to both of them. And one in the eye for Jeanie, who Ian was pretty sure had had no hand in it at all. There were couples who managed to get together without her help, which would probably make her furious. He must remember to tease her about it next time they met. Ian was very pleased for Nigel and it was something of a relief that he wasn't coming with them today. Nigel would have had the day planned to the last second. He'd probably have brought a clipboard and a finely tuned itinerary. They were going to collect information and needed to get people talking. Nigel's presence would probably have made them clam up.

'Where are they going for their date?' he asked. Greyport wasn't an obvious venue for romantic trysts.

'Lunch at the Seven Ringers in Brechin,' said Molly. 'They do a very good all-you-can-eat carvery at the weekends.'

'Bit of a busman's holiday for Joy, isn't it?' Would she be able to keep her hands off the beer pumps if they were having a busy day? For Nigel's sake he hoped she would.

'They're going to do a tour of the cathedral as well,' said Molly. 'Her family come from around there somewhere and she wants to see if any of them are buried in the graveyard.'

Fair enough. Looking at gravestones could be fun, if one

was into that kind of thing. He should go there himself. His own family hailed from Angus. There'd probably be Skairs buried there as well.

Molly had packed a picnic in a red-and-green-striped cool bag, which she lifted out of the back of her car and started to load into Ian's. 'It's always really expensive to eat at places like that,' she said. 'And mostly junk food.'

'Put it on the back seat,' he said. 'We don't want Lottie scoffing it before we get there.'

Ryan giggled. 'Will there be ice cream?' he asked.

'Not for Lottie,' said Ian. 'It's bad for dogs.'

'Why is it?'

'I don't know, but Prince George was ticked off by the RSPCA a year or two ago when there was a photo in a newspaper of him feeding ice cream to his dog.'

'But I can have some, can't I?'

'If you're good and eat all your sandwiches,' said Molly.

'Will I have to eat all my sandwiches too?' Ian asked.

'Of course,' said Ryan. 'No ice cream until you've eaten the first course.'

Well, that put him in his place, he thought as he lifted Lottie into the back of the car. He climbed into the driver's seat and tapped Murray Leaf into his satnav while Molly strapped Ryan in and settled herself next to Ian.

'Are we nearly there?' asked Ryan as Ian pulled out of the village and onto the Stirling Road.

The kennels seemed okay. Lottie had a small pen to run around in and a wooden lean-to at one end with a bowl of drinking water. Ian left her having a good sniff around and she didn't look too worried as he locked the gate behind him.

The kennels were free but entry to the wildlife park itself was not, even though they'd qualified for a family ticket. He wasn't sure they were entitled to it, since only Ryan and Molly were related. But Molly reassured him that it didn't mean they had to be actual family. It was all to do with numbers and ages. In any case it would be added to Stamper's expenses. And thinking about how much it must cost to house, feed and care for dozens of exotic animals, it was probably good value.

'Where do we start?' Molly asked, looking around as they walked through a turnstile and into the park.

They could see green fields in one direction and a group of buildings in the other. 'We know that Andy worked as a cleaner,' said Ian, 'so we can probably leave the animals that are roaming free until later. There's a train that drives through their enclosure.'

'Can we go on it now?' Ryan asked.

'We can go on the train after lunch,' Molly told Ryan. 'Ian and I need to talk to someone first.'

'Come and look at the map, Ryan,' said Ian. 'This is where the train goes.' He ran his finger along the track on the map. 'There's a station near the animal enclosures and another at the far end of the field.' He pointed to a line of footprints on the map. 'I think you are supposed to follow these,' he said. 'They lead us through the animal pens and then over to the first station. Your mum's right. It makes sense to get the train after lunch and look at all the other animals first. Rhinos are the nearest ones and I should think they need a lot of cleaning. So that would be a good place for us to start asking questions.'

Ryan stood on his tiptoes to see the top of the map. 'Penguins are next,' he said. 'They make lots of mess. I saw it on David Attenborough. People scoop the poo off the rocks and they use it for... I've forgotten what they use it for. Grandad would know. Shall I phone him?'

'No,' said Ian and Molly firmly at the same time. 'You can ask one of the keepers.' That could be a good way to get a conversation going about Andy Meade. Perhaps poo-scraping had been one of his jobs. In which case Ian didn't blame him for decamping to alpacas.

They leant on the fence of the rhino enclosure and watched as a man raked bales of hay from a flatbed truck and hurled them into the field. In the distance they could see half a dozen rhinos chomping grass and not looking very interested in their next course.

As the hay flinger offloaded his final bale, Ian walked over to him. 'That looks like hard work,' he said.

'Too right,' said the man. 'And the ungrateful beasts don't even show an interest. Same every day. They'd be just as happy eating grass through the summer.' He flung his pitchfork into the truck and sifted through his pockets for the keys.

'Worked here long?' Ian asked.

'Just a few months,' he said as he climbed into his truck and started the engine.

'Is there anyone I could talk to who has been here a couple of years or more?'

The man shook his head. 'There's a quick turnover of staff, what with students and interns. Most of us are only here for the summer season. I suppose you could try Fred. He's been here for years.'

'Where can I find him?'

'He'll be over by the penguins doling out fish.'

The truck pulled away and Ian looked again at his map. 'This way,' he said, waving towards some sheds. 'Let's go and see some penguins.'

They found Fred wearing waders and yellow rubber gloves. He was standing by a blue pond feeding fish to the penguins from a bucket. *Very polite penguins*, Ian thought. No clamouring or shoving, each one just waiting for its turn. Ian didn't know what kind of fish penguins ate but was surprised by how large they were. Each penguin took one from Fred's hand, swallowed it whole then waddled back towards the pool and slid into the water. A crowd of children stood on a low wall near the pond and clung to the bars of a fence for a better view. Ian lifted Ryan onto his shoulders where he had the best view of all.

Once the bucket was empty, Fred made his way to a gate in the fence, unlocked it with a key and let himself out, locking the gate behind him. Ian put Ryan down and made his way towards Fred. 'Got time for a quick word?' he asked.

'Interested in penguins?' Fred asked, pulling off his gloves, pushing his bucket into the back of a van and closing the door.

'I'm interested in the work that's done here.'

'Aye, it's a good place to work. We're building up a programme of conservation and enrichment. You'll have seen programmes on TV about global warming and changing habitats?'

Ian nodded. 'Have you worked here long?'

'Five years or so. I was working in an insurance office in Glasgow. Dullest job in the world.'

Ian imagined it might have been, although he didn't know a lot about the insurance business. 'So you fancied a new job. Something in the open air?'

'More to it than that. I did a degree in zoology and conservation. Worked here on day release and then stayed on full time.'

In five years he'd probably seen a good many employees

come and go. 'Do you remember a guy called Andy Meade? Worked here a couple of years ago.'

'Oh yeah, I remember Andy,' he said with a sour expression.

Obviously not a happy memory and Ian wondered why. 'You didn't like him?'

'Proper troublemaker he was. Drank too much and got into fights. He turned up one day drunk and let the meerkats out. Hell of a job rounding them all up again. Ever tried herding meerkats?'

'I can't say I have, no.' He'd only seen meerkats on television, cartoon ones. The ones he'd seen spoke with Russian accents and talked about insurance. They were probably very different from the real ones that lived here. 'Did he get into trouble for letting them out?'

'He was sacked on the spot. No idea what happened to him.' He didn't look as if he cared very much either.

'He went to work on an alpaca farm,' said Ian. 'Not far from here, actually.'

Fred looked surprised. 'The one that some pop star runs?'

'That's the one. Have you been there?'

'Don't have a lot of time for alpacas. I prefer the llamas we keep here.'

Ian wasn't sure of the difference between an alpaca and a llama but wasn't going to get into a discussion about it right now. 'I think Andy worked as a groundsman. He probably didn't spend a lot of time with the animals.'

'Is he still there? Or did they sack him as well?'

'Neither,' said Ian. 'He died.'

'Oh yeah?' said Fred, without a hint of surprise. 'Did someone murder him?'

'He had a heart condition,' said Ian, avoiding the question, interesting though it was. 'Why would someone want to murder him?'

'As I said, he wasn't liked.'

Ian had got that. But on the whole most people avoided those they didn't like rather than killing them. What was he not being told about Andy Meade? 'That's not really a reason to murder him, though. What had he done that made him so unlikable?'

'He had some scam going. Something to do with investing in vintage whisky. He lost a lot of people a lot of money.'

'Did the fraud squad know about it?'

'Couldn't tell you that. Didn't have anything to do with it. But I suppose not, since he managed to walk into another job. Jammy bastard.'

Ian was having doubts about Stamper's employee vetting processes. Did he know nothing about Meade's past?

Fred seemed to have read his thoughts. 'He had a smooth tongue on him. Knew how to turn on the charm and I wouldn't put it past him to cobble up some fake references. Why are you interested? If he's dead there's not much anyone can do now.'

'Just making some enquiries,' said Ian.

'Well, I'd better be getting on,' said Fred, opening the driver's door of the van. 'I've got fruit to cut up for the monkeys.'

'Thanks for your help,' said Ian as Fred slung his gloves onto the passenger seat and climbed into the van.

Ian had picked up some useful information and looked around to see where Molly and Ryan were. They hadn't gone far and were gazing into a snake pit. Ian joined them and peered over the wall of the pit. 'Have you seen any?' he asked.

'I told Ryan he needed to be very quiet if he wanted to see the snakes.'

'You heard what Fred told me then?'

'Yeah, interesting. It sounds like there was a motive for wanting him dead. We should try and find some of his victims.'

She was right, but they could be making a lot of extra work for themselves. 'Any idea how we can do that?' he asked.

'People who've been scammed tend to keep quiet about it except with others who've also been scammed. I should think there'll be online support groups. I'll see what I can find when we're back in the office.'

But what did it have to do with the threat to Lucia? Was there a link between Andy Meade's death and the anonymous letter? 'See if you can track any of the victims to Dundas Farm. I'll try to find a link to Lucia. Do you think she could be involved in some kind of financial scamming? She's been out of work for a while.' It didn't seem very likely though. How would a well-known opera singer, who lived in London, cross the path of a disreputable zoo cleaner living six hundred miles away? It was something that was going to worry him until he found the answer, but there wasn't much he could do about it right now. 'Let's put it all to one side for today,' he said, noticing Ryan jumping up and down with impatience. 'We're here to look at animals.'

'Is it time for lunch?' Ryan asked hopefully. 'And ice cream,' he added.

'It's only half past ten,' said Molly.

'But I'm hungry.'

'Me too,' said Ian. 'Why don't we go and get a cup of coffee and a bun and then have a ride on the train?'

'What do you think, Ryan?' said Molly. 'They might have

hot chocolate. And the café is just over there by the insect house.'

'Okay,' said Ryan. 'But only if you promise to stop talking about work.'

'It's a deal,' said Molly, laughing. 'No more work until Monday.'

A day out in an animal park with a seven-year-old was exhausting. By the time they headed back to the kennels to collect Lottie, Ian reckoned he'd seen every animal he'd ever heard of, and a few he hadn't. Who knew about capybaras? Or pangolins?

Ryan had pocket money to spend and they stopped at the shop on the way out to buy a kit of cut out animals. *Just add glue, scissors and patience and you'll have your very own zoo,* it said on the cover. Ian was relieved it wouldn't be *his* patience that was needed. Thank goodness for Nigel, who would be more than happy spending Sunday with scissors and glue. That is, assuming he wasn't otherwise occupied with Joy from the Pigeon.

8

There was one more week before they moved everything up to Dundas Farm for the two weeks of the opera camp. Right now, it was heads down for both of them, finishing off all their ongoing cases before they left. Nothing very interesting but a mountain of admin in terms of reports, invoices and archiving of files. As he was getting stuck into it all and hoping the week would pass quickly, Ian had a call from Duncan.

'I've a report from forensics about your anonymous letter,' said Duncan.

'That was quick,' said Ian. 'Does it mean they didn't find anything of interest?'

'On the contrary. You were in luck because the office was open all weekend expecting some evidence to turn up, but it didn't so they worked on your letter instead. I've just picked it up from them with their report. Can you meet for lunch? I can give the letter back to you and go through the report at the same time.'

Could he spare the time? Duncan could email the report and there was no hurry to get the letter back. On the other hand, it would be good to talk through what had been found with Duncan. There could have been similar cases that might help him understand the mind of the sender. And it would be useful to have the letter back in case there were any more over the next two weeks and they needed to compare them. 'Pub in the village?' he asked. He could take a short lunch break and catch up with office work this afternoon.

'Sure,' said Duncan. 'I'm coming in that direction. Shall we say one o'clock?'

Ian agreed and put the phone down.

'Off out again?' said Molly, looking, he thought, rather irritated.

'I won't be out for long,' he said. 'Duncan's got the report back from forensics. It'll be useful to talk it through with him. You don't mind, do you?' It shouldn't matter to him whether she did or didn't mind. He was the boss, after all. But he didn't want to come back to a disgruntled employee this afternoon.

Molly shrugged. 'I suppose not. I'll probably get on with the paperwork faster without you anyway.'

'If you don't mind,' he said, hoping there was a hint of irony in his voice. Was he imagining it or was Molly becoming tired of her assistant role? Now she was licensed, was she thinking of expanding her career? He couldn't really blame her. He just hoped it wouldn't be too soon before he needed to replace her.

'I don't mind,' she said, sighing. 'I'll be fine on my own.'

'I'll take Lottie,' he told her. 'It'll save me having to walk her later. And I'll work on into this evening and help get this lot finished.'

'Bring me a sandwich,' she said, with a look that must have been common among mill workers who weren't allowed time for a lunch break. 'I'll have a late lunch at my desk.'

Duncan had bought him a pint. 'There you go,' he said. 'You look like you might need it. Can't have one myself so I'll have to enjoy watching you.'

Ian sank into a chair and downed half of his pint in a single swallow.

'Anything wrong?' Duncan asked. 'You look a bit grumpy. Woman trouble?'

'In a way,' he said. In several ways, actually. Caroline had called last night, and he'd told her he was about to go away again for two weeks. Work, he'd assured her. She hadn't taken it well. Since when did they get like that with each other? Uncommitted friendship, they'd agreed. Fun together but the freedom not to be in each other's pockets all the time. And then there was Molly, who was getting stroppy and demanding the pick of the exciting cases and whinging about being left in the office while he swanned off to lunch. He was worried about Lainie, too, but that was one worry too many. He'd think about that when he got back from Dundas.

'You've only yourself to blame. If you'd listened to Jeanie you'd now be safely married,' said Duncan, taking a swig of his lemonade.

How on earth would that help? Ian shook his head. 'It will pass,' he said, thinking of two weeks steeped in opera during the day and in Elsa's company every night. No, that had come out wrong. Thank God he hadn't actually said it out loud. He felt himself blushing inwardly. What he'd meant was that Elsa would be good company while he was on diva watch, Mickey too of course. No more than that. Definitely not. 'I'll order some food,' he said, needing to do something other than sitting there listening to lectures about his private life. 'Pie and chips?'

'Excellent,' said Duncan. 'But not a word to Jeanie. She's got me on salad lunches right now.'

Nice to know Duncan got his fair share of nagging as well. 'I won't spill the beans if you promise to stop going on about the women in my life.'

'It's a deal,' said Duncan, laughing. 'I'll have a side of onion rings as well. If I'm going to break the rules I may as well do it properly.'

Ian went to the bar and placed his order. He smiled at Joy as she rang it up. 'We don't usually see you here at lunchtime,' he said.

'I've changed my shift,' she told him. 'I'm off to the cinema this evening.'

'With friends?' he asked, thinking that he already knew the answer.

'Just one friend.' She started to take another order, then turned back to him. 'You know Nigel, don't you? Doesn't his daughter work for you?'

'Molly's worked for me for a while now, yes.'

She leaned a bit closer to him. 'Do you find her okay? Only she's been a bit off with me. I don't think she likes me seeing her dad.'

'She's been a bit short-tempered with me as well recently, but I really don't think it's anything to do with you and her dad. More likely she's getting a bit fed up with working for me. She's ambitious and I'm afraid I might lose her to one of the big PI companies in Edinburgh or Glasgow.' And he'd have no way of stopping her. Not that he'd want to stand in her way. Her father wouldn't either, and Molly would probably be pleased that, if she moved away, she wouldn't be leaving him on his own again. And if that was what she was planning then he'd just have to start the hunt for a new assistant.

'As long as it's nothing personal,' said Joy, reaching for a duster and giving the bar a vigorous polish. 'Your food will be about fifteen minutes. I'll bring it over when it's ready.'

Ian returned to the table and sat down. 'Fifteen minutes,' he said. 'So time to look at the report on the letter.'

Duncan opened a large manila envelope. The letter itself was now in a plastic evidence bag. 'Keep it in that,' he said. 'You can still read the letter itself and the envelope through the plastic. But they managed to extract some fingerprints and DNA.'

'DNA?'

'Yup. It's an old-fashioned envelope. Not the kind with a ready glued strip. Whoever sent this had to lick it.'

'Interesting,' said Ian. 'I'm looking for someone who has a stash of obsolete envelopes and doesn't know about DNA. I don't suppose it's on record?'

'No, and neither are the fingerprints. But they discovered one or two things that could point you in the right direction.' He opened the report and handed it to Ian. 'The letters were cut from a magazine about knitting and stuck down with nail polish.'

Ian stared at him. 'Nail polish?'

'So they say. Made by Max Factor and in a colour called crimson blush. Probably quite an old bottle. Max Factor doesn't make that colour anymore and as the polish gets older it also gets stickier. New nail polish would have been crisper, and the letters would have been more likely to peel off. It makes much better glue when it ages. I bet you didn't know that.'

Of course he didn't. He hadn't given a thought to nail

polish since Stephanie left him. In any case, the amount she wore it wouldn't have had the chance to get old. She got through bottles of the stuff as if addicted to it. Maybe she was. 'How can they possibly know that? And how can they tell which magazine was used?'

'You'd be amazed what they can do. There's some software they use to analyse typefaces and connect them to different publications. And I suppose there's some kind of chemical analysis they can do with nail polish.'

'So our letter sender looks like an elderly woman with bright red nails who knits.'

Their food arrived. Duncan pushed the folder to one side and reached for a knife and fork from a stone jar marked *McKenna's Beard Wash* that was sitting in the middle of the table.

'Why elderly?' Duncan asked.

Ian fed a chip to Lottie and cut a slice of his own pie. 'Out of date envelopes,' he said, imagining an antique bureau with pigeonholes like the one his grandmother had in her living room.

'Fair enough,' said Duncan, spearing an onion ring. 'But men knit as well, you know. Think of Tom Daley at the Olympics.'

'I doubt if he wears nail polish.' The only things he'd seen Tom Daley in were very small swimming trunks.

The meal deserved their full attention and they continued eating it in silence. 'Well,' said Duncan after ten minutes or so, by which time they had scraped their plates clean. 'I'd better get back to work.' He finished his drink and fed some remaining crumbs of food to Lottie.

'Me too.' Ian couldn't have Molly commenting on the length of his lunch breaks. *Hell,* he thought. *Who's the boss here? I can take as long as I like for lunch.* All the same, he didn't want Molly to think he was leaving her with all the work.

He left the pub and tied Lottie up outside the shop, where he popped in and bought her a prawn and avocado sandwich, the priciest they had on offer.

As he was walking up the hill back to the office he had a thought. *Alpacas.* People knitted things from alpaca wool, didn't they? They'd need knitting patterns and magazines with ideas about what to make. The letter had been delivered by hand, so the chances were that it was from someone local. Ian wondered if they sold magazines in the shop at Dundas Farm. He'd visit the shop as soon as they were installed there, find out who bought knitting magazines and no doubt pick up a lot of other gossip at the same time.

9

'I hope it's not going to rain,' said Molly, looking at the camping equipment that was piled up in Ian's hall, waiting to be loaded into her car. She'd made a list of everything she and Ryan would need for two weeks of camping, and Ian ordered it from a shop in Dundee. It had been delivered yesterday and was making access in and out of his house extremely difficult. They'd already decided it wasn't going to fit into Molly's car, but he wasn't taking very much, just a change of clothes, a toothbrush, the laptop and Lottie's bed. There was still plenty of room left in *his* car. Why hadn't they asked the delivery people to load it all in while they were down at the bottom of his garden instead of lugging it up the path only for him to cart it back down again?

Ian clicked on a weather app on his phone. 'It's looking good. No rain forecast for the next two weeks.'

'We're taking wellies just in case, and waterproof coats. They can go in my car along with the rest of our stuff. Gav said he'd reserve me a pitch close to the barn, so we won't have far to go for meals.'

Hopefully with a parking space, Ian thought, not wanting to drag it all through a field. 'That's thoughtful of him,' he said.

'And he's letting us use a shower in his house, so we don't need to worry about the communal washrooms. I went to Tartan Heart once when I was a student, and the washrooms were awful. And that was only for two days.'

Ian could only imagine it, never having been a festival-goer himself. 'We'll be able to come back here when we're not too busy. I want to make sure Lainie's okay and we can clean up and do our laundry at the same time.'

'And I need to pop home to check up on Dad.'

Why? Ian wondered. Nigel had lived on his own for years. Was she wondering what he'd be getting up to with Joy from the pub? 'Your dad's okay, isn't he?'

'He's fine, but he's been used to having me and Ryan around and… well, you hear about men of his age taking up with unsuitable women who are only after their money. And now he's going out with a woman for the first time since Mum died.'

'You're not worried about Joy from the pub, are you? She seems like a lovely person.'

'I suppose she's okay. She's lived in the village for ages. It's not like they met online, is it?'

'No,' he said, unable to imagine Nigel looking for his soulmate on a dating website or flicking through photos on an app. *Time to change the subject,* he thought, feeling uncomfortable discussing details of Nigel's private life. 'Looks like we're all done and ready to go,' he said.

They'd had a good week. All their cases were now done and dusted, or postponed until they got back. And it was still only midday on Friday. 'Take the afternoon off,' he told Molly. 'I'll see you at Dundas on Sunday.'

An afternoon off appealed to him as well. He thought of calling Caroline and suggesting a long dog walk followed by a meal somewhere. But she'd snapped at him the last time they spoke, so he bundled Lottie into his car and took her to the dog friendly beach near St Andrews, where she could run in and out of the waves chasing sticks and pieces of seaweed. Then he'd called in at the farm shop on the way home and treated himself to some expensive delicacies.

Sunday was going to be busy. Rehearsals would begin in the barn first thing on Monday morning, so the campsite would be heaving with families staking claims to the best pitches, putting up tents and finding their way around. Most of the campers brought cooking stoves and boxes of groceries but it also looked like being a bonanza week for the bistro, which had taken on extra staff and was gearing up to provide early breakfasts as well as the usual brunch and evening meals.

Stamper had invited Ian and Molly for lunch to meet Lucia Pedro Morales and George Strike, two of the professional singers who, along with Stamper himself, would take the leading roles. He had also set a room aside for them to use as an office and Ian would leave Molly to sort it out while he spent the afternoon staking out the barns and chatting to the resident security staff.

The bistro should be straightforward. The staff wore uniforms and name badges. Ian had been given a list of who they all were and which hours they worked. They'd all been checked out by Stamper's admin team, although how much trust they could place in them was doubtful after the obviously cursory check they'd done on Andy Meade. But unless one of the caterers was a covert poisoner, they could probably rule out the bistro as a murder scene. The theatre could be a problem, though. 'It's a simple set-up,' Stamper had told him. 'Don't expect Covent Garden. There's very little backstage apart from the props room, a green room for the orchestra and dressing rooms for the soloists. The chorus costumes and changing rooms are in a marquee at the back of the barn. There's a relay system so that they can hear what's happening on stage. They don't need to hang around inside the barn at all.'

It sounded simple enough, but Ian would feel more relaxed about it all when he'd seen it for himself. There wasn't much in the way of security. People could come and go as they wished. He'd suggested issuing name tags on lanyards for anyone taking part, but Stamper had been against it. It would ruin the free and easy atmosphere of the camp and in any case, he'd said, if Lucia or anyone else were in danger it was more likely to be from someone already involved in the opera rather than a stranger wandering in from outside. And after a few days everyone would know everyone else and a stranger with evil intent would be noticed. He'd given Ian a plan of the farm and the barns compound and Ian had to agree that it did look secure. The campers would be given a code to unlock the gate into their field and a swipe card for the washrooms. He'd set Ian up with a meeting with his security team to discuss monitoring entry to the theatre and the bistro. And his own house was only accessible through the tunnel using a magnetic pass. Anyone swiping in or out would be noted by his computer system.

'What about the windows?' Ian had noticed picture windows in the side of the hill and at this time of year when it was warm, they were left open most of the time.

'Not a problem,' Stamper told him. There's an electric

fence all around the grounds. Anyone trying to cross it would set off an alarm.'

Stamper had been a security risk for years. His own security was second nature for him. A pity, then, that he didn't want Lucia staying in his house. It was probably the safest place for her.

Molly's car was already parked by the barn when Ian and Lottie arrived. She had a reserved place in the campsite, so he supposed there was no need for her to rush there. Ian opened the door and let Lottie hop out of the car. She must have remembered their earlier visit because she headed straight for the tunnel. She'd remember the biscuits, of course, and was obviously less keen to go in the other direction and pass the time of day with the alpacas. They walked through the tunnel. Ian swiped the card Stamper had given him and waited for the door into the atrium to slide open. Once inside, he found Stamper and Molly drinking glasses of sparkling wine, and Ryan playing with a remote-controlled buggy, steering it, skilfully, Ian thought, around the plant pots.

Stamper shook Ian's hand warmly and smiled down at Ryan. 'Thought I'd get the little chap a treat to play with while the grown-ups have a boring chat,' said Stamper.

How well had he and Molly got to know each other? Ian wondered. She'd been up here for a day earlier in the week going through staff lists with him, during which time they appeared to have become best friends. 'A lot of the chorus and orchestra like to bring kids with them,' Stamper continued. 'I've hired a firm of entertainers to keep them busy during rehearsals.'

'Molly told me about that. Circus skills, isn't it?'

'Among other things. There's a whole team of them. Very experienced children's entertainers who run summer camps and activity weeks all over Scotland. They're putting up a marquee for them at the far end of the camping field.'

'And they've all been vetted?'

Stamper slapped him on the back. 'I can see I've employed the right person. Good to know you're taking the job seriously. And yes, they've all been checked. The company does that themselves. Can't be too careful these days.'

How things had changed. He and his brother had roamed wild and mixed with all sorts of dubious types when they were kids. It was surprising they'd survived into adulthood at all. *The Saville effect,* he thought sadly. 'Aren't there children onstage?' he asked, remembering the performance he'd watched.

Stamper nodded. 'In act one. Street children playing at being soldiers. Hey,' he said, turning to Ryan, who had been eavesdropping intently. 'Would you like to join them?'

'And be a soldier on the stage?' Ryan's eyes were wide with excitement.

'Yes. There should be six kids, all children of chorus members. But one of them broke an arm last week. We were going to get by with five, but if Ryan would like to...'

'Oh, yes please,' Ryan said, jumping up and down. 'If I'm a soldier, can I have a gun?'

Stamper shook his head and ruffled Ryan's hair. 'There've been some nasty accidents recently with prop guns and now the law is very strict. We're only allowed one and that has to be locked up all the time. The stage manager has a key to a special safe and only he knows the backup code. It's only used on stage for a very short time in act three, when José takes a pot shot at Escamillo, and then it's locked up again.'

'Not a real gun, surely?' Ian asked.

'No, it's a replica, but even those come with a mass of regulations. There are people who steal them and turn them into real guns.'

'Are the smugglers armed?' Ian asked, becoming interested in possible dangers from onstage.

'They have cudgels and the soldiers in the chorus have holster belts but nothing in them.'

Ryan was becoming impatient and tugged at Molly's sleeve. 'Mum, can I be a soldier on stage?'

'Isn't he a bit young?' asked Molly.

'He'd be the smallest,' said Stamper. 'But it's just kiddies playing. Nothing difficult. He'll get a toy trumpet or a drum, and he'll need to learn a song.'

'I don't know,' said Molly. 'He's not done much singing and no acting.' Ryan looked at her indignantly. 'We sing every day at school,' he said. 'And I know how to be a child. I won't have to act.'

Stamper laughed. 'That's a good point,' he said, turning to Molly. 'They'll be working with a singing teacher from the local school for an hour in the mornings. Then onstage when act one is rehearsing. I'll give you a schedule but it's no more than a couple of hours a day at most. The rest of the time they'll be in the play tent doing fun circus stuff. He'll be well looked after, and it would leave you free to talk to cast members and that.'

'Will he need a costume?' Molly asked. 'I don't know if I'll have time to make him one.'

'No problem. There'll be one ready for the other kid. There's a Mrs McFee in charge of costumes. She'll get it altered in moments. Like I said, it's just ragged shorts and a shirt.'

'Well, okay,' said Molly. 'If you're sure he won't be a nuisance.'

'Not at all,' said Stamper. 'He might just discover an ambition to be an actor when he grows up.'

'I'd probably rather he stuck to zookeeping,' she said. 'But it will be fun for him for a couple of weeks.'

At that moment Stamper's phone rang. 'That'll be Lucia's driver,' he said, answering the call. 'They're at the barn. So they'll be here any minute. I've booked lunch for her driver at the bistro. Shall I ask him to come here this afternoon so you can talk security with him?' he asked Ian.

'Please,' said Ian. 'I'm meeting the whole team later to go through arrangements before we drive up to Inverbank. I said she'd be there for dinner this evening.'

'And you'll be staying up there with her?'

'I will,' he said. 'With one of the security team and the driver. One of us will be close to her at all times. We'll take shifts overnight and escort her back here when she's needed.'

'I'm impressed,' said Stamper. 'She should be safe with three of you.'

'She'll be fine at the hotel, but the roads are quiet up there. I want to make sure we aren't followed, and I want to keep an eye on anyone coming and going who isn't connected to the hotel. We don't want to risk any kind of ambush, so I'll need to know when you want her here.'

'I'll give you a copy of the schedule as well.'

'Molly's going to be based here,' said Ian. 'Her job is to get to know everyone and watch out for anything unusual. She'll be running the office.'

'Sounds like you've got it all under—' Stamper was

interrupted when the door was flung open and a dark-haired woman appeared, a short, chubby man following in her wake. The woman was wearing a tight-fitting black suit and red, high-heeled shoes. She surged forward and embraced Stamper in a waft of perfume.

'Darling Gavin,' she said, ignoring everyone else in the room. 'Lovely to see you.' She kissed him on both cheeks. 'Such a boring drive,' she sighed. 'Why do you have to live so far from any civilisation? And what are all those silly-looking animals?'

'They're alpacas,' said Ryan, who was the only one in the room not left speechless. 'They are a camelid species originating from South America.'

How the hell did he know that? Ian was impressed. How old was he? Seven?

The woman, Lucia Pedro Morales, Ian assumed, since no one had yet introduced her, let go of Gavin and stared down at Ryan. 'And who might you be?' she asked.

'I'm Ryan Burrows,' he said. 'And I'm going to be a zoologist when I grow up.'

Lucia looked unimpressed. 'Never wanted children myself,' she said, turning back to Stamper. 'You've not gone and adopted him, have you?'

'Ryan is here with his mum,' said Stamper, pulling Molly forwards. 'Molly Burrows.'

Molly held out her hand, but it was ignored.

'Molly and Ian here are the investigators looking into that letter you were sent.'

Ian didn't bother proffering his hand. He was fairly certain she wouldn't shake it. He stepped forward and nodded to her, hoping he didn't look too deferential. 'Ian Skair,' he said. 'I'll need to talk to you about why you thought the threat was aimed at you.'

'How tiresome,' she said. 'But I suppose I can make room for you between rehearsals tomorrow.'

If you prefer, we can just let whoever threatened to kill you get on with it. Probably best not to say that out loud. He needed the fee this job was going to bring in. But he was beginning to understand why Stamper refused to have her in the house. Why on earth hadn't he found a more genial leading lady? He hoped she wouldn't alienate Mickey Rix as well. He'd never be able to find another room for her with so little notice.

The chubby man crept out from where he'd been standing, pretty much obliterated from sight by the diva. He smiled at Ian and held out his hand. 'George Strike,' he said. 'I'm taking the part of José.' He smiled at Stamper. 'Cara not joining us for lunch?' he asked.

'No,' said Stamper. 'She's, er, got a previous engagement.'

'Cara?' Ian asked.

'Cara Curtis. She's playing Micaëla,' Stamper explained.

Ah, thought Ian, *probably to avoid a cat fight.* He guessed Lucia didn't take well to any possible rivalry.

'Nice to meet you,' said Ian, turning towards Strike with relief. He looked like a far more friendly type. 'You're the guy who falls in love with Carmen, aren't you?'

'That's me,' he said with a grin. 'I can't see why. Poor bloke should have been content with Micaëla, listened to Mummy and not messed around with a woman who was so far above his pay grade.'

Ian laughed. 'Not much of a plot then, though.'

George grinned. 'I suppose not. You can't have a tragic opera without a bit of drama, can you?'

He must check up on George Strike, Ian thought. He seemed a nice enough guy, but if anyone was going to murder the leading lady, the bloke who was playing the part of her actual killer had to be a prime suspect. Or would that be far too obvious? Probably. All the same, he'd keep a close eye on Strike and run a background check. 'How does it feel playing a murderer?' Ian asked.

Strike looked in Lucia's direction. 'Just hope I can restrain myself until act four.'

A woman wearing a maroon jacket came in and said something to Stamper, who clapped his hands. 'Lunch, everyone,' he said, leading them into a dining room, one wall of which was glass with a door leading out onto a terrace set into the hillside. Lunch was wheeled in by more people in maroon jackets on a procession of trolleys; Scottish salmon served with tiny new potatoes and a tomato salad, warm bread rolls wrapped in white damask napkins, cut glass jugs of iced water, and on the final trolley, bowls of fresh raspberries and a pitcher of cream.

They sat down, Stamper at the head of the table like some lord of the manor, which Ian supposed he was. He sat Lucia on his right with Ryan and Molly on his left. Ian and George took the remaining seats further down the table. The chairs were arranged so that they could all enjoy the view from the window, where they could see alpacas munching on grass in the distance on the far side of a tall, heavy-duty wire fence, on top of which Ian noticed a CCTV camera. Stamper had been right. It was very unlikely that anyone could get over the fence that protected the perimeter of his land.

Lucia picked at her food, taking tiny mouthfuls of salmon and pushing her potatoes to the side of the plate. She dabbed at her lipsticked mouth with a linen napkin and leant across George towards Ian. 'Tell me about this place I'm supposed to stay in,' she said, scowling in Stamper's direction.

'We thought you'd prefer it,' said Stamper. 'There'll be too much going on here. You wouldn't be able to rest properly.'

'I expect the alpacas make a lot of noise at night,' said Ryan.

Stamper patted him on the head and looked relieved. 'The lad's right,' he said. 'I wouldn't want to deprive you of your beauty sleep. They probably snore and there are a lot of them.'

'Inverbank is lovely,' said Ian, thinking he should help out. 'They've reserved their most luxurious room for you.'

'Does it have a private bathroom?' she asked.

'Of course,' said Stamper. 'Why wouldn't it? It's a five-star boutique hotel.'

'I don't know, do I?' said Lucia. 'Scotland's so old-fashioned. All draughty castles and brigands. Why do you think Gavin buried himself underground like this if it wasn't to escape the locals?' she added, picking at a raspberry.

'Stupid woman,' Stamper muttered under his breath. 'I'll have you know my house is the last word in environmentally friendly building procedures. Carefully planned to blend in with the landscape.'

Ian was sure that everyone was relieved when the meal was over. Except perhaps Ryan, who seemed to be handling the situation well. He'd have a future as a diplomat if the zookeeping didn't take off. Lucia and George were shown into the music room to discuss something Ian failed to understand about a duet involving a rose. Ryan returned to his buggy in the atrium with a young lad in a maroon jacket, who had waited on them at lunch and who Gavin had tipped to keep an eye on Ryan while Ian and Molly were shown into the room that was to be their office.

It was a nice big room with a window that gave them a

view of a field where people were putting up tents. Ian looked around the room approvingly. It was about the same size as the office in Greyport, but without the clutter. There were two empty desks facing each other, office chairs, a filing cabinet and a cork-lined wall with some fire regulations and a card with a WiFi code pinned to it. Near the door was a keypad attached to a speaker and a list of numbers; Stamper's office, barn, bistro, housekeeper, McLean, and several more that they probably wouldn't need.

'There's plenty of room here,' said Molly, pinning the rehearsal schedule to the cork wall. 'We can keep notes just like we do in Greyport.'

'We'll get people popping in,' said Ian. 'So we must be careful what we put up there. We'll use the filing cabinet for stuff we don't want to share with everyone.' He found two small keys in the lock of the filing cabinet, put one on his own keyring and handed the other to Molly. He opened a small brass trapdoor in the floor and, finding a row of power points, he fed a cable though a hole in one of the desks and plugged in the laptop.

'You can see why they call her the diva,' said Molly, turning on the laptop and connecting it to the WiFi. 'She's a bit fierce, isn't she?'

Ian didn't disagree. 'Perhaps she'll mellow once she's settled in. I liked George, though. But we need to do a bit of background on him. I imagine the opera world is quite cutthroat. We should know if there's any history between them.'

'How does he kill her? In the opera, I mean.'

'He stabs her at the end of act four.'

'Well, he's not going to do that in real life, is he? Not if he hopes to get away with it.'

Ian agreed. However much he hated her, if he even did

hate her, killing her on stage wasn't going to do his career any good. And he'd shown no sign of even mild dislike. In any case, he didn't have the build for violence. He was going to find it hard enough to convincingly stab a woman who was a good three inches taller than he was. But that was a problem for the producer. He and Molly had more serious things to worry about. 'We should plan from day to day,' he said, reading the rehearsal schedule and memorising times when Lucia would be needed in the theatre. 'We'll meet in the afternoon while they're rehearsing and compare notes. The security guys can keep an eye on the theatre.'

'This evening,' said Molly, 'I'll get to know people on the campsite. I haven't unpacked yet so I can play the poor little woman who doesn't know how to put up a tent. Then Ryan and I can eat in the bistro and get chatting to people.'

'That's if Ryan doesn't monopolise them with learned facts about alpacas,' said Ian.

Molly laughed. 'I sometimes wonder if he spends too much time with my dad,' she said. 'He's seven going on eighteen and geeky.'

'He put the diva in her place, though,' said Ian. 'I was impressed.'

'Tomorrow I'll start checking on George. I'm guessing I'll have the house pretty much to myself. Gav's going to be welcoming everyone in the barn. Then the chorus are rehearsing on stage until lunchtime.'

'The soloists?' Ian ran his finger down the list. 'Ah, duet sessions with the voice coach in the music room here. More shouting, I suppose. Lucia's not needed until after lunch so I'll stay up at Inverbank with her and try to get to know her a bit.'

'Good luck with that,' said Molly. 'Do you think this voice coach bloke will shout at her as well?'

'I might eavesdrop for a bit and find out,' said Ian. 'And once she's safely singing duets I want to go over to the shop and have a read through their knitting patterns. Let's meet here at, shall we say, four-thirty for a catch-up?'

'Fine,' said Molly. 'It's great that Ryan's going to be involved. That's going to make it so much easier for me.'

And Molly herself was a lot less grumpy since they'd arrived. He left her happily sorting out the office while he went to meet the security team. Stamper had a team of three ex-coppers like himself, although retired rather than invalided out as he had been. There was also a driver drafted in with his car from a local upmarket limousine company. Ian suspected he was also ex-police as they all seemed to know each other. They were a cheerful bunch who regarded being on Stamper's team as a cushy number – well paid and with very little to do. Ian hoped these two weeks were not going to be a shock for them. He also hoped he wasn't going to have trouble remembering who was who. They were all in their late fifties, well-built and rugged-looking with similar close-cropped haircuts. And harder still, they all had very ordinary names. Tom, Rob, Bill and Dave. Rob at least wore a chauffeur's peaked cap so he would be easily recognised, except of course when he wasn't wearing it. Dave had a beard and Ian had to stop himself from forbidding him to shave it off in case he didn't recognise him. Tom and Rob, he gathered, lived in the same street so he decided they would become part of his team up at Inverbank. The other two would carry on as normal while being extra alert to the apparent threat to Lucia.

10

Some people were horse or dog whisperers. Mickey Rix, Ian decided, was a diva whisperer. Within minutes of her arrival, he had Lucia Pedro Morales eating out of his hand.

He was standing at the hotel entrance to meet her, Ian having called ahead to say they were on their way. They drove from Dundas in a convoy because Inverbank was isolated by a drive through narrow lanes and up steep hills. Ian led the way in his car, making sure the other driver didn't get lost. If they had, he could almost hear Lucia's complaints in his head and the last thing he wanted was for her to arrive too bad-tempered to be polite to Mickey.

He needn't have worried. Mickey held out a hand and led her up the steps into the hotel as if she were stepping onto a red carpet. He snapped his fingers, and a young man called Jock appeared instantly to carry her luggage, and he escorted her upstairs himself. Ian followed with a music case that she'd left on the back seat of the car.

'Such an adorable room,' she said, looking around as Mickey threw open the door to the Rose Room. She picked up a pink glass bottle from the dressing table and used the tasselled bulb to treat her wrists to what Ian assumed was rose perfume.

They were followed into the room by Jock with her suitcases, which he put on a stand near the door. 'Would you like someone to unpack for you?' he asked.

'That won't be necessary,' she said, giving him a look that suggested she suspected he was intent on looting her luggage.

Jock nodded politely and walked out of the room, slowly and backwards with glances towards Lucia's handbag.

'I'll see about tips when I leave,' she said. 'If everything is satisfactory until then.'

Would they all line up by the door as she left? Ian wondered. Hat in hand and holding out hopeful palms?

'We'll leave you to settle in,' said Mickey. 'Just ring if you need anything.' He pointed to a silk cord that hung near the bed. 'Would you care to join me for dinner?' he asked. 'Or would you prefer something on a tray?'

'I'd love to join you for dinner,' she purred at him. Then she turned to Ian. 'I shan't be needing you again tonight,' she said. 'Be ready to leave at eleven-thirty tomorrow.'

That put him in his place. He wondered if he should wear a cap to doff at moments like this. 'I'll let your driver know,' he said, trying not to sound irritable.

He and Mickey returned downstairs, and Ian cheered up considerably when Elsa appeared. 'All settled in?' she asked. 'Is she a nightmare?'

'Not if you know how to handle her,' said Mickey. 'She's joining me for dinner. Could you ask them to prepare the table in the alcove by the window? It's not been booked, has it?'

'I'll reserve it,' she said. 'We'll eat in the kitchen,' she told Ian. 'What's the name of her driver and the bloke that came with them? I'll make sure we have a meal for them as well.'

'The driver is Rob, and the security man is Tom. The three of us will be taking shifts overnight sitting in the cars on the drive. One awake and the other two sleeping.'

'That doesn't sound very comfortable. We have a chalet that's not occupied yet, so do tell them they can use it. There's a couple of beds, a small shower room and a kitchen with tea and coffee-making stuff.'

'I know they'd appreciate that,' said Ian. 'But make sure you invoice Stamper for it.'

'And what about you?'

'I can sleep in my car when I'm not on watch, or we can do shifts with the beds.'

Elsa took his hand. 'I think we can do better than that,' she said.

The next morning, his alarm waking him at seven, Ian walked Lottie and then ate a large breakfast cooked by Flora. He was standing with Tom and Rob on the drive promptly at eleven-thirty. It was five to twelve when Lucia appeared, having ordered breakfast in her room at eleven-fifteen. Ian glanced at Stamper's rehearsal schedule and hoped that he'd allowed for his star to arrive late.

She nodded curtly at him as he held the car door open for her. 'Have someone fetch my music case for me, would you?'

A 'please' might have been nice, but he didn't want to hold things up any longer, and at that moment Mickey appeared with the case and placed it on the seat next to her. *Just as well,* Ian thought. At least they'd set off with the diva's temper soothed by Mickey's attentions. Elsa waved and winked at him as he got into his own car and set off.

He delivered Lucia safely to the barn, where they had cleared the stage of chorus members ready for a run-through of the duets with the rehearsal pianist, a stern-looking woman with horn-rimmed spectacles who was drumming her fingers impatiently on the piano lid. George Strike and a young woman Ian assumed was Cara Curtis, AKA Michaëla, were standing on the stage. Quentin Lyle, the shouty voice coach, was sprawling in a seat in the front row, ready to stand up and shout, Ian supposed, if anything wasn't to his liking.

The pianist placed her hands on the keys but had played no more than a couple of introductory chords when Lucia marched onto the stage from the wings. Quentin buried his head in his hands and the pianist stopped playing and scowled at her over the top of the piano lid.

'I need to do the Habanera first,' said Lucia, all but pushing Cara out of the way and smiling flirtatiously at George. 'I warmed my voice up in the car. I can't risk my throat getting cold.' She wrapped a silk scarf around her neck as if about to ward off an imminent blizzard. Then strode to the front of the stage and glared at the pianist. 'Ready,' she said, snapping her fingers at the woman, who flicked crossly through the pages of her score and sighed loudly.

'Make up your flipping minds,' she muttered, finding the correct page and wedging it onto the music desk as if she'd just taken it hostage and didn't plan on freeing it until someone had paid her a large ransom. Or agreed to send a helicopter to rescue her from what could well become the worst day of her working life. Ian assumed that her usual work consisted of playing hymns on a wheezy church organ and bribing reluctant children to practise scales.

Stamper, no doubt alerted by the sound of no one actually rehearsing anything, appeared from the wings. 'Everything okay?' he asked.

'Just a teeny change in the schedule, darling,' said Lucia, smiling sweetly at him. 'No one minds a bit, do they?' She glanced around as if daring anyone to say that they minded, which Ian was fairly certain they did. Quentin still had his head buried in his hands and seemed to have given up any idea of voice coaching, the pianist looked mutinous, Cara had ambled sulkily off the stage and was now sitting in the auditorium with her eyes shut. Only George looked unfazed, sitting on the edge of the stage with his legs dangling down into the orchestra pit as if waiting for the next part of the plot to unfold.

Ian decided he couldn't stand around waiting for them to resolve things and start rehearsing. He needed to find Molly and see how she was getting on. She'd probably have life histories from most of the chorus and orchestra by now. He headed to the bistro and picked up coffee and muffins for both of them, which he carried away in a cardboard tray, Lottie at his heels.

He found Molly in their office with the laptop open in front of her. Ian put the tray down on her desk and she looked up at him. 'Hi,' she said. 'Ooh, coffee, just what I need.' She took a sip of coffee and a bite of her muffin. Lottie put out a paw and tapped her hopefully on the leg. 'No muffin for you, Lottie, you'll get fat.'

'Come here, Lottie,' said Ian, reaching into one of the

desk drawers where he had left a stash of dog biscuits. He threw one to Lottie and she settled herself under the desk at his feet and started to chew. 'Been busy?' he asked.

'Just reading an email from Duncan,' she said. 'Some interesting stuff about Andy Meade.'

Ian sat at his own desk and Molly turned the laptop round so that he could read it.

Hi you two, enjoying yourselves? Found out one or two things about your man Andy Meade. He was arrested but not charged after a drunken brawl outside a pub near Murray Leaf a couple of years ago. He spent a night in a cell sobering up but no one was hurt so they let him go the next morning. He was also a person of interest in a fraud case about eighteen months ago. No charges but a lot of ill will. Something to do with selling fake vintage whisky. Let me know if you need more and I'll get hold of the case notes for you.

'That could be a motive, don't you think?' said Molly. 'If he'd lost all their money for them, they might have felt like killing him.'

'I suppose they might,' said Ian. How likely was it, though? They didn't even know that Andy Meade *had* been murdered. But there must have been suspicions about last year. Why else would someone link it with a threat to Lucia? Or was that just coincidence? Someone had it in for Lucia, and as far as they were concerned, it wouldn't hurt to remind her that people died during opera camp. On the other hand, if someone planned to kill Lucia, why warn her first? Didn't that just make it more difficult? Or was it someone who knew about the threat but wanted to warn her? Withholding that type of knowledge was a serious offence, so it could only have been someone close to the potential killer. Or was there actually no threat at all – someone just didn't want Lucia there? But she was there so that had failed. The only person who knew whether the threat was genuine was Lucia herself, and so far she'd proved less than helpful about it. So he was back to trying to link her with Andy Meade.

'We need to know who remembers him from last year,' he said. 'You're good at getting all the gossip. See if you can find anyone who had a grudge against him.' But there were so many people there; not just those involved in the opera, but their families, members of staff, members of the public...

'I need to narrow it down,' said Molly, who must have read his mind. 'I put together a little questionnaire and handed it round after Gav's welcome this morning. I asked if they'd had any experience of opera camps before, and how they'd heard about this one. I was just sorting through them. I can probably leave anyone who is here for the first time. There are twenty-four in the orchestra and fifteen, not counting the children, in either the chorus or playing minor roles. Only sixteen of those were here last year. Six in the orchestra and ten onstage. I don't know how many of them were here with families, but I thought I could ask about that when I talk to them.'

'Excellent,' said Ian. 'Any of the same people in leading roles last year?'

'Just Cara and George. And Gav, of course. Some of this year's chorus had minor solo roles last year. *HMS Pinafore* is much easier to sing, apparently. That's why Gav chose it. He knew it would be difficult to get professionals when lockdown had barely ended.'

'Do we know how many behind the scenes and front of house people were here last year?' Ian asked.

'There are ten altogether. Most already work for Gav on the farm or in the office, and all but two were here last year.'

'That's another eight we should keep an eye on. Andy will have known them better than the musicians who are outsiders.'

'But if they'd wanted to do him in, they could have done it any time. Why wait for the opera?'

'A good point. Lack of opportunity, perhaps. It's not easy to inject someone with a lethal dose of something when you're working out in the open. It would be a lot easier backstage in the dark,' said Ian. 'See what you can find out about the backstage people and I'll try to discover why our diva thinks she's also under threat.'

'If she's not just being temperamental and does have a reason to think someone's out to get her, then we should be trying to find a link between her and Andy.'

What kind of link could there be? 'I can't think how there could be,' said Ian. 'I don't think she's ever been to Scotland before and they hardly share the same interests, do they?'

Molly drained her coffee and wiped some muffin crumbs from her fingers. 'What do we do next?' she asked.

'I'm going to try and find out who wrote the letter. It was hand delivered so we're probably looking for someone local.'

'That might be where we find our link. A sender who knew both of them,' said Molly. 'The shop here would be a good place to start.'

'That's what I was thinking. And remember, Cara is local. Didn't Gavin tell us she had family nearby?'

'Do you think Cara could be involved? Andy sounds like the type who might have made unwelcome advances.'

'Possibly, but would she also have it in for Lucia?' Although, thinking about this morning's spat in the theatre, she could have all manner of reasons for hating Lucia.

'She might be jealous,' Molly suggested. 'It's all quite cut-throat, isn't it? Perhaps they've gone for the same roles or something like that.'

'We'll add her to our list of people to check,' said Ian. 'She's been working with Edinburgh Opera, so have a look at their website and see what kind of roles she's doing. And try to find out exactly where she was when Andy died and what she was doing half an hour or so before that.'

'That should keep us both busy this afternoon.' Ian looked at her warily, but he could see none of the grumpiness she'd shown in Greyport. Hopefully whatever had been bugging her a day or two ago had now passed and she was back to her usual energetic, helpful self. It must help being here; both Molly and Ryan were throwing themselves into things. Not just the work but socially. 'What's on the schedule for this evening?' He studied the timetable Molly had pinned to the wall. 'Band call after dinner from eight to ten. That will just be the orchestra, won't it?'

'With the MD,' said Molly.

'MD?'

'Musical director. We met him the day we visited. You remember. Quentin the voice coach.'

'Oh yeah, bad-tempered guy. He was in the theatre looking glum when I arrived. Was *he* here last year?'

Molly checked her list. 'No,' she said. 'He did some coaching before the camp started but wasn't here once they'd started rehearsals.' She ran her finger down the list. 'But it says here that an Oliver Lyle was the MD. Do you think that's his brother?'

'That's interesting,' said Ian. 'Can you ask Stamper? If they are brothers, we'd better check out both of them.'

He printed Duncan's email and locked it in the filing cabinet. Then he looked around for anything else that shouldn't be on general view. But it was all very tidy. Molly was doing a good job. He hoped she was taking some time off, not just spending every minute in the office. 'If it's only the orchestra rehearsing this evening, what will everyone else be doing?' he asked, hoping there would be something social that Molly could join in with.

'From what they told me about last year, people hang around chatting in the bistro, some walk to the village pub, there's a group that likes to sing madrigals, and sometimes they have a barbeque on the campsite.'

'Sounds fun,' he said, with a slight twinge of regret that he was going to miss it all. 'I've not had orders from the diva yet, but she's taken to her host at Inverbank so I'm guessing she'll want to go there for dinner. It looks as if Lottie and I will be stuck up there for the evening, but it's a good area for walks, isn't it, Lottie?'

'Are Tom and Rob good company?' Molly asked.

'They're fine, but of course one of us is always on watch so we don't get much time to socialise. The hotel staff are very friendly though, and the food is great.'

Molly laughed. 'I won't feel too sorry for you then.'

'Any idea what the stars will be doing without Lucia causing mayhem?'

'Cara looks like the type to sing madrigals, don't you think?'

Ian had no idea what a madrigal type looked like and perhaps Cara might have done enough singing for one day and would just go home.

'Quentin doesn't live far away and he's not very sociable,' added Molly. 'I expect he'll just go home. I'd imagine Gav and George will be here in the house.'

Probably, Ian thought. He wondered why there was no Mrs Stamper. Or perhaps there was, and she just kept out of the way. Or perhaps the role of Mrs Stamper was an impermanent one, there having been several in the past, but right now Gavin was between wives. Ian could almost feel sorry for the man if he lived in this beautiful house on his own, miles from anywhere with only alpacas for company and a career long ago finished. But from what he'd seen of Stamper so far, he was a jovial type who appeared to be enjoying his current life with or without a significant other. He seemed to be free of the drug or alcohol addiction and general angst displayed by music stars at the wrong end of their careers. Perhaps Stamper had always wanted to be a Scottish farmer and his boy-band days had just been a step towards his ambitions; a way to make enough to fund it all.

11

Ian and Molly grabbed a quick lunch in the bistro. Ryan bounced in and then out again, saying he was having lunch with his new best friend, whose family was conveniently staying in a tent very close to his and Molly's. 'He's adapting well,' said Ian.

'He's loving every minute. We both are,' said Molly, taking a bite of salad-filled brioche.

'Good,' said Ian. 'There's nothing like getting stuck into a case that's a bit different to lift the spirits. Lovely place as well, beautiful scenery, good food and lots to occupy us. What more could we want?'

'It's Gav that's really made it for me,' she said.

'Of course, your teenage idol. Is he all you expected?'

'It's only partly that.'

'Oh, yeah?' he said, giving her what he hoped was a knowing, fatherly look.

'I should have explained,' she said. 'I'm sorry, I was feeling a bit off before we came up here. I was in a foul mood.'

'That's okay. We all have off days. Were you worried about your dad?'

'No, not really. Well, only that if this thing with Joy gets serious, Ryan and I may have to move. But that's not a problem. Dad's not going to throw us out. Ryan and I can find a place in the village. No, this was because of Caroline. And I feel bad about that.'

'Caroline? You've fallen out with her?'

'No, not at all. She didn't tell you what happened?'

'I haven't seen her for a while.'

'No, of course, it was when you were in France.'

'What happened?' What kind of unfeeling, selfish idiot was he? She'd called him and all he'd said was that he'd be away for two weeks.

'Her ex turned up one evening saying he wanted a reconciliation. She told him to get lost and he tried to force his way in, so she punched him.'

Good for her, he thought. But maybe not such a good idea. Could this guy have her up on an assault charge? 'Is he still hanging around?'

Molly shook her head. 'She'd made a note of his car registration and called Duncan. He traced the car back to the border, so it looks like he was heading south. But she was a bit scared, so she came and stayed with us for a couple of nights. Dad got straight on to the solicitor who had dealt with me and Tel and now there's a restraining order against him.'

Ian pulled out his phone and tapped in Caroline's number. There was no reply. 'Where is she now?' he asked. 'She shouldn't be on her own.'

'She's staying with her sister in Perth until they're sure he's back in London and aware of the restraining order.'

Ian looked at the panini on his plate and no longer felt

hungry. 'I feel terrible. I should have been there for her. But I don't see why you should feel bad. You and your father took her in. It seems to me she's lucky to have you both as friends.'

'The trouble is that she made me realise that I could be in the same position. Tel, my ex, will be up for parole in a few months. I didn't feel I could talk to Dad about it. He's been so good to us already. Caroline has her own problems. I was losing sleep worrying about what I'd do if he came for Ryan.'

'You didn't think you could talk to me?'

'I was worried about my job. I was afraid you wouldn't want me working for you if Tel could turn up at the office and threaten me.'

'Rubbish,' he said. 'Molly, you and I are a team. I'll do anything I can to protect you. We've still got nearly two weeks here, but when we get back, we can think about what we need to do to keep you safe.'

'It'll be a few months and there's a good chance he won't even get parole. But what's really made me feel better is talking to Gav. That day I was here last week, I got a bit tearful and poured it all out to him. He got straight onto his legal people, who found a family law firm and we called them. They told me I could get a file together and object to the parole and after I told them what had happened to us, they were sure I'd have a good case. I was worried it would all be very expensive, but Gav's going to give me some work. Just some stuff I can do at home. It won't take time away from working with you. And he'll cover the legal costs.'

Well, that was quite a mouthful. But good for Stamper for making Molly feel better. He suspected the work he gave her would be nowhere near enough to cover legal expenses. But if it allowed her to accept help without her feeling like a charity case, then he was grateful to Stamper for his sensitivity. And to Stamper, any financial contribution would just be a drop in the ocean. 'I'm glad he was able to help,' said Ian, wondering if he should thank him or whether it was better to keep quiet. 'And remember I'm here to help as well, okay? Don't keep your worries to yourself.'

'Thanks,' said Molly, looking embarrassed and glancing at her watch. 'I'd better get back and start checking people.'

'I'll go to the shop and chat about knitting. I'll see you back in the office before I head off to Inverbank.'

Ian strolled across the car park, stopping to pass the time of day with some alpacas on the way. He stood by the fence, Lottie cowering at his feet, and worried about Caroline. He should have known something was wrong. She'd called him and he'd more or less brushed her off with all his talk about the time he'd be spending at Dundas. Jeanie had been right. He should have done more to nurture their friendship. *Was it too late?* he wondered. He tried calling her again. Still no answer, but this time he left a message. Perth was not far from Dundas. Why not drop in for a chat? Then, trying to keep the mood light, he suggested it could be a good time for her to get to know some alpaca friends of his. He put his phone away and, to Lottie's obvious relief, strolled across to the shop.

There were a few people browsing inside. They were wearing walking boots and carrying maps, so presumably weren't from the opera camp. A woman in a purple cagoule was trying to choose an alpaca wool rug, insisting half a dozen should be unfolded and spread out in front of her. An impatient husband, Ian assumed, stood to one side, sighing and looking at his watch.

Ian found several books about alpacas, tartan boxes of fudge, whisky-flavoured chocolate, and pens with pictures of alpacas stamped on them. Nothing about knitting, which knocked his theory that the letter had been put together by someone directly connected to the farm on the head. The rug-buying couple eventually made their choice and a woman, whose badge suggested that her name was Margot, wrapped it up for them. As the couple left, she sighed and started refolding rugs and stacking them back onto their shelves. 'Can I help you, love?' she asked.

'I don't think you can,' said Ian. 'I was hoping to find something about knitting with alpaca wool.'

'We don't sell anything like that,' she said. 'You need to try the shop in the village. They have knitting magazines. Quite popular, I think.'

Ian could believe it. He imagined a village packed with women like Lainie, all knitting furiously. 'Is it far?' he asked, not remembering driving though a village on his way there.

'Turn right out of the car park. It's about half a mile down the road. You'll not have seen it if you drove up from Perth.'

Ian thanked her and, keeping Lottie on her lead, followed Margot's directions to the village.

It was a pleasant walk along a quiet lane with wildflowers growing along the verge and a whiff of what Ian imagined was alpaca wafting on a gentle breeze. He might well have been inspired to try his hand at poetry if he'd been able to think of anything that rhymed with alpaca. Lottie, still suspicious of the strange, curly-haired creatures that stared at her over the fence, kept close to his side. As they neared the first houses in the village, Ian looked out for signs of a shop. He spotted an advert for ice cream about a hundred yards in front of him and headed towards it.

Arriving at the shop, he found a sign that announced *Gregory's Handy Stores – if we don't stock it, you don't need it.* Below the sign was an iron rail next to a drinking bowl with a pattern of paws along its edge. Dog walkers, he supposed, were frequent visitors to the shop. He fastened Lottie's lead to the rail and opened the door with a ping of an old-fashioned bell on a coil of wire. It was quiet and dark inside. A maze of tall shelves piled high with cans of food, packets of cereal, cakes in boxes and biscuits in tins. It was impossible to see from one end of the shop to the other, so he made his way along the rows, past baskets of fruit and vegetables, packets of soap and detergent, kitchen utensils, packets of aspirin and throat lozenges, eventually making his way to a checkout where he spotted, among bars of chocolate and packets of chewing gum, a rack with newspapers and magazines.

At the checkout Ian found a man – Gregory himself? – whose age he was unable to guess. Although he looked lean and fit, he also looked well beyond retirement age, but his eyesight must have been okay. He was sitting behind the cash register knitting something sludge-coloured on very large needles. It reminded Ian of one of his great-aunt Elsie's dishcloths. Ian was the only customer in the shop, and he coughed gently to attract the man's attention.

'Can I help you?' Gregory, if that's who he was, asked.

'I'm looking for knitting magazines,' said Ian, glancing at the rack of publications and not seeing anything about knitting. 'Do you stock any?'

'You knit as well?'

'No,' Ian admitted. 'I'm just asking for a friend.' Well, if he bought a magazine, he was certain Lainie would give it a good home.

'I don't keep any in stock,' said Gregory. 'I can order them when anyone wants one.'

'Have you ordered any recently?'

Gregory pondered this for a moment. 'Aye, I've a regular order. Comes in monthly. Last one was a couple of weeks ago.'

'For yourself?' Ian asked, nodding at the knitting.

'No,' he said with a chuckle. 'I don't use patterns and the like. This is just a dog blanket. Plain knitting, nothing fancy.'

Ian was just wondering if Gregory also owned the dog who was about to be treated to a new blanket, when an extremely ancient dog pottered out from the behind the counter and sniffed at his shoes. It was grey muzzled and walked stiffly. If any dog deserved the comfort of a warm blanket, it was this one. Ian bent down to pat it, and was rewarded with a weak wag of its tail.

'Old Jesse,' said Gregory. 'Suffers from arthritis something chronic.'

'Poor old thing,' said Ian. He watched as the dog returned creakily behind the counter. They were getting rather off-topic. 'This monthly order,' he asked. 'Is it for someone in the village?'

'Aye, who else would it be for?'

A good point. 'Can you tell me who?'

'Maudie Croft. Lives in one of them cottages over there.' He waved vaguely towards a row of houses a few yards further down the road. 'The one with them stupid men in the garden.'

'Stupid men?'

'Yeah, you know. Can't remember what they're called. Got beards and pointy red hats.'

'Oh,' said Ian, suddenly realising what he was talking about. 'Garden gnomes.'

'Can't see the point of them myself.'

'And she's a keen knitter, this Maudie Croft?'

'Suppose she must be. Busy right now though. Her granddaughter's staying with her.'

'She's an elderly lady, then?'

'Yeah, she's registered to collect her pension here.' He waved at a glassed-in cubicle, which Ian assumed was the post office part of the shop. 'Or she was until they started paying it into her bank account. She's not going to win any glamorous granny competitions so I'm guessing she's somewhere around my age.'

Next to the post office counter was a rack of envelopes and writing paper. *Not a big seller,* Ian guessed, looking at the labels, which were turning brown with age. No one wrote letters any more or bought many stamps, he supposed. And pensions were all paid online now so post offices were little used these days. The only trade he could think of was people posting parcels of stuff they'd sold on eBay.

He didn't think he could leave empty-handed so he picked up a bag of sherbet lemons from the rack of sweets, then added some extra strong mints. 'Thanks for your help,' he said. He tapped his card onto the machine and left to retrieve Lottie.

As he walked back to Dundas, he thought over what Gregory had told him. Had he found his anonymous letter writer? A granny with a regular order of knitting magazines and access to old-style notepaper and envelopes. He hadn't asked about the nail polish, although he had spotted some on his walk along the shelves. Had it been old? Very likely, he thought. Everything else in the shop was. Including the owner and his dog.

He'd need to talk to Maudie Croft, but he could hardly barge in on her and accuse her of sending threatening letters. He'd ask Molly to find out a bit more about her first. A more pressing problem right now was how to persuade the diva to tell him why she had been sent the letter. A problem as Lucia, apart from giving him orders, was very reluctant to talk to him. Stamper might be able to persuade her, he supposed. Or would it be better to wait until she was back at Inverbank, where she seemed a lot more amenable?

12

As he passed the barn on his way back, Ian could hear shouting. Three voices, he thought. One he knew was that of Quentin Lyle, whose shouting he had heard before. Of the other two he recognised Lucia, who didn't exactly shout but who had a voice that could penetrate triple layers of glass and would probably have the ability to shatter anything thinner. And there was another woman's voice; less of a shout and more of a disgruntled whine. It was the tone of voice that Stephanie had used when he committed a serious sin such as loading the dishwasher incorrectly or when he insisted that he was unable to afford a better car. He couldn't make out what they were saying, but it didn't sound like a discussion about tempi or balance, or whatever it was that singers needed to discuss. Lottie pulled back on her lead as if reluctant to go any closer. Ian was inclined to agree with her.

George Strike was leaning against a wall of the barn, sucking a lollipop. He waved it at Ian. 'Menthol,' he said. 'Keeps the vocal cords lubricated. Tastes vile though.' He stopped sucking and stuck it top first into a pot of hydrangeas.

'What's going on?' Ian asked, nodding towards the barn.

'Just a tiff among the gypsies.'

'Sorry?'

'You know the scene at the tavern? Carmen and her two gypsy mates dance for the soldier bloke. It's just a run-through with the pianist but Lucia said the two gypsy girls were encroaching into her sweet space on stage.'

'Sweet space?' He obviously had a lot to learn about theatricals.

'It's the area on stage where she feels the most energy from the audience.'

'I've never heard of that,' said Ian.

'Not sure it really exists. It's just a bit of hype put about by temperamental performers with big egos.'

'Seems to be causing a lot of trouble.'

'She was exerting her status and accused them of being incompetent amateurs. One of the girls, Marylin I think she's called, started arguing. Believe me, no one argues with Lucia and survives. If we weren't in the back of beyond, Marylin would be out on her ear by now.'

'I thought you and Lucia were friends?' Ian was puzzled by the off-stage politics, the cast sniping and gossiping behind each other's backs.

'We are, dear boy,' he said. 'I'm very fond of Lucia. Most of the time.'

'How long have you known her?' he asked.

'Must be more than ten years. I met her when I was just emerging as a soloist. She was already well established but we hit it off somehow. I was no threat, I suppose, and she quite liked having me around, a gay best friend. A lot of women like to have one of those. I was someone she could gossip with and share secrets.'

'And did you?'

'What, share secrets? Yes, we were both quite good at getting entangled with the wrong kind. Lucia issued marching orders to a couple of my unfortunate liaisons. That was before I grew up and became more discriminating. She's not had to do it recently.'

'And did you do the same for her?'

'Just the once. Mostly her affairs didn't last long, but there was one I saw through right away. He was only after Lucia as a route to UK citizenship.'

'He planned to marry her?'

'He did. It was all about to happen, but I tipped off the immigration people and they put a stop to it.'

'How did Lucia respond to that?' Not well, he assumed.

'She was furious. Didn't speak to me for months. But then we heard he'd tried the same thing with a number of other women, and she realised I'd done her a favour. Not that she ever admitted it. Made out she'd seen right through the guy and broken it off herself.'

They were interrupted by more shouting. A man's voice this time. 'Sounds like Quentin is giving them an earful as well,' said Ian.

'No change there, then,' said George as Stamper appeared through the tunnel. George looked him and smiled. 'Just in time to stop the cat fight,' he said.

'Oh, good God, they're not at each other's throats already, are they?'

'I'm afraid so. I was about to go and do my shmaltzy rose-sniffing bit and get press-ganged into joining the smugglers. But they won't get to that before the tea break at this rate. Might as well go and put my feet up with a good book.

Far be it from me to question your choice of leading lady, mate. I admire Lucia as much as anyone, but it's going to need a miracle to get this production together by the end of the week. Text me if I'm needed,' he said as he disappeared into the tunnel.

Stamper sighed and grinned ruefully at Ian. 'I'd better go and calm things down,' he said.

'Good luck,' said Ian. He made his way to the house and into the office, where Molly was making lists.

'Possible suspects,' she said. 'Two lists, actually. One of people who had it in for Andy and one for Lucia haters.'

Ian studied the lists. 'What are you basing it on?'

'Bits of gossip I've picked up. It may seem like a relaxed, friendly set-up but it's seething with resentments under the surface.'

'Yeah, I've just seen an example of that. What have you discovered?'

'Women who say Andy rejected them. Women who couldn't get rid of him. Men who accused him of making out with their wives or girlfriends.'

'In other words, a pain in the backside. Motives for murder, do you think?'

'Not sure. We need to know more about them.'

Ian tapped a name on the list. 'What's he doing there? He wasn't here last year, was he?'

'Quentin Lyle? Not as MD. He came in to do some voice coaching. I checked with Gav. As we thought, Oliver and Quentin are brothers and Oliver was MD last year. There's a rumour that he gave Andy Meade a lot of money for some whisky scam he was running.'

'Sounds like a motive. We'd better add Oliver to your list.'

'I've done a bit of a check on the two of them. They both

taught at a posh boys' school not far from here. Quentin's still there but Oliver left a few months ago.'

'Do you know exactly when? And why?'

'Beginning of March.'

'Mid term? A bit unusual, isn't it?'

'I got chatting to one of the mums, whose youngest is in the chorus with Ryan. Her older son is at the school, and she told me there were rumours of some scandal that was hushed up. Something to do with misuse of school funds the previous academic year.'

'So the year they did *Pinafore,* Oliver was here as MD and Andy Meade was working backstage. That could be interesting.'

'Can we ask Duncan if Oliver Lyle was involved in the fraud he mentioned? It would link him to Andy Meade.'

'I'll call him later,' said Ian. 'Is there anything to connect him to Lucia?'

'Only through his brother, who is this year's MD. I don't think Quentin's worked with Lucia before and I don't think they like each other very much now.'

'Lucia seems to hate everyone apart from Stamper. Oh, and Mickey Rix has managed to charm her. She's involved in a slanging match with Quentin right now, along with a couple of gypsies.'

'It makes the opera itself feel quite tame, doesn't it?'

'The leading players certainly seem to be at each other's throats. Stamper's trying to sort them out.'

'I don't know how he stays so cheerful. George, too. And he's the one that turns into the murderer.'

'He was just telling me he's known Lucia for years. Quite close friends, I think. Did you find out anything about him?'

'Nothing incriminating. He's had a steady career and is

well liked. He's got a Facebook page where there are lots of complimentary posts about him.'

'Twitter?'

'Very little. He did something on TV during lockdown and no one posted any unpleasant tweets.'

'So he's not on either of your lists?'

'No. He seems to have been well liked last year as Frederick,' said Molly. 'One woman said she thought he was a bit chubby for the part of a young cabin boy. Nothing worse. They all liked his voice.'

'He's rather vain, but he'd hardly have taken murderous offence to being described as chubby, so he's probably not planning to do anyone in this year. And there's nothing to suggest he had anything against Andy Meade. Or even knew who he was.'

'What did you find out at the shop?'

'They don't sell knitting magazines there. I had to go to the village shop. They don't sell them there either, but there is one woman who orders one every month. Could you check her out? Her name's Maudie Croft and she lives in a cottage with a garden full of gnomes. She currently has her granddaughter staying with her. I'll go and talk to her, but I'd like to know a bit more about her first.'

'Okay, I'll get onto that tomorrow. I'm about to nip back to Greyport while Ryan's busy in the kids' tent. He's run out of clean clothes. Do you need anything?'

Ian shook his head. 'Just check that Lainie's okay.'

'I was planning to. She might need something from the shops. What are you doing this evening?'

'I'll get back to Inverbank as soon as Lucia's finished. I'm gearing myself up to talk to her this evening and she seems nicer when she's not here.'

Molly patted the pocket of her jacket to make sure she

had her car keys, then tidied away some coffee mugs and muffin wrappers and locked her lists into the filing cabinet. 'I'll see you tomorrow, then,' she said, slinging her bag over one shoulder and heading towards the tunnel.

Ian looked at his watch. Half an hour and he'd be on his way back to Inverbank. It had been a good day. He'd discovered a possible source of the letter, they'd learnt a lot about how an opera production worked and a fair bit about artistic temperaments. And no one had been murdered. Shouting and threats, but all rather trivial. It was a bit like dogs snarling at each other before deciding whether a fight would be worth the effort.

He checked the board to make sure they hadn't pinned up anything they wouldn't want to share. Not much danger of that as the door would be locked, but he didn't want to chance someone like a cleaner leaving it open for anyone to wander in and see what they'd been doing. Deciding that everything was in order, he looked at the schedule and checked day two. Soloists on stage in the morning for act four, rehearsing the murder. That would be interesting. Chorus and children with the orchestra in the afternoon. Did that mean Lucia was on the loose? Would she stay and watch that? Probably not. She didn't have a lot of time for anything she was not involved in. He'd better prep Tom and Rob. Who knew where she might want them to drive her to?

13

Tom and Rob knew the way to Inverbank now, so there was no need for Ian to lead the way. Instead, he drove behind them at a distance far enough for him to spot if anyone was following them. At one point, he'd pulled up at a junction and had to wait for a small, red car to pass before he could turn out into the main road. Not a big problem; the road was otherwise deserted, and he had a clear view of Rob's car up ahead. Then, just before the turning to Inverbank, the red car suddenly pulled over to the right and swung left into a narrow lane that led up into the hills. Ian had to brake suddenly and swerve to avoid hitting it. He hooted angrily and made a mental note of the registration number. *Just some tourist*, he thought. Visitors didn't know the lanes well and were often caught out by concealed turnings. Apart from that, the drive was uneventful and they arrived at the hotel a few moments later.

Ian wasn't looking forward to that evening. He was going to have to insist that Lucia told him more about herself and why she was so certain the letter had been aimed at her. Yes, it had been addressed to her, but it was no good her prancing around saying someone wanted to kill her unless she came up with a bit more information about who and why. It would make it a whole lot easier to intercept anything threatening if he knew what the threat was. He'd have to talk to her that evening. He wasn't sure how. If she didn't want to talk to him there wasn't much he could do about it. Molly had already tried, and she was usually very good at getting people to talk to her. But when approached, Lucia had given her a look that suggested she was merely one of the servants, a person of no consequence, and she waved her away impatiently. But if Lucia wanted them to keep her safe, she was going to have to give them an idea of what she wanted to be kept safe from.

Mickey was waiting for them at the entrance with a rose he had cut from his glasshouse and a suggestion of cocktails in the orangery. An invitation Lucia accepted with a flutter of her eyelashes. What did Mickey have that the rest of them lacked? No matter, Mickey was the answer. If anyone could get her talking, he could. He'd suggest that the three of them met for an after-dinner liqueur. Lubricated with a cocktail, wine during dinner and a glass of Mickey's most exclusive, she'd talk to them. Whether what she said would make any sense was another matter, but it was worth a try.

Once Lucia was safely in the orangery with Mickey to take care of her, Ian went with Tom and Rob to their chalet, where Elsa had organised drinks and snacks for them.

'I need a drink,' said Tom. 'Something strong and right now.' He sank into a chair with a sigh.

Ian investigated the drinks Elsa had left for them in the tiny kitchen. 'A nice single malt?' he asked, picking out a bottle of Glenmorangie and pouring three glasses. 'Bad day?'

'Thirty miles of pure hell,' said Rob. 'Open the windows, shut the windows, turn up the aircon, turn it down because it dries her throat. Slow down, speed up, stop talking so she can sleep.'

'And that was just this evening,' said Tom. 'This morning it was half an hour of voice exercises. Sounded like my grandad's pigs being slaughtered.'

Ian laughed. 'I hope Stamper is paying you well.'

'Can't complain about that,' said Rob, taking a slug of his whisky. 'And they're looking after us well here. Could be worse, I suppose.'

'I hate to break it to you lads,' said Ian. 'But you're going to be doing extra time tomorrow. She's not needed in the afternoon. What do you say to getting her away from the place?'

To say they didn't look enthusiastic was an understatement. Tom poured a second glass of whisky and Rob stared out of the window as if trying to remember an urgent appointment tomorrow afternoon. Anything preferable to more hours with Lucia. Root canal treatment, perhaps, or sitting in a barrel of ice for charity.

'You could take her to do a bit of sightseeing or shopping and drop her back here in the evening,' he suggested. 'There are some leaflets at reception. There might be something she fancies doing.'

'What she likes doing,' said Rob, 'is making everyone's life miserable.'

'You could ask Mickey. He probably knows a few aristocrats she could go and have afternoon tea with.' He drained his glass and stood up. 'You've got an hour or two free now. She'll be having dinner and then I need to talk to her.'

'Thank God for small mercies,' said Tom, eyeing the whisky bottle.

'Enjoy your evening,' said Ian. 'I'll let you know when she goes to her room.'

'Fine,' said Rob. 'We'll take the first two watches. You okay to take over at four am?'

It was the reverse of what they'd done last night, which was fair enough. He'd catch a few hours of sleep and then take Lottie for a walk round the grounds to wake himself up. He'd taken to leaving her with them while they were on watch. She enjoyed the attention and Ian knew she would bark and wake them up if they happened to nod off.

He strolled back to the house and found Elsa in the kitchen. 'Join me for a meal?' she asked. 'If you don't mind eating in the kitchen.'

'Not at all,' he said. He'd been hoping she'd ask him to join her again. 'Could you just have a quick word with Mickey? I need to get the diva talking and she's more amenable when he's there. Can he tempt her with his most expensive liqueur, do you think? We could meet when she's finished her dinner.'

'I'll go and ask him now. He's just delivered her to the dining room for what he's named his operatic special. It's a seafood dish that he told her was designed by an Italian chef to nurture the vocal cords. It's not on the menu. He had the chef make it just for her and deliver it to her in person.'

'Operatic special? Did he make that up?'

'Probably. But she's tucking in. She even smiled at the chef.'

Smiling didn't come naturally to the diva. She produced a smile on a limited number of occasions to a small and select group of favoured people. 'What is it Mickey has that the rest of us lack? Although, come to think of it, she's like that with Stamper as well.'

Elsa shrugged. 'No idea. Perhaps they're both used to dealing with prima donnas.' She stood up and uncorked a bottle of wine, which she pushed in his direction. 'I'll go and have a word with Mickey now, then we can eat. Help yourself to a glass of wine.'

Ian felt relaxed and well fed later that evening when he joined Mickey and Lucia, who were sitting in a quiet corner of the orangery. The diva, Ian noticed, had tucked Mickey's rose into the collar of her dress and patted it gently as he poured her a glass of vintage Remy Martin from an expensive-looking cut-glass bottle.

She took a sip. 'Ah, exquisite,' she said. Then she looked up and noticed Ian. She scowled at him, looking for a moment like Kezia Wallace, the DCI who dropped into his life now and then, and was not usually good news.

'I told you I don't need you until the morning,' she said, waving a dismissive arm in his direction.

Not a good start. But Mickey wasn't letting it go that easily.

'Dear lady,' he said, leaning forward in his chair with a wink at Ian that she didn't notice. He indicated that he should pull up a chair and join them. 'Ian is the top detective around here. He's caught murderers, you know.'

Ian smiled modestly.

'He is making your safety a priority right now,' Mickey continued. 'I know you've had a long and arduous day, but if you could spare him a moment, it would put all our minds at rest.'

Lucia sighed. 'Very well. I can spare you a few minutes. What is it you want?'

Ian sat down between them, and Mickey handed him a glass of the brandy. It looked like it was now or never. Lucia would be in a mellow mood, full of specially cooked food and warmed by expensive brandy.

'It's the letter Mr Stamper forwarded to you,' Ian said. 'It would be a great help to us if you could say why you think it's aimed at you.'

She stared at him in silence for a moment. Then took a sip of her brandy. 'It was addressed to me. You are supposed to find out who sent it.'

'And I'm making progress there,' said Ian. 'But what I want to know is why it was sent.'

'Isn't it obvious?' she said with an impatient sigh. 'It was a threat. Someone wants to kill me.'

'Do have any idea who would want to kill you?'

'I can't give you a name, if that's what you mean, but there have been death threats before.'

Interesting, he thought. That *would* make her nervous. 'Were the threats letters like the recent one?'

'Not letters, exactly, but there's been a lot on social media.'

'There's always a lot of that on social media about people who are in the public eye. Especially, I'm afraid to say, women.'

'You're saying I'm making it up?' She stared at him angrily.

'No, not at all. Some of these people do carry out threats. What I'm saying is that it's difficult to trace them.'

'So you're not up to the job.'

'Of course he's up to the job,' said Mickey. 'He solved the Lansman murder.'

'The hotel owner?' For the first time since he'd met her, Lucia looked at him with a glimmer of respect. 'I stayed at one of Lansman's hotels once. It was in Milan. I was singing at La Scala.' She turned to Mickey. 'Do you know Milan?'

'Never been there,' said Mickey. 'I hear it's very beautiful.'

'Oh, it is. You really should go there.'

'I'm sure I will,' said Mickey. 'But to get back to…'

'Oh, yes,' she said, in a way that suggested she had forgotten Ian's presence. 'You can find who is trying to murder *me*.' It was a statement, not a question.

'As I told you,' said Ian, hoping he wasn't about to lose patience with the woman, 'we have some interesting leads but perhaps if you can't say *who* it is, it would be a great help to me if you could give me a motive. Why would anyone want to murder you?'

'Revenge,' she said in a tone that suggested he should already know that.

'Revenge for what?'

'It's not important. I don't wish to speak of it.'

He was getting nowhere. If she wasn't going to tell him anything, how on earth was he going to get to the bottom of it? 'Okay,' he said, deciding on a different tack. 'I read that you fell down some stairs at a theatre in London. Do you think someone might have pushed you?'

She stared at him and gasped. 'How did you know that?' She pulled a lace handkerchief from her sleeve and twisted it round her fingers. Suddenly she was no longer the difficult diva. She was a frightened woman. Genuinely scared.

'Tell me what happened,' he said kindly.

'I'd been held up in my dressing room. A call I had to answer. By the time I'd finished everyone else had left. The dressing rooms were on the second floor with a stone staircase down to the stage door. The lights were on timers. By the time I reached the second staircase the light had gone out and I had to feel around for the switch. One of those push button things. You know?'

Ian nodded.

'I remember feeling along the wall for it and then I tripped and suddenly I was falling. Luckily for me I must have screamed, and the doorman heard me. He was the one who called the ambulance.'

'Did you have any feeling that you were not alone on the stairs before you fell?'

'I heard what I thought was one of the dressing room doors shut while I was walking down the first flight. I turned round to check but it was dark at the top of the stairs. I thought I saw movement, but it could have just been shadows. And something tugged my dress while I was trying to find the switch. The police found a piece of it on the stair rail. They said I must have caught it and that was what tripped me.'

'You reported it to the police?' That was good. It would be on record somewhere.

'They came to see me in hospital. The doorman had called them because he had to log it as an incident.'

'So they searched the staircase?'

'Not until the next day. That's when they found the fabric from my dress. The doorman said he searched as soon as I left in the ambulance, but there was no one else in the theatre by then.'

'And the police called on you in hospital and took a statement?'

She shook her head. 'They visited, yes, but they didn't believe I had been pushed. They asked if I'd been drinking. I told them I hadn't, but I don't think they believed me.'

'That was just before lockdown?'

'Two weeks before. Then everything was in chaos. I caught covid while I was in hospital. Luckily not badly. It didn't affect my lungs or my voice. My leg was broken in two places and they had to operate on it. It was in plaster for four months.'

'How did you manage?' Mickey asked, reaching for her hand.

'I could hobble around on crutches in my flat. I had food delivered and I was able to practise my singing every day. But it was only the beginning of a bad time for musicians. I've had very little work since then. That's why I accepted Gavin's invitation.'

'Let's suppose,' said Ian, 'that someone pushed you down the stairs. Do you have any idea who it might have been?'

'It could have been a person paid to do it.'

'You seem very sure of that. Do you know who would have paid them?'

'No.'

'And yet you say someone is after revenge.'

'It's complicated.'

Wasn't it just? But she wasn't going to say any more. He'd have to dig deeper into her past.

Mickey poured her another glass of brandy. 'I'll take this to my room,' she said.

'Just one more question,' said Ian.

She sighed and leant back into her chair.

'Is there anyone at the camp that you've met before?'

'Gavin, of course, and I've known George for years. It's possible Cara might have been singing in a chorus in one of my productions, although I don't remember her. No one else.'

'Not Quentin or Oliver Lyle?'

'I don't think so.'

That was enough for tonight. There was plenty there that Molly could start researching. 'I'll let you get to bed,' said Ian. 'But can you just tell me how you know Gavin Stamper?'

'You should ask Gavin. I'm too tired tonight.' She picked up her glass and left them.

Ian took out his phone and called Rob, telling him it was time to take up his post outside Lucia's window. He looked at his watch and could hardly believe it was nearly eleven-thirty.

He wandered through to the kitchen, where Elsa was checking an inventory before closing it down for the night. 'Cup of tea?' she asked, plugging in the kettle.

'Just a quick one. I need to catch a few hours' sleep before I relieve Tom.'

'Did it go well with Lucia?'

'Not bad. Mickey was a great support. I don't think she'd have opened up the way she did if it had just been me on my own. She still mistakes me for one of the lower order of staff. How is she with you?'

'I don't think she's aware that I exist at all. She treats me a bit like a telephone and just barks orders at me. I assume she's a wonderful singer or no one would put up with her.'

'When she's on stage she's a different person. I've only watched her rehearse but she's wonderful.'

'Sounds like you're smitten.'

'Only when she's in character. The rest of the time she's a complete pain.'

'Did you get the information you needed from her?'

'Partly. She's given me enough to expand my enquiries. And I'm hoping Gavin will be able to elaborate.' He yawned and rinsed his mug in the sink. He wouldn't want Elsa to think he wasn't house-trained, although she probably didn't care one way or the other.

The alarm on his phone woke him at three-thirty, rousing him from a dream in which women in red dresses tumbled down flights of stairs. He dressed quickly and made his way to the car park, where Tom was reading a thriller and Lottie was perched on the back seat wagging her tail at him.

Ian tapped on the window and Tom looked up. 'All quiet?' Ian asked.

'Yeah, nothing to report. A few guests returning late from somewhere although God knows where they go. Must be miles to the nearest civilisation. Rob told me Madame's light went out at midnight so I'm guessing she's sound asleep. Did you get some sleep yourself?'

'Aye, a couple of hours.'

'This middle shift's a killer. I'll head off and try to get back to sleep myself. Rob's snoring like an old pig, I suppose?'

'He was. He must have come in very quietly. Neither of you woke me when you changed shifts.'

Tom climbed out of the car and headed off towards the chalet. Ian led Lottie to his own car and settled them both down with cushions and blankets to watch the dawn.

14

Trailing Rob and Tom in his car back to Dundas the next morning, Ian thought over what Lucia had told him. He could understand now why seeing the letter had scared her. She'd had one frightening experience, and no one had taken it seriously. He was convinced her fall down the stairs was no accident, although he was possibly the only person who thought so. Shouldn't the people who ran the theatre have at least shown a little concern? If only to check the lighting on the stairs and who else had been in the theatre at the time. According to Lucia's account, the police hadn't been any better. Okay, she was a difficult, temperamental person, but that shouldn't mean no one believed her. But everything had been in turmoil around then. The country was verging on lockdown with all the worries of ruined economies and lost jobs. A short time later the theatre, all the theatres in fact, were closed for no one knew how long. All actors and musicians were suddenly out of work and one more or less for whatever reason didn't make a lot of difference.

But Ian believed her. There were too many inconsistencies for him not to, and if he could, he was going to get to the bottom of what had happened. She was a fit, healthy woman who swore she hadn't been drinking. He believed her. She'd just performed a long and exacting operatic role for which she'd have needed a clear head. Even if she'd had a drink at the end of the show, she was only ten minutes or so behind the rest of the cast. She'd enjoyed her glass of brandy last night, but he'd not seen her the worse for drink. She could handle it, and anyway, there'd not been not enough time to drink so much that she was unsteady on her feet on a flight of stairs she had used many times before.

Then there was the matter of the light going out. She'd probably be able to find her way down even in the dark, but a sudden change from light to dark could have thrown her off balance, however well she knew the way. Was it possible to override a time switch? Unless she was going very slowly, and who would do that late at night in a more or less deserted theatre? The light had gone off too soon. Time switches are carefully programmed. People were going up and down those stairs all the time. If there'd not been enough time, there would have been complaints. He made a mental note to find out more about time switches and ways of manipulating them.

So what caused a healthy woman to stumble and fall on a staircase she used every night? Lucia said she had tripped over something but that nothing had been found on the stairs after her fall. He made a note to ask Duncan to search for police records. He'd also contact the theatre. Accidents like that had to be logged and there must also be a record of everyone who came and went through the stage door.

He must talk to Gavin, who knew her well, although Ian still didn't know when and how they'd met. He wasn't sure of the best time to do this. Gavin was fully occupied with the production and was always on stage either as producer or singer. But this afternoon, Ian remembered, it was chorus and children onstage for act one, with the school singing teacher and Quentin doing sound checks. Escamillo wasn't in the first act. Nor was he going to be occupied with Lucia. Mickey had turned up trumps again and arranged for her to take tea at Balmoral. The royal family were not in residence, but he'd managed to contact one of the equerries, an ex-army major who was there preparing horses for an upcoming state visit, which involved a carriage drive to the local Highland games. The major, Mickey had discovered – and how he'd done that Ian couldn't begin to imagine – was an opera fan who attended Glyndebourne every year. He would, Mickey told him, be delighted to entertain a world-famous opera singer for tea. This arrangement would also please Tom and Rob, who would drive her to Balmoral as soon as she'd finished her lunch and would return her to Inverbank in time for dinner. There'd be no reason for them to stay there. Balmoral, even without the royal family present, was one of the most secure places in the country. They'd have at least three hours free to explore the local countryside or take tea in Ballater.

~

George had just driven his knife into Lucia's chest for the fourth or fifth time when it was decided to break for lunch. Apart from the stabbing, the morning had gone well. Musically it had been a straightforward run-through. The chorus had been well trained, and the few logistical problems had been quickly sorted. But the stabbing still wasn't working. George had been unable to position the knife correctly and it looked too contrived. It was a standard prop dagger with a blunted plastic blade that was supposed to retract on a Spring when inserted between the folds of Lucia's dress. She should then collapse into Escamillo's arms before drawing her dying breath. But it wasn't working. After several attempts both George and Gavin had dissolved into fits of giggles and Lucia flounced out, swearing that she'd never acted with such a bumbling pair of cack-handed idiots in her entire career. It was decided to leave the scene for now.

Ian intercepted Gavin on his way out of the barn.

'Okay, mate?' said Gavin. 'Making any progress?'

'Some,' said Ian. 'But I wondered if I could talk one or two things over with you this afternoon.'

'Don't see why not. I can leave act one to Quentin. I'll see you in your office after lunch.' He disappeared into the tunnel and Ian went to the bistro, where he bought himself a smoked salmon sandwich and found Molly and Ryan trying to decide between a trumpet and a drum for this afternoon's rehearsal.

Ryan was wavering between the two. 'You need to choose, love,' said Molly. 'You have to be ready to rehearse in fifteen minutes.'

Ryan pouted at her. 'If I'm a soldier I should have a sword or a gun.'

'Gav explained to you,' she said. 'Guns and swords are too dangerous to use on stage.'

'George has got a gun,' he objected, 'and a knife.'

'They're not real,' said Ian. 'And the gun's only allowed to be out of the safe for a few minutes.'

'Anyway,' said Molly. 'George is grown up and a very experienced actor.'

Ryan sighed and shrugged. 'Don't care which I have. They're just stupid toys.'

'George's knife is just a toy,' said Ian. 'That's what you

use when you're an actor.' He picked up the trumpet and blew down it. Nothing happened. 'I'd go for the drum if I were you. You can make a real noise on that.'

'Okay,' said Ryan.

He picked up the drum just as Mrs McFee appeared. 'Just rounding up our little army,' she said. 'You ready, sweetheart?'

'He's just choosing his props,' said Molly.

'Good choice,' said Mrs McFee, giving the drum a tap. 'Give it to me after the rehearsal and I'll write your name on its bottom, so we know it's yours.' Ryan giggled. 'Okay if I hang on to him for a wee while after the rehearsal? I need to see if his costume fits.'

'Keep him as long as you want,' said Molly.

'Gav's joining us in the office,' said Ian. 'I want a bit more background on Lucia. You able to join us or have you got something else planned?'

'I'll join you. Then I'm planning to do a bit of research on Cara like you suggested. After that I thought I'd walk to the village and get some gossip on Maudie Croft. I'll take Ryan to the playground when Mrs McFee is done with him. That's always a good place to chat to other mums.'

It was the school gate all over again. By supper time that evening Molly would have made friends with every mother in the village.

∼

'Quiet in here,' said Gavin, grabbing a chair and sitting down at Molly's desk. 'Not like the rest of the place.' He grinned at them in a way that suggested that being surrounded by noisy musicians was exactly how he liked things. 'And I don't need to worry about Lucia causing mayhem. That was a brainwave your friend had. She'll be full of how she hobnobbed with the aristocracy when she gets back.'

'Mickey's a genius,' said Ian. 'And Lucia adores him.'

'She not causing too much fuss at his hotel, then?'

'Not at all. As long as Mickey's around, she's all sweetness and light.'

'I'm going to owe that guy big time when all this is over.'

'It won't be doing his business any harm either. I expect he'll fill the place with photos of her and exploit her for publicity.'

'Fair enough. I can't see her objecting to that. But how are you and Molly getting on? Cracked the case yet?'

'We've found out a few things,' said Ian, not wanting to commit to anything just yet. 'I'd like to know a bit more about Lucia, though.'

'So she really is under threat?'

'We're not sure yet, but I'm suspicious about that fall she had.'

'You think it might not have been an accident? That someone's still got it in for her?'

'From what she told me,' said Ian, 'the police didn't take it seriously. And there are a couple of things that don't make sense.'

'Like?'

'The light on the stairs going out suddenly, that she's sure something tripped her and yet nothing was found, and she thinks she heard someone as she left her dressing room.'

'Interesting,' said Stamper. 'She'd not said much to me about it.'

'It happened more than two years ago. If she hadn't been

sent that letter, she'd probably have thought no more about it.'

'What have you found out about the letter?'

'I had it checked by police forensics. I think it could have been sent by someone in the village.'

'Who would she know in the village? She's never been here before.'

'That's what we're working on right now. How well do you know her? Is there anything in her past we should know about? Anyone who might have a grudge against her?'

'I can't think of anyone in particular. There've been a few rumours, but she's a very high-profile star. People will always gossip.'

'How did you meet her?'

'I've known her since the band was at its most famous. She was having a seriously steamy affair with a young bloke ten years her junior. About my age, in fact. She'd got tickets for one of our gigs as a birthday present for him and arranged for him to meet us after the show. Took us all out to dinner at the Black Duck in Wapping. Do you know it?'

Ian had heard of it. It was the kind of place that served tiny dishes of unlikely paired ingredients – spinach ice cream came to mind – on slate slabs for three times the average weekly wage. It was booked up for years ahead and you could rub shoulders with A-list film stars and oil magnates from the Middle East. Once it was the haunt of Russian oligarchs, although recently not so much.

'Well,' Gavin continued. 'We hit it off, nothing sexual, more like brother and sister. I told her I'd always wanted to sing opera and she gave me the name of a woman who would train me. I couldn't take lessons then. It would have ruined my band voice. But once we'd split up, I got in touch with her again and she fixed it up for me.'

'And how long did her affair with this young man last?'

'For a couple more months, I think. There was some talk of them actually getting married, but no one really expected it to last. Least of all Lucia, probably. She doesn't go for long-term commitment. Except to her singing, of course. Mind you, it lasted longer than most of her affairs.'

'I don't suppose you remember his name?'

'I do, as it happens. He was Turkish, name of Kasra Mansour. Looked a bit like Freddie Mercury.'

'Was he a singer?'

'No, at that time he was a student at the London School of Fashion.'

'And did the affair end amicably?'

'Shouldn't think so. They didn't usually. I doubt if he'd have let it fester for ten years and then shoved her downstairs though.'

He was probably right. They were looking for a much more recent grudge.

'Do you know what happened to him after they split up?'

'He went back to Turkey and is now a successful fashion designer.'

'You kept tabs on him?'

'No, I met him by chance last year in Edinburgh. He was over here for Edinburgh Fashion Week. It was a few days before we started *Pinafore* rehearsals. I'd been sent tickets.'

'Do you have an interest in fashion shows?'

'Not really. People send me tickets for all kinds of things. I wouldn't have bothered with it but, well, you've noticed how fashion-conscious Cara is? She'd been working hard with me and Quentin for a couple of weeks and we both needed a break. I thought she might enjoy it. Turns out she'd met Mansour before. He was in London just before lockdown and Cara had been filling in for some singer who'd gone sick. Don't know what the show was or how they met.'

'Did you talk to Mansour?'

'Briefly. He remembered meeting me all those years ago. We went through one of those "must meet for a drink some time" type conversations. Can't imagine we ever will though.'

Not much to pursue there, Ian thought. As Stamper said, he'd hardly be back to settle a ten-year grudge. He obviously had a thriving career and had probably not given Lucia another thought.

'Do the Lyle brothers have any connection to Lucia?' Ian asked, changing tack.

'Not as far as I know. I didn't know them myself until I started a little glee club up here when I first moved in.'

'There was a bit of bother, wasn't there? At the school where they taught.'

'Quentin still works there. Oliver left last year. Never said why and he didn't want to MD here again this year. Pity. He was better tempered than his brother.'

'Did he get on with Andy Meade?'

Gavin thought about that for a moment. 'No one got on with Andy, poor bloke. Not once the drink took hold. And he had a habit of breaking up marriages, which isn't really the way to make friends. I do remember seeing him and Oliver in the bar together occasionally. Are they – what is it the police say? – persons of interest?'

'Not sure yet,' said Ian. 'We're looking into everyone.'

Gavin looked at his watch. 'Hope that's helped,' he said. 'I need to be getting back to the barn. I said I'd sit in on Cara and George rehearsing once the act one chorus has finished.

Keep up the good work. And let me know if you need anything.'

'We will,' said Molly. 'And thanks for getting Ryan involved. He's really enjoying it.'

'He's a good kid,' said Gavin as he opened the door and left them.

Ian turned to Molly. 'How have you been getting on this morning?' he asked.

'I dug a bit deeper into the whisky scam,' she said. 'I emailed Duncan and he sent me some records. Oliver and Andy were definitely involved in it. Duncan thought Oliver could have been a victim rather than a perpetrator. He'd got himself into trouble over it and bailed himself out using school funds. But no arrests were made. Duncan thinks Andy was a middleman and they were hoping he'd lead them to someone higher up, but it all fizzled out after he died.'

'Where's Oliver working now?'

'Nowhere. He does some private coaching, plays the piano on cruise ships, accompanies choirs, that kind of thing.'

'If he'd lost his job because of Andy, he'd have a motive for killing him,' said Ian.

'But Andy died *before* Oliver lost his job.' Molly reached for a pen and some paper. 'How about this?' she said, writing a timeline.

*Some time before the opera camp last year, Oliver gets involved with Andy and loses a lot of money he can't afford. He kills Andy, thinking it will let him off the hook, but finds himself threatened by someone higher up in the chain who puts pressure on him to pay up or be reported for murder. Oliver gets the money and pays him off, but the school authorities discover it and kick him out.'

'Why not press charges?' Ian asked. 'It sounds like they had enough evidence.'

Molly sucked thoughtfully on a sherbet lemon. 'Perhaps the real villain is someone high up in the school, a governor maybe. If he pressed charges, he'd have come under suspicion himself.'

It was a theory, Ian supposed, but an impossible one to prove. They still didn't know for certain that Andy hadn't died of natural causes. 'And where does Lucia come into it? And why send that letter?'

'She couldn't have been involved as well, could she?' Molly asked. 'She's a highly paid opera singer, at least she was until covid hit. Why would she need to scam people out of their money?'

'It all comes back to the letter,' said Ian. 'I think it's time to go and visit Maudie Croft and her gnomes. Want to walk to the village with me?'

'Ryan's rehearsal will be winding up and I should probably pop in on his costume fitting in case he's being awkward. Can you wait a bit?'

'I'd rather get it done now. I'll let you know everything she tells me. And you'll probably get more out of your mums if I'm not hanging around.'

'Okay,' said Molly. 'I'll see you in the morning.'

'Come on, Lottie,' said Ian, reaching for her lead. 'Another walk for you.'

Lottie knew the way now. Through the tunnel, past the barns and across the car park to the main gate, pausing at one of the fences for a quick growl at the alpacas. 'What did they ever do to you?' said Ian, pulling her away from the fence and out into the lane. There were few things Lottie disliked; postmen and delivery people in general were about her limit. So what had alpacas done to upset her? One of them shook its curly head at them and for a moment it reminded him of Stephanie after a disastrous session with her hairdresser. She'd come home with a headful of ginger curls and a bad temper, which she took out on him for several days. And no doubt she continued to have bouts of bad temper, even after she left him. Had she had another unfortunate experience with a hairdo gone wrong? And did Lottie remember it? He rather hoped so.

Maudie's cottage was easy to recognise. Gregory had been right about the gnomes. Ian counted six of them in the front garden alone. Lottie walked up to one of them and sniffed at it. Was she hoping for a reaction? If she was, she didn't get one and quickly lost interest in it. Gregory was right. Pointless things.

Ian knocked on the door and waited. Perhaps Maudie Croft was a bit deaf. He knocked again more loudly, and a woman's head appeared from a window of the house next door. 'No use making that racket. She's not in.'

'Don't suppose you know when she'll be back?'

'She took the bus to Perth. She'll not be back 'til the bus returns this evening. About half past six usually. I can give her a message if you like.'

Ian thought about that. *Just popped in to see if she was the writer of anonymous letters.* 'No,' he said. 'I wouldn't want to trouble you. I'll come back another day.'

'It's no trouble.'

He was sure it wasn't. A chance to nose into her neighbour's affairs, no doubt. 'It's fine. I'm staying quite close. I can easily pop back another day.' He turned, walked back down the garden path and left before she had a chance to say any more.

He and Lottie walked back towards Dundas. There was no rush and he let Lottie sniff at interesting smells – well, he assumed they were interesting. Only Lottie had a good enough sense of smell to know. But it was a nice sunny afternoon, and he was enjoying a gentle stroll with no distractions apart from some birds tweeting and a few bees exploring the flowers along the side of the road. He'd just passed Greg's stores when he heard the sound of a car. The first there had been for a while. He bent to clip on Lottie's lead then had to jump onto the verge, pulling Lottie with him, just as a red car appeared around a bend in the road and drove towards them at speed. Ian scowled at the driver, who seemed not to have noticed them as he drove on into the village and pulled up in front of the row of cottages. *Idiot,* Ian thought. He strained to read the number plate, but the car was too far away. He'd not had much time to see the driver. All he had was an impression of dark hair and sunglasses. There must be hundreds of small red cars in Scotland, but this could have been the car he'd seen near Inverbank. He needed to find out who owned it. He reached into his pocket and found the slip of paper he'd written the number on. He took a photo and texted it to Duncan, asking him if he could find out who it belonged to.

15

Ian arrived back at the barn while Cara and George were rehearsing the scene in which Micaëla delivers a letter to José, begging him to return home to his dying mother. He was surprised by Cara's interpretation of the role. In the production he'd streamed, Micaëla was sweet and gentle, appealing to José's better nature. But the emotion she was expressing here was one of contempt. A valid way of viewing things, he supposed. José had deserted her for a voluptuous gypsy, deserted his post in the army and turned smuggler. On top of that, he'd taken a pot shot at Escamillo. Micaëla had every right to be royally fed up with him and being dispatched to fetch him home was probably the last straw.

Gavin had been wandering round the auditorium, pausing to listen and make notes. When the scene finished, he jumped up onto the stage and put his arms round the two singers. 'Spot on,' he said. 'Balance is perfect. We may need to tweak one or two things when we go through it with the orchestra. But for now, it's coming across beautifully. Interesting interpretation, Cara.'

So Ian had been right. It hadn't been the usual way to sing the duet. He could give himself a pat on the back for knowing more about opera than he'd thought. In the past it had just been a pleasant way to pass the time and listen to some lovely music. But now he was realising how much work went into it and how much each character could change just with a shift of emphasis on a particular phrase, or a subtle change of expression.

'What gave you the idea?' Stamper asked.

Cara shrugged. 'The blighter deserves it, don't you think?'

'As long as it's not personal,' said George. 'Not reading too much into the character, are you? Remember it's José you've got it in for, not poor old me.'

Cara scowled at him, grabbed her jacket and flounced off the stage.

'What's got into her?' said George. 'She was such a sweet little thing last year as Josephine.'

'Search me,' said Gavin, sighing. 'I thought one diva was enough. Want me to have a word with her?'

'Nah, she'll be okay. Wish I'd known she was going to change it, though. I need to work on José's response.'

'I thought your look of bemused surprise handled it nicely. What did you think of it, Ian?' Gavin asked.

'Well, I don't know much about opera,' he said, feeling flattered to have been asked. He took a breath and prepared to explain his theory. 'She's got a lovely voice and I suppose Micaëla would be a bit fed up trekking backwards and forwards trying to get José to go home. She probably feels like nothing more than an unpaid messenger.'

'Interesting,' said Gavin. 'I think you could be right. I suppose José's reaction might be one of irritation.'

'Easily done,' said George. 'It would certainly come from the heart.'

Gavin turned to the piano where Quentin was marking some details onto his score. 'What do *you* think?' he asked.

'A bit unexpected,' said Quentin. 'I'll need to make notes for the orchestra. But it works well enough, and I can't fault her singing. You too, George, but then you're easy to work with.'

'My God,' said George, fanning his face with both hands. 'Unexpected praise.'

'The rest of the scene was fine,' said Gavin, as the stage manager took the gun from George.

Ian assumed the poor man had to hang around every time the gun came out of the safe. Just as well, though, with a potential murderer among them.

'I've made a few notes,' Stamper was saying, 'but there won't be any drastic changes. The shooting was good, George. You're better with a gun than a knife.'

'You don't want me to shoot Carmen, do you?'

'No, we'll stick with stabbing. It's more authentic.' He looked at his watch. 'The bar will be open. Let me buy you all a drink.'

'Not for me,' said Quentin. 'I've things to do.'

'How about you, Ian? Do you have time? When are you expecting Lucia back?'

'The lads are going to call me when they're on their way to Inverbank. Hopefully she and the major will have hit it off and he'll invite her to stay for dinner.'

'Did anyone else know she was going to Balmoral?' Gavin asked.

'Only Mickey and Elsa at Inverbank. And Molly.'

'No security threat, then.'

'Shouldn't be,' said Ian. 'I assume Balmoral is as safe as

anywhere. But I'm a bit wary of the roads around Inverbank. There was a red car driving erratically up there the other day. Probably nothing, but I'd like to keep an eye out for it.'

'An easy afternoon for Rob and Tom,' said George.

'They deserve it. By all accounts, she's the world's worst back seat driver. That's when she's not warming up her voice.'

'All part of the job,' said Gavin. 'I'm paying them well for it.'

The bar was quiet. Besides the three of them, there were only a few members of the orchestra. 'Where is everyone?' George asked. 'It's usually heaving at this time of day.'

'Costume fitting,' said Gavin. 'For the chorus and kids.'

He'd not met Molly on his way back from the village so it must be taking longer than she'd expected. He hoped that was not because Ryan was being difficult and insisting on full army uniform with a red coat and a helmet with a spike on top. But whatever the reason, it meant that she hadn't caught up with the village gossip yet. She probably wouldn't go this evening. Not much point. The playground would be empty apart from a few teenagers hanging out. And if his experience of teenagers was anything to go by, sharing cans of elicit alcohol and smoking. But perhaps teenagers around here were different from the ones he'd dealt with in his Leith days. Perhaps they sat around and chatted about bird-watching or school work. Probably not. But it meant that neither of them had picked up anything useful in the village and they would need to try again tomorrow.

He'd just finished his drink when his phone pinged with a text from Duncan. *Car belongs to a hire company operating out of Edinburgh airport* was all it said. As Ian had thought, just tourists.

16

As Ian studied the rehearsal schedule the following morning, he wondered why they were going backwards. On Monday he had watched José struggling with the knife. That was act four. The very last moments of the opera. Yesterday it had been act three with José firing a gun at Escamillo, and Micaëla's plea for him to return to his dying mother. Today it was act two and the tavern scene in which Escamillo makes his first appearance. In each act they ran the chorus numbers first and then concentrated on the soloists. It gave the whole thing a disjointed feel. Maybe that was intentional. It meant they worked on the music without being distracted by the plot. Ian looked at the schedule again. It was tight; a short time in which to stage a complete opera. Tomorrow, Thursday, would be the first time they started from the beginning and ran through the scenes consecutively, and Ian began to see the logic of the breaking up the schedule into shorter sections. Tomorrow, for the first time, everyone would be there for the whole day, apart from the children who were only needed at the start of act one, after which they'd be led away for a fun day of circus skills at the bottom of the camping field. Just as well for the adults in the cast. There would be a lot of stopping and starting and, he imagined, a lot of worn-out, bad-tempered people by the end of the day. Lucia and George were in every act and Ian felt he was about to discover the stamina needed for being an opera singer. But from what he had seen of the soloists' rehearsals so far, he thought that they were well prepared. The solo numbers should run smoothly.

On Friday they would run through the whole opera in the morning with no stops. They'd take a lunch break to absorb Gavin's notes and run over the whole thing again in the afternoon. And on into the evening for any particularly sticky patches. Saturday would be a technical and costume rehearsal, and on Sunday a dress rehearsal. Monday was a free day, although Gavin told him they would need to go over any scenes that were still causing problems. Then performances would run from Tuesday to Saturday.

Having seen Lucia safely delivered to the barn on Wednesday morning, he strolled over to the office and found Molly already at her desk. 'I thought I'd check out Lucia's fall,' she said. 'There'll be reports about it on opera pages and social media, maybe even news websites.'

'I'm going to do a bit of research on Cara,' said Ian. 'But I can do that this afternoon, while you're in the village chatting to mums. I guess you didn't have time to go yesterday.'

'No, we finished quite late. I'll take Ryan after lunch to let off a bit of steam. Why Cara?'

'I watched her rehearse with George yesterday and I've a feeling there's more to her than we know about. But you do your research this morning. I'll come back and do mine this afternoon. And then we can compare what we've found.'

As Molly would be monopolising the laptop all morning, Ian thought he'd go and watch the rehearsal. What he'd seen yesterday suggested that watching what was going on in rehearsals might give him an insight into the character of some of the players. This morning would be gypsies and smugglers. A busy scene for the chorus, so they planned to include the soloists and run through to the afternoon.

This had to be Lucia's favourite part of the opera. She certainly looked set to enjoy it. It was a chance to show off her dancing as well as her voice. Although not in costume, she was managing to look seductive. She was all in black, a red shawl tied around her waist and her hair tied loosely at her neck. Even in rehearsal she was mesmerising. Ian sat back in his seat and enjoyed every minute of her opening song and dance.

This was a big moment for Gavin as well – the first appearance of Escamillo. Gavin, Ian thought, was made for the role. Full of boastful bluster as he enthralled the crowd with an account of his exploits in the bullring. Not so different from the noisy fans he'd remember from his boy-band days. Adoring young girls and mildly jealous boyfriends. Ian couldn't help feeling there was a weakness in the plot at that point. George made his appearance as the downtrodden soldier José, now released from prison where he had been held for letting Carmen escape arrest. He had an amazing voice and was no mean actor, but why Carmen should choose the pathetic José over the dazzling Escamillo, only Bizet's librettist knew. But then George pulls out the rose Carmen had given him in act one and gives her a look that would melt ice. George had never struck Ian as a sentimental type, but he had won him over, so may have had a similar effect on Carmen. Either that or the librettist knew nothing about women.

Not only was George a brilliant singer, he was also a highly convincing actor. Had he and Lucia worked together before? They had a presence on stage that suggested they knew each other extremely well. And of course, they had an offstage history too. Was George, by any chance, in the theatre the night Lucia fell down the stairs? It wouldn't be too difficult to find out. There can't have been that many performances of *Aida* in London that night. He'd add it to his research for the next day. Had George sent the letter hoping she'd pull out of the production? Perhaps he'd wanted another singer to play Carmen. A girlfriend, perhaps – unlikely, wasn't he gay? But surely he didn't have any kind of grudge against Lucia. George was one of the few people who got on with her. Ian couldn't imagine him being that manipulative. He simply didn't match the stereotype of the highly strung opera singer. Although there was no doubt he was a very convincing actor. Could he be a seething mass of hate under all that laid back geniality?

Both Gavin and Quentin were strict about time. The rehearsal broke for lunch on the dot of twelve-thirty. The orchestra put their instruments away in double-quick time and climbed from the pit while most of the singers were still on stage, and headed for the bistro. There was always a queue for lunch and the orchestra had the advantage of not having to change their clothes. Quentin looked set to join them and Ian followed him as he left the barn. Something puzzled him about Quentin and now seemed like a good time to ask him some questions. He joined the back of the queue and they edged towards the food together.

'Mind if I join you?' Ian asked as he loaded a plate with food and looked around for somewhere to sit. 'There's a table over there by the window.'

'Sure,' said Quentin. 'I could do with getting away from temperamental singers for a while.'

They were just in time. The queue had grown and now tailed back almost as far as the car park. 'Hope they won't be late back this afternoon,' said Quentin, looking at his watch. 'We've a lot to get through.'

'You control them with an iron hand,' said Ian. 'Or should that be an iron baton?'

'More like an iron voice,' said Quentin, laughing. 'I know I shout a lot. Sometimes it's the only way to get results.'

'I certainly remember you shouting at Gavin the day I first came here. He didn't seem to mind.'

'He's a good sort, Gavin. The trouble with having been so famous is that he's used to getting his own way. Not sure how much discipline there is in a boy band, but I've had to be firm with him. You've seen how disciplined Lucia and George are. Hours of practice, endless voice exercises. But even they have their moments.'

'And they get their fair share of shouting from you?'

'When it's needed, yes. They understand that it's necessary.'

There didn't seem to be any danger of him exploding into a fit of bad temper right then. He was just a mild-mannered musician enjoying a good lunch. Was it all an act? Ian wondered. Perhaps he was gentle and quiet at home, saving the fireworks for when he was working. But this didn't really work as a theory. The idea that Quentin was two different people; one at home, one at work. 'There's one thing that puzzles me,' said Ian.

Quentin was coming to the end of his plate of lasagne. He pushed it aside and reached for the apple and Mars bar he'd left on his tray. 'Oh, yes?' he asked, peeling the apple. 'What's that?'

'I've never heard you shout at Cara. Even when she went completely against what had been agreed in her duet with George.'

'No, that's right.' He unwrapped the chocolate and took a bite. 'I don't shout at Cara.'

'Want to tell me why?'

'You're thinking of yesterday? In that instance I agreed with what she was doing. Micaëla would be pretty hacked off with José, don't you think? She's usually played as a meek little thing. I think Cara's way works better.'

'She really looked as if she hated him.' Was that good acting or did she have reason to hate George? If she did, George didn't seem to have noticed. Or was he pretending he hadn't noticed? Sometimes, Ian thought, working with actors was very difficult.

'She overdid the anger a bit. We may need to tone that down, but she's on the right track.'

'Do you always agree with her? You say you don't ever shout at her.'

'It's because I'm sorry for her. She's had enough going on in her life without me adding to it.'

Odd, Ian thought. Quentin didn't appear to have much time for anyone else's personal life. Was there something between him and Cara? He'd not noticed it. If they were a couple, they were very discreet about it. Was there a reason for that? It must be difficult directing someone close to you. Was it a way to keep private and personal lives separate? He'd need to be tactful. 'You know her well?' he asked.

Quentin's answer surprised him. 'She was nearly my sister-in-law. My brother broke off the engagement during last year's camp.'

'Do you know why? If you don't mind my asking.'

'I do, as it happens. Not something I care to discuss.'

Fair enough, it was an intrusive question. 'I heard he lost his job as well. Something to do with some money?'

'He made a stupid mistake, tried to cover it up but was found out. Oliver's never really got over it. Hides himself away. Too ashamed to face people, even though the school let him off lightly.'

Ashamed or guilty? Guilty not only because of the money but because he'd got his revenge on Andy Meade. But how? Did he have any medical knowledge? Could he have found a way to exacerbate Meade's heart condition? Would he have had the opportunity to slip something into a drink backstage? 'Oliver was the musical director last year, wasn't he?'

'That's right,' said Quentin. 'And Gavin would have had him back this year, but Olly couldn't face everyone after what he did.'

What he did? Did Quentin have any idea what that might have been? 'Were *you* here much last year?'

'A few sessions as a voice coach, yes. Mostly before rehearsals started. I didn't have anything to do with the production itself. But I'd got to know Gavin quite well and when Olly refused the offer this year, Gavin asked me to take over. And of course, I was honoured to be working with Lucia.'

'She must be very difficult to work with.'

'Temperamental, certainly, but I can't fault her musicianship.'

Ian couldn't argue with that. He'd seen both her temperament and her musicianship. He'd also seen her softer side when she was with Mickey and, of course, her fear. He could only admire the way she didn't let this interfere with her performance. A diversion perhaps. Once she was on stage she was in a role. Not herself any more and able to forget what had happened to her, and what might still be lurking out there waiting for her.

~

Returning to the office after lunch, Ian found Molly printing something she had found on the Internet.

'It's the transcript of a podcast from an online music magazine,' she said. 'It's called *Working with a Diva*. It was written quite soon after Lucia had her accident.'

'Is she mentioned?'

'Briefly, but not by name. It talks about a production of *Aida* that was running in London just before lockdown. The star apparently was known for taking against singers in the chorus and having them removed from the production.'

That sounded like Lucia, but perhaps all divas did that kind of thing. It was becoming more and more obvious to Ian that the world of opera was a cut-throat one. 'Do we know for certain it was Lucia?'

'There can't have been any other productions of *Aida* in London at the same time, can there?'

He'd no idea. Knew very little about what went on in London. 'Probably not, but see if you can find details. Which company was it? Who else was in it? Which theatre was it and who was on the stage door that night?'

'Being chucked off a production could be a motive for pushing her downstairs, couldn't it?' said Molly.

'It's a bit extreme, but who knows what these arty types are capable of.'

Molly clicked into Google while Ian emailed Duncan to ask for a police report about Lucia's fall. 'We need to go over what we've got so far,' he said. 'I'm beginning to think there are two investigations. One about threats to Lucia and the other about Andy Meade.'

'Do you still think he was murdered?'

'I think it's possible. And I think I have a suspect.'

'Oliver Lyle?'

'Yes. Quentin told me a lot about him. He was badly affected by the whisky scam; furious with himself for being taken in by it. He'd messed up and couldn't get over it. And on top of that, it had lost him his job.'

'But that was after last year's opera, wasn't it?'

'He stole the money after it, but Meade could have been putting pressure on him well before that.'

'Enough for Oliver to kill him?'

'Maybe. Once Meade's dead, Oliver discovers whoever was using him was even more of a threat, so he stole the money to get rid of him.'

'I can see why he went to pieces after that,' said Molly.

'There's something else. He was engaged to Cara until last summer. He broke it off during the opera camp.'

'*He* broke it off? Not Cara?'

'That's what Quentin told me.'

Molly tapped her pen on the desk. 'Andy Meade was a known womaniser. Could he have tried it on with Cara?'

'And Oliver finishes him off out of jealousy?'

'Then he'd have two reasons for wanting Meade out of the way,' said Molly. 'But why break it off with Cara if Meade's out of the picture?'

'Guilt, I suppose. Or perhaps Quentin's wrong and it was Cara who finished it.'

'There's no evidence, is there?' said Molly. 'And even if that *is* what happened, it doesn't help us with the threat to Lucia. We still don't know who sent her the letter.'

She was right. The more they found out, the more complicated it got. The letter implied that Andy Meade had been murdered and that Lucia was now a target. That is what had set it all off. That must be his priority. Find out who had sent the letter and perhaps things would start to fall into place.

17

Thursday was run-through day and Lucia wanted to arrive early. She was having breakfast with Gavin to discuss one or two problems they'd had with the smuggler scene. Ian saw her safely through the tunnel and then walked with Lottie to the village to see if Maudie Croft was at home. He steered a path round the gnomes, which had been joined by a pink tricycle and a doll's pram. He knocked on the door, which was promptly opened. Maudie Croft was not as old as Ian had expected. In her seventies perhaps, and sprightly. 'Can I help you?' she asked.

Ian handed her his card. 'I wondered if I could have a quick word.'

'You're a detective? I've not done anything wrong, have I?'

Most people asked that. It was usually a sign of a clear conscience. 'Not at all.' He would have to be careful. He couldn't just ask if she'd been sending anonymous letters. 'I've been up at Dundas Farm. At the opera.'

'Oh, yes?'

'Yes, it's quite busy up there,' he said conversationally. 'A lot of people camping. I wondered if you'd seen any of them in the village.'

'They come down to the pub and the shop sometimes.'

'Got to know any of them?'

'Not really. Don't much care for opera myself. I'd rather listen to a nice bit of Michael Ball. Mind you, I've been kept busy having my granddaughter to stay.'

Ah yes, the owner of the pink tricycle. 'Is she here now?'

She gave him a surprised look. 'Not right now, no.'

'I hear you like knitting,' he said, feeling rather short of suitable questions to ask her.

'Knitting? What's that got to do with anything?'

'I was chatting to Gregory in the shop. Just happened he was knitting a blanket for his dog. He told me you order magazines from him.'

'Look, if it's knitting you want to talk about, why don't you come in for a cup of tea?'

'That would be very nice, thank you.' He glanced down at Lottie. 'Is it okay if my dog comes in as well?'

'Of course. I've often thought of getting a dog myself. One that size would suit me nicely.' She bent down to stroke Lottie, who licked her hand. 'Friendly, isn't she?'

She led them both into a living room. 'I'll just away to the kitchen and put the kettle on,' she said.

Ian looked around the room. The window looked out onto the back garden. It was tidier than the front. No gnomes or children's toys. Just a neat lawn and some flower beds with dahlias. The room was also tidy: a chintz three-piece suite; a tiled fireplace with a mantelpiece; a sheepskin rug – not alpaca, he noticed – and a polished coffee table with a neatly folded newspaper. On the mantelpiece was a row of plastic pots. The kind that pharmacists use, with childproof screw-on lids. He went closer to read the labels. He didn't recognise any of them but took a quick photo on his phone. Sending anonymous letters and taking prescribed medication didn't have any obvious link, but one never knew. At the side of one of the chairs he could see a magazine rack, but he could hear Maudie returning with the tea and didn't have time to look at its contents.

She returned with a tray laden with china cups and saucers, a teapot wearing a bobble hat and a plate of biscuits. Lottie sat up and wagged her tail.

'This is a pleasant room,' Ian said as she poured the tea.

'Yes,' she said, passing him a cup. 'And it's nice and tidy when there are no children here.'

'Do you have many grandchildren?' he asked.

'Just the one,' she said, looking surprised.

She'd said children. But the grandchild would have visiting friends, he supposed. He looked round for photos but didn't see any.

'Did you knit that?' Ian asked, indicating the tea cosy. It was an elaborate affair with coloured stripes and twisting patterns. Ian wished he'd paid more attention to Lainie's knitting.

'I did, yes. I had some odds and ends of wool from the sale bin in the Perth wool shop. Couldn't let them go to waste. It's seed stitch. Do you knit yourself?'

'No, but I have a very good friend and neighbour who does. I don't suppose you have any of your knitting magazines I could look at? She'd be very interested in them.'

She reached into a basket at the side of her chair and pulled out a couple of magazines, which she handed to him. 'They're quite old,' she said, 'but you can have them if you like.'

Ian flicked through them, hoping to find missing pages

or places where things had been cut out, but they both looked intact. 'No, I couldn't do that.' He took out his phone, opened a page with a woman wearing a jumper in a pink lacey pattern, took a photo of it and handed it back to her.

'You can't be taking snaps of the whole magazine, and it's no trouble,' she said, thrusting them back into his hands. 'Take them. I hope your friend enjoys them.'

He rolled the magazines up and pushed them into his jacket pocket. Lainie probably would enjoy them, so it hadn't been a completely wasted trip. 'My friend goes to a knit and natter group,' he said. 'Do you have anything like that in the village?'

'No, I don't think anyone else in the village is interested. Except Gregory and his dog blankets.'

Could Gregory be the letter sender? Ian didn't think that was likely, although it could be worth finding out if he had lost money in the whisky scam. And he didn't wear red nail polish. Maudie Croft wasn't wearing any either, but maybe she did when she was dressing up for something.

He was not getting much, and was just wasting the morning drinking tea when Molly would probably have her head deep in Internet searches, furiously making notes. He finished his tea and stood up. 'Thank you for the tea,' he said. 'And the magazines.'

She walked with him to the gate and waved as he and Lottie made their way down the road.

As he walked back to Dundas, he wondered if he could eliminate Maudie Croft as a suspect. There was no way she could have anything against Lucia. She wasn't interested in opera, so she'd probably never even heard of the woman. But someone had dropped off that letter. Not necessarily anyone from the village. It could have been someone who drove there.

As he strolled back into the car park, he stopped at McLean's shed. It was a sunny day and there was a long queue for alpaca walking tickets. Ian didn't want to wait in the queue. McLean probably wouldn't even remember what had happened the day the letter was delivered. Just as he turned to cross the car park towards the barns, he noticed a CCTV camera aimed at the waiting queue. It was just over two weeks since the letter had been delivered, and he thought it was usual to keep CCTV footage for a month before overwriting it. He assumed McLean wouldn't hand over the tapes to just anyone. Ian would need to go back and get Stamper to ask him for them. He'd come back later, when it was less busy, and spend his evening going through them. He could do that from the laptop in his car. It would while away some of his on-watch hours. And he might just catch sight of someone holding a letter, maybe even handing it over to McLean for delivery to the house.

18

As he expected, Ian found Molly trawling the Internet. 'Found anything useful?' he asked.

'I found out more about *Aida*. It was an Opera For All production at a theatre in Highgate. Ran for two weeks with a number of guest soloists.'

'Anyone we know apart from Lucia?'

'I didn't recognise any names. I called the agent and asked if they had a full cast list, but they don't keep one. They said the chorus members can change from one performance to the next. I was wondering if George was there, but he was doing Pinkerton in *Madame Butterfly*.'

'In London?'

'In Oslo.'

'That lets him off the hook then. But did we really think he might have pushed Lucia downstairs?'

'We don't know much about him really, do we?'

'No, we don't, but he's the only connection we have between the opera here last year and Lucia.'

'What about Quentin Lyle? He was the voice coach last year as well as MD this year.'

'But he wasn't in London when Lucia had her accident, was he? And he only did a bit of voice coaching before the camp started.'

'He was teaching at that school, and it would have been during term time. But I suppose he could have taken a trip down to London. If he flew from Edinburgh he'd have been there and back in a day.'

'The same goes for Oliver. Do we know when Andy Meade's whisky scam started?'

'Do you think Lucia was involved in that?'

'No idea, but it's the only way I can see a link.'

Molly stretched and rubbed her neck.

'You've spent too long bent over that laptop,' Ian said. 'You need to get out in the sun for a while.'

'Did you hear where they'd got to in the theatre? I might go and spend some time with Ryan if I can drag him away.'

'They were well into act two when I passed the barn. They'll have finished with the children.'

'He'll be back with the other kids then. They've got juggling today, I think,' said Molly.

'They keep them busy, don't they?'

'Gavin's got some amazing stuff organised.'

'Must be costing him a fortune,' said Ian. 'But he's not short of money and it means everyone's really focussed when they're on stage and not worrying about their children.'

'I might grab Ryan at lunchtime and take him for a picnic,' said Molly. 'He likes to see the alpacas. Then we can go to the playground in the village.'

'Good idea. Come back fresh this afternoon.'

'Oh,' she said. 'Before I forget, there's a photo I found on an opera page on Facebook. I've saved it on the desktop. It was taken at the *Aida* dress rehearsal curtain call. I don't know if the cast was the same for the whole run, but I should think the majority of them were there the night of Lucia's fall. I downloaded it but it's not very clear. Might be worth sending off to someone who can enlarge and sharpen it up a bit.' She picked up her bag and left just as there was an email ping from the laptop. Ian clicked it open. It was from Duncan.

Not much luck with the Met. Got a friend to check the log for the night of Lucia's fall. She was taken to hospital at eleven forty-five that night. A police sergeant interviewed her the next morning and wrote a report. Just an attention-seeking nutcase, he said. *No further action recommended although Lucia told him she was sure she was not alone on the stairs. That's all I could get, I'm afraid. Wouldn't happen on my patch. I'd have had that sergeant up in front of me for using language like that. Sorry I couldn't be more use.*

Ian replied with a short email thanking him. Then, as an afterthought, he asked for more information on the whisky scam. He knew the case hadn't led to a prosecution, but it was closer to home for Duncan. There would still be a record of it. When he'd asked before, it was only to discover Meade's role in it. Now he asked Duncan to check out other names and listed George Strike, the Lyle brothers and Lucia herself. Then he added Maudie Croft and Gregory in the shop.

He clicked open Molly's photograph. She was right. While he recognised Lucia, the chorus were just a blurry mass of faces. He opened his contacts and scrolled through until he found the name of a police image specialist he had worked with once. He wrote him a short email and attached the photo, not very hopeful that he would be able to do anything with it.

Ian missed his whiteboard. He liked to have everything

spread out in front of him while he tried to work things out. He and Molly had decided that although their office was locked when they weren't there, it would be too easy for people to wander in and see what they were doing. They had been locking all their notes into the filing cabinet, but that was a nuisance. Every time they needed to check something they had to get out sheets of paper and spread them around on the desk. Things got muddled. So now they were using an app Molly had found called *Fact Stuffer*, which annoyed him not so much because of the name but because he needed to wear his glasses to see it. The glasses were new to him and he hated them, but needs must, so he put them on and created a new 'corkboard'. He downloaded the photos he had taken that morning, a page from a knitting magazine and a photo of some pill boxes. The ones that contained whatever it was Maudie Croft was taking. He checked the names of the drugs and discovered they were prescribed to treat low blood pressure. Maudie Croft apparently needed her heart speeding up. Then he searched until he found a font identifier. He loaded in a copy of the anonymous letter and the page from the knitting magazine and compared them. Several hits were recorded which told him that even if Maudie Croft didn't cut out letters from magazines and send them to nervous divas, she did read a magazine that contained letters that had been used.

A productive afternoon, he thought, as he shut down the laptop and packed it into its case. A quick word with Gavin, who had hopefully found the message Ian had left and called McLean, and he could spend the evening trawling through CCTV footage of potential letter deliverers.

The rehearsal would be finishing soon, and Ian was just thinking of seeking him out in the bar when Gavin himself came into the office, looking pleased with himself. He dropped into a chair next to Ian, pulled Lottie onto his lap and grinned. 'Thought I'd pop in and check that everything's okay,' he said.

'A good rehearsal?' Ian asked. Gavin didn't seem to be in any hurry to leave, so Ian sat down again.

'Yeah, not bad at all. It's a relief to have come this far without any disasters. It's all working on stage apart from a couple of small glitches, everyone knows their lines, and no one's died. I'd call that pretty successful.'

'You've finished for the day?' It was earlier than Ian had expected. He'd need to see Lucia back to Inverbank. He assumed she would be in her dressing room as she always changed out of her rehearsal clothes before she left. To impress Mickey, perhaps. Or just a way of winding down and putting the day's work behind her. Anyone else who had the kind of facilities Mickey provided would wait and make the most of the private bathroom, fresh towels and complimentary toiletries. But Lucia wasn't like anyone else. Who knew? Perhaps she would shower and change all over again when she got there. Change into her finery for dinner. He sent a quick message to Rob, telling him she'd soon be ready to leave and that he'd meet up with them in the car park. Rob replied with a thumbs up emoji.

'I've given everyone the evening off,' said Gavin, relaxing back into his chair and putting his feet up on the desk, giving Lottie space to stretch out a bit. 'I've had a cinema screen put up at the end of the camping field. Right now, it's running cartoons for the kids and we're showing the latest James Bond later tonight. Sorry you can't stay and see it, but I can't see Lucia wanting to sit on the grass watching a movie, can you?'

Ian agreed that she wasn't a sitting on the grass kind of person. But he didn't mind at all. He wasn't a James Bond fan and an evening at Inverbank was a far more enticing prospect. He'd have to spend some of it going through the CCTV footage, but he was on the middle watch tonight and could do it then. It would help him stay awake. His watch started at midnight, which gave him a nice long evening. It was Elsa's evening off, and she was cooking for him in her chalet. Definitely something to look forward to. 'Did you have a word with McLean about the CCTV tapes?' he asked. Why did they continue to call them tapes? They were all on flash drives these days. Video tape had gone out years ago.

'All sorted,' said Gavin. 'You can pick them up on your way out. What are you hoping to find on them?'

'I think I may have found the source of the anonymous letter, although possibly not the sender. I suspect it was delivered by someone on foot from the village.'

'And you're hoping to see a guy handing it over to McLean?'

'He doesn't remember anyone delivering it, but we may spot someone leaving it in his mailbox.'

'Bit of a long shot, isn't it? Can you tell what people are putting in the mailbox from a grainy CCTV video?'

'It could be a wild goose chase,' Ian admitted. 'But I might just spot someone. I can zoom in and hopefully get a shot that I can pass around. Someone might be able to identify them.'

'So you'll be watching all this footage while everyone else is enjoying James Bond?'

'Can't be helped,' said Ian. 'It could help crack this case.'

'You're very conscientious. Both of you,' he added as Molly came in and smiled at him.

'That open-air cinema is a brilliant idea,' said Molly. 'I can't drag Ryan away. I've just popped over for a takeaway from the bistro. Is there anything that needs doing before I knock off for the evening?'

'Nothing more to be done today,' said Ian. 'We'll get the *Aida* photo back tomorrow. I'm getting it printed and couriered here. They can enlarge it and the images will be clearer in a hard copy. We can check if there's anyone we've seen before. You've got to know the campers pretty well, you can start looking for faces you recognise.'

'I'll try, but the chorus aren't professional singers, are they? So it's not very likely they'd have been on stage in London two years ago.'

'Probably not, but take a look anyway. And show them to the orchestra. There might be people they knew as students. Perhaps one of them had friends there.'

Molly sighed. 'But that would be no use. We're looking for someone who is here now.'

'Indulge him, Moll,' said Gavin. 'Musicians are great networkers. It could just throw up a useful connection.'

'Okay,' she said, smiling at him. 'I'll do it as soon as the photo comes back.'

Molly was probably right, Ian thought. It was extremely unlikely that anyone who sang in *Aida* two years ago would be up here right now. Interesting, though, that while she argued with *him*, she'd probably do anything Stamper asked of her. A bit of lingering hero worship probably, or gratitude. Either way he was grateful for it.

'Oh, by the way,' said Molly. 'I chatted to one or two people at the playground when Ryan and I had our picnic.'

'Any interesting gossip?'

'Could be,' she said. 'I've added a corkboard in *Fact Stuffer* about it. It's the one called *Playground*.'

'I'll take a look when I've been through the CCTV stuff,' he said, hoping she hadn't typed it up in the kind of text that would require his glasses. 'I'm taking a break this evening, though.'

'He's got a hot date,' said Gavin, winking at Molly. 'I can tell. Look, he's blushing.'

'I'm definitely not,' said Ian, noticing that his face did feel rather hot. 'Just planning a quiet meal while Tom and Rob are on watch.'

'Are you coming to the movie?' Molly asked Gavin.

'Nah,' he said. 'Saw it at the premiere. George and I have a date with a bottle of single malt up on the roof terrace tonight. The bistro will be nice and quiet with everyone drooling over Daniel Craig.'

'Probably only half the audience will be drooling,' said Molly. 'The other half will just be envious.'

'Not sure you've quite done the maths there, Moll,' said Gavin. 'But it's a beautiful evening. George and I can watch the flickering lights from the movie and catch a whiff of distant alpaca.'

'Sounds idyllic,' said Ian. 'You sure you wouldn't like me to leave Lucia here to join you?'

'Too risky, mate,' said Gavin with a hoot of laughter. 'Wouldn't put it past either George or me to shove her over the edge.'

Molly giggled. *Not funny,* Ian thought. It was tempting fate. Not that he believed in that sort of thing. But someone may have already pushed her downstairs and sent her threatening letters. *He* was familiar with Gavin's black humour. He wasn't sure anyone overhearing him would be.

His phone and Molly's beeped almost simultaneously. Molly's with a message from the bistro to say her order was ready. His from Rob telling him that Lucia was installed in the car ready for the drive to Inverbank. Ian retrieved Lottie from Gavin's lap and picked up the laptop bag. The three of them walked through the tunnel together.

'Enjoy your evening,' he said with a wave, as he headed towards his car and flashed his lights at Rob to signal that he was ready to leave and follow them up to Inverbank.

~

Arriving back at Inverbank, Mickey was waiting at the door with his usual cocktail for Lucia. She swept out of the car and gave him a peck on the cheek. 'Just what I needed, darling,' she said, taking a swig.

Mickey was amazing, the way he had Lucia eating out of his hand, Ian thought. The man deserved a medal. He must remember to reserve a seat for him at one of the performances and make sure Gavin showed his gratitude in some way above and beyond settling the invoice. It was still early, so he decided to take Lottie for a long walk. He'd not really had time to enjoy the countryside around Inverbank, which was a shame as people paid huge amounts of money to do just that. Not all of them, of course. Inverbank was pricey but there were campsites and youth hostels not too far away. They often passed groups of people trudging along in hiking boots, carrying their worldly possessions, well, their holiday possessions, on their backs. There were holidays around here for all budgets and yet *he* had taken very little advantage of the fresh air and glorious scenery.

He set off down the drive and joined the road that ran beside the stream at the bottom of the valley, stopping to take a deep breath of sweet, peaty air. Very refreshing after the smell of barbeques at the camp site with a background aura of alpaca. One doesn't notice that alpacas smell until they are no longer there. Not an unpleasant scent; a bit like goat but not as pungent. For the rest of his life he was going to associate the aroma of alpaca with threats of murder and the tension this case was generating.

As he looked up the valley towards the purple heather, heard the bees buzzing and the ripple of water, he felt the tension lift. There were no cars on the road. No one had followed them up here. He watched Lottie jump joyfully into the water, then emerge to shake herself all over him. He threw sticks for her until she slumped down next to him, resting her muzzle contentedly on her paws. The weather had been dry recently and it was pleasantly free of the midges that blighted so many summer evenings in the Scottish countryside. It was warm and peaceful. Lottie was snoring softly, and nothing was trying to eat him. He almost nodded off himself, until the thought of an evening with Elsa drew his mind back to the hotel.

He stood up and brushed some twigs from his clothes, turning to see if any had stuck to his back. As he did so he caught a glimpse of light in the distance. Something up on the hill on the far side of the river. He stood still and stared across the water. Had he imagined it? No, there it was again. Something reflecting the setting sun. What would do that? The only thing he could think of was a pair of binoculars trained down on Inverbank. Someone spying on the hotel. It was a chilling thought. Had someone been watching them since Lucia arrived there? But he wasn't going to rush up into the forest in search of people with binoculars. He was being paranoid. It was probably just a birdwatcher and he'd scare them to death, not to mention the birds. All the same, he needed to warn Tom and Rob.

19

The evening had been lovely, and if he hadn't been on watch he'd probably have stayed a lot longer. But work was work and if he missed his watch, chances were that it would be the exact moment that some as yet unknown person scaled the wall outside Lucia's window and carried out his evil plan. And having spotted a potential spy made him nervous. He'd mentioned it to Tom and Rob, but they agreed it was probably just a birdwatcher out for a bit of evening twitching. There had been talk in the hotel of sightings of a Scottish crossbill. Ian wouldn't know a Scottish crossbill from one of any other nationality, but by all accounts it was a rare and nervous bird that people would walk miles to see. So a birdwatcher was the most likely explanation. All the same, they agreed they should be extra alert tonight. And besides, he had CCTV footage to watch before tomorrow. Molly would need the laptop and would have no patience with him trawling through hours of footage when she could be putting it to much better use. No, he had to do it tonight. At the very least it would help him stay awake. So he reluctantly left the cosiness of Elsa's chalet, not to mention the enjoyment of her company.

'Anything to report?' he asked Tom, who had been watching Die Hard on his iPad.

'All quiet,' he said. 'Lottie started growling about an hour ago so we took a little walk around, but there was nothing to see. After that she quietened down again, so it was probably just a badger or something. A couple of guests came in around half-eleven and I asked if they'd seen anyone on the road, but they hadn't.'

'Sounds like a false alarm then,' Ian said. 'I'll let you get to bed.'

'Okay then, but call if you need any backup.'

'Sure,' said Ian, taking Lottie on a quick and uneventful patrol of the car park, then settling them both in the back of his own car. Lottie curled up and went to sleep, but she was a light sleeper and would alert him if there was any sign of life. He booted up the laptop, plugged in the first of the flash drives and prepared himself for a long night of trawling through some very boring footage.

He went through it several times and found very little of interest. It was, in fact, even duller than he'd anticipated. The camera covered the area around the ticket office and about halfway across the car park. He watched families unload picnics, dogs and small children. He watched them queueing up to buy tickets and then walk out of view, presumably towards the gate where they would exchange the ticket for an alpaca on a lead. He didn't know the set-up. Did they walk in groups, with a guide, or were they trusted to go where they pleased? He'd not taken a lot of notice and assumed convoys set off at intervals. Fifteen-minute gaps seemed reasonable. Time enough for plenty of punters without them getting entangled with each other. He very much doubted that you could just rent one and go free range with it. They were valuable animals. Stamper wouldn't risk them being kidnapped or mistreated.

The day the letter was delivered, a few days before Ian's first visit to Dundas, had been pleasant and sunny, ideal for a nice day out with the family and for a walk with an unusual and attractive animal. Probably a day for loading phones with photos and boring one's friends on social media. Gavin thought the letter had been collected from McLean along with the day's post, at around twelve-thirty. There was a mailbox near the door of the hut, which his PA emptied once a day. Occasionally packages and letters that needed a signature were handed to McLean, who kept them behind his counter until the PA collected them. So the letter could have been delivered any time from the day before, when the mailbox had last been opened. Ian began the replay from midday, when he had a clear shot of Gavin's PA opening the box and retrieving a pile of mail. From then on there was a steady stream of ticket-buyers until four-thirty when the last walk of the day set off. No one posted anything. Even the postman appeared to be taking the day off. Ticket buying was quick and efficient. None of the customers spent more than a couple of minutes at the kiosk.

McLean closed his hut at five o'clock and pulled down the shutters. The mailbox, however, was still accessible so Ian fast-forwarded through seven hours when very little happened. His hopes were raised when, at around midnight according to the timer, a car drew up and parked close to the hut. But no one got out, and Ian assumed it was a young couple doing what young couples usually did at midnight in parked cars. The only other activity was a fox exploring one of the rubbish bins close to the hut and running off with what Ian thought was a half-eaten hamburger. The alpaca walks kicked off at ten the next morning, and from then until the mailbox was opened again there was a steady stream of people buying tickets. Since the pandemic, very few people paid for anything in cash and all the tickets were paid for using a card machine. Once again, transactions were quick and efficient. Ian didn't see a single thing being handed over to McLean, so the letter must have been dropped into the mailbox and he hadn't seen it happening. Had he been too focussed on the ticket kiosk itself and not on the mailbox? He ran through the recordings again and no one went anywhere near it, let alone put anything in it. Then he realised he'd missed something. He rewound back to nine-thirty and took another look at a woman with a small child on a tricycle. They had stopped near the mailbox while the woman unwrapped an ice lolly for the child who, unable to ride a tricycle and eat at the same time, sat in the saddle and licked the lolly while the woman leant against the side of the hut, looking at her phone. When the child had finished the lolly, the woman took a packet of tissues out of her bag and wiped its fingers. Then she turned towards the bin and threw the used tissues away, putting the packet back into her bag. As she closed the bag, she turned away from the bin and Ian could see she had something in her hand. Another tissue, he thought, but as she hefted the bag onto her shoulder and steered the tricycle away from the bin, she slipped it into the mailbox.

Ian paused the recording and took a screenshot. It was dark and his eyes were tired from staring at the screen, but it hadn't been a waste of time. He had an image of someone posting something into the box. All he had to do now was identify her and find out whether she was the letter writer or just the messenger. He checked the time on his phone. It was almost four in the morning and only five minutes until

Rob was due to take over from him. He saved the picture and closed down the laptop. He'd get a few hours' sleep and take a closer look in the morning. During his watch there had been no strange visitors with or without binoculars. No people creeping past with torches and no footsteps crunching on the gravel. He'd been occupied with the CCTV footage, but not so much that someone could have sneaked past him and into Lucia's bedroom. And even if he had missed that, Lottie would have woken up and barked.

He was still suffering from eye strain, or possibly lack of sleep, when he crawled out of his bunk and made his way to the kitchen for an early breakfast.

'You look like you need this,' said Elsa, pouring him a cup of strong coffee. 'I shouldn't have kept you so late last night.' She looked bright-eyed and energetic, but then she hadn't spent the night watching boring videos.

He'd not left her chalet until one a.m., when he had to take over from Tom. He'd had three hours sleep and badly missed the other five. Was he getting too old for this? Usually he would have dozed for an hour or two before his shift, but instead he'd been tempted by a delicious meal, a bottle of Mickey's best and Elsa's company. It had been worth every minute of lost sleep. He smiled at her. 'I'm fine,' he said, yawning. 'It was a very enjoyable evening.' How pathetic did that sound? It had been more than enjoyable. A whole lot more.

'We should do it again some time,' said Elsa.

He'd not argue with that.

'Do what again?' asked Mickey, as he came into the kitchen and poured himself a coffee.

'Mind your own business,' said Elsa, winking at Ian in a

way that made him rather weak in the knees. Or perhaps that was the effect of strong coffee and lack of sleep.

'How's the opera coming on?' Mickey asked.

'Gavin seems pleased,' said Ian. 'He's ready for a run-through this morning and as long as that goes well, it's all set for the dress rehearsal on Sunday.'

'Don't forget our tickets,' said Mickey. 'You an opera fan, Elsa?'

'Wouldn't miss it for the world,' she said. 'Seeing one of our guests on stage is exciting.'

'Not many opportunities to sit in a barn and watch a world-famous star,' said Mickey. 'I can't wait.'

'It's a converted barn,' said Ian. 'Proper seats and lovely acoustics. There are a few straw bales to stop the audience falling into the orchestra pit, but otherwise it's definitely more theatre than barn.'

'No expense spared with its conversion, then,' said Mickey. 'But that's what I'd expect from Gavin Stamper. He's not the type to skimp on expenses.'

'Takes one to know one,' said Elsa, flicking a tea towel in his direction.

'Can you come on Saturday?' Ian asked, envying the easy way they got on with each other. Were he and Molly like that? He wouldn't have thought so last week, but since they'd been here, they'd both been more relaxed. Perhaps that meant he was getting better at being an employer. 'I'm told final performances are usually the most exciting,' he said. 'There's a particular buzz on the last night.' There would be speeches and bouquets, and of course the after-show party. And hopefully nothing like last year's death to spoil the festive atmosphere.

'Saturday would be great,' said Mickey. 'I'll arrange cover for the evening.'

Ian made a note on his phone to remind Gavin about the tickets. Then he tucked into a plate of bacon and eggs that Flora put in front of him.

Rob's car turned out of the Inverbank drive ahead of Ian. He was about to follow when a red car shot past in the opposite direction at a speed not usually recommended for Scottish lanes. He had time to register the fact that it was the same car he'd seen a few days ago and he managed a glimpse of the driver, but dark hair and sunglasses were all he caught. Probably nothing to worry about. He already knew it was a hire car and there were plenty of those about at this time of year. Flying to Scotland was cheap. It was easier to do that and pick up a hire car at the airport than to face a long drive. No passengers, though, so not a family holiday. Could this be their birdwatcher out to catch an early morning sighting of the elusive Scottish crossbill? Ian had no idea what the crossbill's habits were. Was it a lark or an owl (so to speak)? Nocturnal, or chirpy participant in the dawn chorus? He wouldn't worry about it now. The car was going away from Inverbank and in a different direction from themselves so no immediate threat to Lucia. He'd keep it in mind on the off-chance it was a less immediate threat, and warn Tom and Rob to look out for it. Not much more he could do, so he turned his car in the direction of Dundas and hoped he'd catch up with Rob before they arrived.

20

McLean called to Ian as he made his way through the car park. 'Package for you,' he said. 'Special delivery.' He handed Ian a large brown envelope with a stiffened carboard back. On the front, in red letters, it said PHOTOS DO NOT BEND. McLean had already signed for it, so Ian took it from him and made his way through the tunnel to the office.

He sat at his desk and opened the envelope. It was the enlarged and enhanced photograph of the cast of *Aida*. He put his glasses on and took it over to the window, where the light was better. He looked at the date the photo had been taken and compared it with the dates that *Aida* had run for. The dress rehearsal must have taken place a couple of days before the opening night. There were a lot of people in the chorus, and he assumed that not everyone in the picture took part in every performance, but that probably meant that everyone who was there the night Lucia fell would be in the picture. He turned again to the article Molly had found. *A certain singer who was known for having members of the chorus removed.* Was there someone in this photo who had been ejected from the cast by Lucia? And if so, were they here at Dundas waiting to get their own back, having failed to kill her by pushing her down the stairs?

He was still studying the photo when Molly arrived. 'Do you recognise any of these people now it's been enhanced?' he asked, handing her the picture.

Molly took it from him and frowned. 'It's really hard with all that make-up and the Egyptian headdresses. We could go and watch the rehearsal this morning and see if we can match anyone.'

A waste of time, probably. They had better things to do than sit through a rehearsal. 'Most of the chorus are local and wouldn't have been in London two and a half years ago,' he said.

'What about the minor characters? The two gypsies and the smugglers?'

That was more likely. 'Didn't Gavin mention that they'd taken photos of everyone for the programme?' Ian asked. 'Do you know where they are?'

'Stacked up in boxes behind the ticket desk. Shall I go and ask if we can have one?'

'Yes,' said Ian. 'And grab a couple of coffees at the same time.' They could browse through them here in the office. Much easier to match faces to photographs than staring at them on stage.

A few minutes later, Molly returned with two cups of coffee in a cardboard tray, and a copy of the programme tucked under one arm. Ian opened the programme and studied each photo, which had a short biography underneath.

'Those are helpful,' said Molly. 'We can rule out both smugglers because one was working in Canada and didn't come back to the UK until a couple of months ago, and the other was working in an amateur group in Glasgow.'

'What about the gypsies? Lucia had a run-in with one of them a couple of days ago for upstaging her. Perhaps she recognised her.'

'Wouldn't she have tried the same thing? If she recognised her from *Aida* she could have had her removed before that happened.'

'Perhaps she's softened,' Ian suggested.

'If this is a softened Lucia we're seeing, I hate to think what she was like before,' said Molly.

'You're probably right. And we need to remember that she and Gavin are friends. She'd make less of a fuss because of that.'

'Anyway,' said Molly. 'They don't look anything like anyone in the *Aida* photo. These two are far more... well, buxom. All the *Aida* slave girls look really skinny.'

She was right. But people had put on weight during lockdown. Molly dismissed it with a laugh. 'Not that much weight. They might have got a bit chubbier, I suppose, but these two are quite a different build.'

'I suppose that's something casting directors take into account when they audition. A chorus of slave girls could hardly look as if they dined in style every night.'

'What about this soldier bloke?' she said, pointing to the man whose role was to arrest José in act one. 'He's fairly athletic-looking and he could have been a soldier in both productions.'

Ian looked along the line of soldiers in the photo, but was unable to match any to the man in Gavin's programme. 'I don't see Lucia targeting the men,' he said. 'She's too much of a flirt. I think if she had it in for anyone, it would be one of the slave girls.'

Molly turned back a page and studied the leading players. 'Look,' she said, folding the programme back and lining it up with a face on the *Aida* photo.

'Well, well,' he said. 'I think you could be right.' He looked at the two pictures. One a slave girl with dark hair falling around her shoulders. The other was Cara, who had short, fair curls, but in her role as Micaëla was wearing a long, dark wig.

'We need to talk to her,' said Ian. She was already implicated in the Andy Meade scam because of her relationship with Oliver Lyle, although Ian had never suspected her of harming Meade. On the other hand, hadn't Meade been instrumental in her breakup with Oliver Lyle? He still couldn't see how Lucia's accident and Andy Meade's death could be connected. But if this was Cara in the *Aida* photograph, surely her being around at both incidents couldn't be a coincidence.

They tried to catch her at the end of the rehearsal but were told she'd left in a hurry. 'It will keep,' said Ian. While he waited for an opportunity to talk to Cara, he'd try to find out the name of the woman with the pushchair who had delivered what he suspected was the anonymous letter.

21

Ian clicked the screenshot he had taken of the woman with the letter, enlarged it as much as he could before it became unrecognisably fuzzy, and printed two copies. One for himself and one for Molly.

'Ask around,' he said, 'and see if anyone recognises her. I'll go and see McLean and if he doesn't know who she is I'll go and ask in the village.' He looked at the child's tricycle, wondering if it was pink like the one he'd seen in Maudie Croft's garden. No way to tell, of course, as it was a black and white picture and there were probably many children in the village with similar tricycles. But it could be a place to start if McLean didn't recognise her.

McLean was taking an early lunch break when Ian arrived at his kiosk. A woman had taken his place selling tickets while McLean himself lounged in a deckchair at the side of the hut. He had his feet up on a wooden packing case and was reading a newspaper while eating a pasty and, Ian suspected, keeping an eye on the woman who was selling tickets in his place. Ian showed him the picture. 'Do you know who this is?'

McLean gave it a cursory glance. 'Nah,' he said. 'We weren't open. You can see the closed shutters.'

'But that might not have been the only time she was here. Perhaps she came back when you *were* open.'

McLean shrugged. 'Don't recognise her. Alice,' he called to the woman behind the counter. 'Do you know who this is?'

Ian passed her the picture.

'I've seen her around the village,' said Alice. 'Don't know her name.'

Well, that was a start, he thought. 'Does she live in the village?'

'Couldn't tell you, I'm afraid.' She passed it back to him.

'No problem. I'll go and ask around.'

'Try the shop,' she suggested. 'Old Greg knows everyone.'

'Thanks,' said Ian. 'I'll do that.'

He and Lottie walked across the car park towards the gate. Lottie, as usual, dragged her lead around his legs, keeping him between her and the alpacas. 'Don't you understand fences?' Ian said as Lottie peered suspiciously through the wire. Perhaps she needed dog therapy to cure her of her alpaca phobia. Was it just alpacas? he wondered. She was fine with sheep and goats, who were the only other woolly animals she might have experienced. She'd yet to meet llamas or camels, but Ian doubted that she ever would. She'd probably not have a lot to do with alpacas either once they'd left here, so perhaps he didn't need to worry about therapy for her.

By now they had safely crossed the car park and were walking along the road into the village. Ian kept close to the verge in case the red car appeared, having seen him leave Inverbank, made a quick U-turn and followed him here. That would be alarming because it meant that the driver was not only a threat to Lucia but knew where she was day and night. But there was no sign of the car, so the one that had forced him and Lottie onto the verge was most likely some tourist who didn't have the good manners to drive slowly though the village. Plus, they didn't have anyone with dark hair and sunglasses on their list of suspects.

Ian didn't feel it was necessary to zigzag his way around the various shelves in the shop and found a short cut by squeezing himself through a gap between the tinned veg and the bottles of fizzy drinks. Greg was still sitting at the checkout, knitting. The sludge-coloured blanket was growing fast and had now gained a few rows of red stripes. Ian didn't feel he could only come into the shop to ask questions, so he picked up a packet of garibaldi biscuits and a bunch of over-ripe bananas that were on the shelf closest to the checkout. Then he reached into his pocket for his wallet. Greg weighed the bananas and searched the packet of biscuits for a price. 'Not been priced up,' he muttered. 'Shall we say two quid for both?'

Sounded reasonable, Ian thought, tapping his card onto the machine.

'Need a bag?' Greg asked.

'No, thanks,' said Ian, eyeing a rather grubby selection of used plastic bags on the counter. He stuffed the biscuits into his pocket. The bananas felt soft in his hand and were destined for the nearest litter bin. 'Do you know who this is?' he asked, showing Greg the photo of the woman with the child. He wasn't hopeful. He guessed from the state of his knitting that Greg's eyesight was not that of a young man. But Greg reached into a drawer, rummaged around for a while, and found a pair of brown, plastic spectacles held together with pink Elastoplast. He balanced them on his nose and stared at the picture.

'Aye,' he said. 'Her name's Sandy something. Works as a cleaner somewhere. Don't know where, but I've seen her waiting for the bus.'

'That's the bus to Perth?'

'It's the only bus that goes through the village. Leaves here at 9.45 every morning.'

'So she lives in the village?'

'Not sure. She leaves her kiddie with Maudie Croft sometimes while she's working, so she probably doesn't live too far away.'

Maudie Croft. That was interesting. Maudie Croft uses one of her knitting magazines to compose a threatening letter and gives it to Sandy to deliver. But why?

He walked up to Maudie's cottage, but no one was in and there was no tricycle outside. He walked back to the bus stop and studied the timetable. It was twelve miles to Perth. He could hardly drive the route stopping at houses along the way and asking if they employed a cleaner called Sandy. The bus returning from Perth arrived at six-thirty in the evening, which seemed like a long working day. Perhaps Sandy's employer was only a couple of stops away and she was able to walk back. But he had no idea what time that would be. Then he had an idea. He crossed over to Greg's shop and studied the postcards and notes people had put in the window. It was an interesting selection. There were things for sale from garden furniture to cleaning equipment, dog walkers, childminders, a man who cleared gutters and someone who baked cakes for weddings and christenings. Then he spotted it. A card in the bottom left-hand corner of the window which read, *Careful, thorough cleaner looking for work. Call Sandy. No cats.* Then it gave a number. Ian tapped it into his phone and called her. She answered quickly, sounding breathless. He introduced himself and told her there were a few questions she might be able to answer for him.

'A private detective?' she said. 'Why? Is someone spying on me?'

An odd question, he thought. Unless she had reason to be worried about who might want to spy on her. 'Do you think they might be?' he asked.

'I'm not sure.' She sounded nervous.

'If you're not sure,' he said, 'then maybe the best thing would be for you to talk it through with me. I might be able to help.'

'It's probably nothing, but...'

'Where are you now?' he asked. 'Can I meet you somewhere?'

'I'm walking home from work, but...'

'You don't want me to call on you at home,' he said. 'That's perfectly understandable. We can meet somewhere safe. In the open where there are people about.'

'I suppose that would be okay. Can you get to Dundas Farm? It's on my way home and I usually pop in with my little girl to look at the alpacas.'

'Perfect,' he said. 'How about meeting at the café in the car park? We can get a coffee and sit and chat.'

'I can be there in about ten minutes.'

'Me too. I'll see you there.' He put his phone away and walked back to the car park. There were some metal tables and chairs outside the café. He chose one a little away from the others, quite close to the alpaca field, which would suit Sandy's little girl if not Lottie, who was already growling through the wire.

He recognised Sandy as she came through the entrance and walked towards the café looking uneasily around. She'd no idea what he looked like, so he waved to her. The little girl was sitting in a pink pushchair looking sleepy, but she perked up when she spotted the alpacas. Then she stretched out a chubby hand and pointed to Lottie. 'Doggie,' she said. Lottie wandered over to her and licked her outstretched hand. The little girl chuckled. *A promising start,* Ian thought.

'Can I get you a tea or a coffee?' Ian asked. 'And something for the little one?'

'A cup of tea would be nice. I've a drink for Tian in my bag, but she'd like a biscuit.'

Ian tied Lottie's lead to a table leg, went inside and bought two teas and a packet of digestive biscuits, realising as he paid for them that he already had a packet of garibaldis in his pocket. Oh well, he could take those back to the office with him. He found a battered metal tray with a picture of a cheerful if red-faced bloke advertising MacKinlay's Scotch Whisky, grabbed some sachets of sugar and a couple of plastic tubs of milk, and returned to the table, where Lottie was doing her usual excellent job of breaking the ice.

Ian handed a cup to Sandy and opened the packet of biscuits. He offered one to Tian, and broke off part of another for Lottie. Then he took out the screenshot of Sandy at the letter box and spread it out in front of her. 'This is you, isn't it?' he asked.

She nodded. 'Did I do something wrong?'

'What makes you ask that?'

'There was something about that bloke. And I was worried about the woman,' she said. 'But I was on my own with Tian and I was scared to say no.'

'Perhaps you should start at the beginning,' Ian suggested.

'I was on my way to work,' she said. 'Sometimes I leave Tian with Maudie Croft but that day, when I called in to drop her off, she had a dreadful cold. And you can't be too careful, can you? Not with covid still around and old people suffering so badly with it. So I told her I'd take Tian with me. The woman I work for doesn't mind. I think she quite likes the company, and she still has some toys that her own children played with. And when it's sunny Tian can play in the garden.'

'Is that where you've been today?'

'Yes, I just do a couple of hours early on a Friday. I only leave Tian when it's several hours. It isn't worth paying a childminder if it's not a full day's pay.'

'So you pay Maudie Croft to look after Tian?'

'Yes, she's a registered childminder.'

'Not just company for her granddaughter?'

Sandy looked puzzled. 'No. I've never met her granddaughter but from what Maudie Croft has told me, I don't think she likes children very much. I try not to leave Tian during the opera.'

Ian felt he was getting out of his depth and away from what he really wanted to talk to Sandy about. 'The opera?'

'Yes, that's when Maudie Croft's granddaughter comes to stay.'

'Does she have a son or a daughter in the opera?'

'Who, Maudie Croft? No, I've never met anyone else in her family. It's the granddaughter who is in the opera.'

Ian looked at her in surprise. 'How old is this granddaughter?'

'No idea, about thirty I should think, why?'

'Not a small child, then?'

Sandy laughed. 'Why would a small child be in an opera?'

'I've obviously misunderstood. I saw some toys in her garden and she mentioned a granddaughter. I suppose I just assumed... but that's not what I want to talk to you about.' He tapped the photo. 'Can you tell me what you were doing at the postbox that morning?'

'Posting a letter,' she said, giving him a look that suggested he was a few eggs short of an omelette. To be honest, he was wondering the same himself.

'A letter to Gavin Stamper?'

'No, to some woman. Lucy, some name like that. But it did say *care of G. Stamper*.'

'So it wasn't a letter you had written yourself?'

'No, I told you. The woman gave it to me.'

'Which woman was that?'

'The one in the car with the bloke.'

'The one that scared you.'

'He made me feel uneasy rather than scared. Like I said, there was no one else about.'

'So this woman who was in the car just what, leaned out, handed you the letter and asked you to deliver it?'

'No. The car pulled up a few yards ahead of me. I think they were quarrelling. I could hear raised voices and it looked like the man had grabbed her arm. But then the car door opened, and she fell out onto the verge. Then he drove off very fast.'

'And where were you when this happened?'

'Just turning into the car park. Tian was in a strop because she couldn't stay and play at Maudie Croft's. It was still early so I thought I'd buy her an ice lolly and she could look at the alpacas for a bit.'

'And the woman was pushed out of the car close to the entrance. Do you think she was on her way here?'

'I think,' said Sandy, 'that she wanted to get out, perhaps to go to the barn or the shop, and the bloke in the car was trying to stop her.'

'Was she hurt?'

'She was sitting on the grass rubbing her leg, so I asked her if she was okay. She said she was, but she wanted to get home before the man came back. She gave me the letter and asked me to take it to the office where they sell tickets for the alpacas. When I got there, it was closed. I hung about for a bit and bought Tian an ice-lolly. But I decided not to wait and left the letter in the postbox.'

'And what did she look like?'

'As I said, late twenties or early thirties. She had fair, curly hair. Quite pretty.'

'Did you get a look at the man?'

'He looked a bit foreign. Not coloured, but quite dark-skinned, black hair and flashy clothes.'

'He was wearing a suit?'

'No. A kind of foreign-looking shirt, linen I think, with one of them Indian-looking collars. And he had posh sunglasses.'

Ian wouldn't know posh sunglasses from any other kind, but he took her word for it. 'Did you notice what kind of car it was?'

She shook her head. 'Don't know much about cars.'

'What colour was it?'

'Red.'

'I don't suppose you had time to notice the registration number?'

'No, sorry. Did I do something wrong?'

'No, not at all. Had the woman gone when you got back to the car park entrance?'

'Yes, and I didn't see the car again.'

'And you've not seen the woman again? In the village, perhaps?'

She shook her head.

Ian handed her one of his cards. 'Could you call me if you see either of them again?' he asked.

'Can I go now?' she asked, putting his card into her purse.

'Yes, of course. And thank you. You've been very helpful.'

He watched as she strapped Tian back into her pushchair and walked back down to the road, turning towards the village.

22

'How did you get on?' Molly asked when they were both back in the office. 'I didn't have much luck. No one on the campsite recognised the woman.'

'I discovered quite a lot,' said Ian, feeling rather pleased with himself and telling her about his chat to Sandy.

'We need to find out who the couple in the red car were,' said Molly. 'If they were driving out of the village, do you think your friend in the shop would know them?'

'He might. I'll have to go back and ask.'

'I've not seen a red car here. I don't think it belongs to any of the campers.'

Ian opened the packet of garibaldis and offered one to Molly, who shook her head. He sat at his desk nibbling one of them thoughtfully. 'How would you describe Cara?' he asked.

'Bad-tempered,' said Molly, without needing to think about it.

'Bad-tempered or scared?'

'Why would she be scared?'

'Just a thought. Tell me what she looks like.'

'You know what she looks like. You've seen her rehearsing.'

'Just imagine you've been asked for a description by the police.'

'Why?'

'Because that's what you'd do if you'd just seen her for a moment, perhaps in a difficult situation.'

Molly sighed. 'Average height, thirty-ish, fair hair, quite pretty.'

'And that's almost exactly how Sandy described the woman who gave her the letter.'

'Of course,' said Molly. 'That makes sense. Cara could have made the letter using bits cut out from her gran's magazine and was on her way to deliver it when she got waylaid by the man in the red car.'

'What do you mean, her gran's magazines?'

'You said she'd got knitting magazines.'

'I said Maudie had some.'

Molly sighed. 'And Maudie is Cara's grandmother. I told you.'

No, he wouldn't have missed something like that.

'It's in *Fact Stuffer*,' said Molly. 'I made a corkboard called *Playground*. Didn't you look at it?'

Damn, he'd been too busy with the CCTV footage, theories about birdwatchers and other distractions at Inverbank. He clicked on the corkboard and read what Molly had written. It looked as if they might now have a suspect. 'Cara's been here since before the camp started,' he said thoughtfully. 'She came early to practise with Quentin. The letter was written a couple of weeks ago. Easy enough to check if her practice coincided with the letter being delivered.'

'And we know she was in *Aida*, so do you think she pushed Lucia downstairs?'

'I'm beginning to think so. If Lucia had her kicked out of *Aida*, she'd have a motive. And once she knew Lucia was going to be here as well, she might have sent the letter hoping to stop her coming.'

'So can we stop worrying about Lucia? Cara might have sent her the letter, but if it was just to make her pull out of the production...'

'Maybe, but we don't know that. If she did cause Lucia's fall, she could still have plans to do something violent to her.'

'We need to talk to her, don't we?' said Molly.

'We do indeed.'

The rehearsal broke for lunch as planned on the dot of one o'clock. Ian and Molly were in the barn, waiting for Cara. Gavin clapped his hands. 'Well done, everyone,' he said. 'Back here at two sharp for notes. Then we'll run through things that didn't go so well this morning. Soloists, lunch with me at the house. The rest of you, get out and enjoy the sun. See you all later.'

Ian didn't want to talk to Cara while they were all having lunch together. He waylaid Gavin as he left the barn and made his way towards the tunnel. Gavin greeted him in his usual good-natured way. If there had been any mishaps this morning, he wasn't dwelling on them. He slapped Ian on the shoulder. 'You're doing a grand job,' he said. 'Any luck tracing our letter writer?'

'Possibly,' said Ian. 'We've one or two leads.' He didn't want to flag Cara up as a suspect. Not just yet, but he did need to talk to her. 'I need a few words with some of your soloists,' he said. 'Just a few questions about anything they might have noticed.'

'I won't need all of them this afternoon. We want to save our voices. There are some bits of business I need to go through, though.'

'Could you spare Cara after lunch?'

Gavin looked at his notes. 'I've a few moves to go through with the opening chorus so I can spare her after that for half an hour or so. We don't need to run her scene with George. Do you need him as well?'

'Some time,' said Ian vaguely. 'But there's no hurry.'

'Before the technical tomorrow?'

'Fine,' said Ian. 'You'll ask Cara to drop into the office when you've finished with her?'

'Will do,' said Gavin.

Ian bought some sandwiches, which he and Molly ate while they waited for Cara in the office.

'What are you going to say to her?' Molly asked. 'You can't just accuse her of sending anonymous letters and shoving Lucia down the stairs.'

'No. There's no real evidence that she did either. In any case, if she did, she's hardly going to admit it to us.'

'What are we going to talk about, then?'

A good question, but before he could answer it there was a knock at the door and Cara came in. Did she look nervous? Hard to tell. She didn't look friendly.

'You wanted to see me?' she asked.

'Just a quick word to set our minds at rest. You know we're here to keep an eye on security.'

She nodded. 'I feel quite secure, thank you.'

'No one's bothering you at all?'

'No, why would they be?'

He couldn't work out her expression. Was it guilt? Fear?

Something wasn't quite right. 'I was a bit worried after talking to someone who said she'd seen a woman of your description being harassed by a man in a red car.'

'Not me,' said Cara. Too quickly for Ian's liking. She hadn't even asked when the incident happened. He was sure she was lying. Protecting someone, perhaps.

'Gavin wants us to make sure everyone feels safe,' said Molly. 'You can tell us if anyone's bothering you.'

'They're not,' Cara snapped at them.

'Gavin tells us you're staying with family while you're here,' said Ian conversationally. 'That must be nicer than sleeping in a tent.'

'It's okay.' She seemed more relaxed now. 'I like staying with my gran. She lives alone and she enjoys having me to chat to in the evening.'

'How long has she lived in the village?'

'She's lived here for years. I can remember coming to stay with her when I was quite little.'

'It must be nice for her to have your company,' said Molly.

'I suppose so. She's a childminder during the day so there are plenty of people coming and going. But she gets lonely in the evenings. I'm not there much. I'm too busy rehearsing, but she waits up for me so we can have a chat.'

'Do you have a car, or do you walk there?'

'Why do you want to know that?'

'Because once the performances start, you'll be leaving here quite late each evening. The road isn't lit, and if there are strange men in cars lurking in the village...'

'I can look after myself,' she said irritably. 'Even when I was in London, I had no trouble walking home at night.'

'You were working in London?'

'Just for a week.'

'Singing?' Molly asked.

'Of course singing. It's what I do. *Aida*, actually. I did a week in the chorus covering for someone who was ill.'

'Were you at the final performance of *Aida*?'

'No, just the dress rehearsal and the first week.'

'And after that did you stay in London?' Molly asked.

'No, I went back to Edinburgh. I don't see...'

'Sorry,' said Molly. 'I always thought it would be nice to live in London for a bit. Just worried it might not be safe. I suppose if you've got friends there, a boyfriend perhaps...'

Quick thinking, Ian thought, *if not entirely convincing.*

Cara didn't seem convinced either, but with any luck she'd think Molly was just being nosy about her personal life. 'Look,' she said impatiently. 'I managed to get myself across London in the dark and I guess I can manage a ten-minute walk through a sleepy Scottish village. Now, if you'll excuse me, I've got work to do.'

'Just remember we're here if you need us,' said Ian, thinking that sounded rather lame.

'What, to hold my hand while I cross the road? No thanks.' She left, slamming the door behind her, which Ian thought was unnecessary, aggressive even.

'What do you make of that?' he asked Molly once Cara was safely out of earshot.

'She's very defensive. It's just as well we didn't actually accuse her of anything.'

'Could that be a sign of guilt, do you think?' Ian wondered.

'I'm not sure what she's guilty of. I don't think she would have told us she was in *Aida* if she had something to hide. And it sounds as if she was there on a short contract. There wouldn't have been time for her to annoy Lucia and get herself chucked out of the production. They'd have been desperate to keep her if she was covering for someone who was ill.'

'It's a bit of a coincidence that she was there, isn't it?'

'Not necessarily,' said Molly. 'Opera is probably quite a small world. And what's her motive? Even if Lucia did have her thrown out of the chorus, that's hardly a reason to push her down the stairs, is it? Anyway, the timing's all wrong if she was only there for a week.'

'We don't know if she was telling us the truth about that.' Cara might be a compulsive liar for all he knew. 'I'd really like to know more about this man in the red car. I'm sure she was lying when she said she knew nothing about him. Sandy told me she was pushed out of the car and I believe her. So why wasn't she kicking and screaming about it?'

'If they were having a row, she might want to keep quiet about it.'

Was that likely? He'd take her word for it. Molly was more familiar with that kind of situation than he was. 'Sandy was sure they were quarrelling, and they were driving out of the village just yards from Maudie's cottage. Would there have been enough time for a quarrel to start unless they already knew each other?'

'Enough time, I think,' said Molly. 'She could have got into the car and realised almost at once that it had been a mistake.'

Once again, he had to acknowledge that Molly knew more about it than he did.

'Perhaps,' said Molly, 'she cut out pages of her gran's knitting magazine and put together a threatening letter to Lucia. She wanted it delivered quickly so she hitched a lift in a red car with a man who then pushed her out after driving a very short distance. She was scared and wanted to get home so she got Sandy to deliver the letter for her. But that's a bit far-fetched, isn't it?'

'Put like that, yes,' said Ian. 'But suppose she already knew red car man and is too scared to admit it. I can't help thinking she's already involved with this man, somehow. We really need to know more about him and his red car. I saw one up near Inverbank the other day. It cut in front of me, and it could have been following Lucia's car. Then I saw the same one this morning, just as we were leaving.'

'How many red cars do you think there are in Scotland? We don't even know the make, do we?'

'The one I saw was a Fiesta. Turned out it was a hire car so probably just tourists getting lost in the lanes. Sandy didn't know what make the one she saw was.'

'There must be hundreds of red Fiestas in Scotland. Even if that's what Sandy saw, there's nothing to suggest it was the same one.'

'All the same, I think we should keep an eye out for it. I'll get McLean to let me know if he sees one. And Tom and Rob are keeping a lookout as well. I'll make sure they all have the registration number in case it *is* the one I saw at Inverbank.'

'Do you want me to get to know Cara a bit better?'

'That would be a good idea, as long as you can do it without making her suspicious.'

Molly raised her eyebrows at him. 'I do know that,' she said.

'Of course you do. I'm sorry. Yes, see if you can get her chatting to you. Does she mix with the campers much?'

'She keeps pretty much to herself. Some of the chorus think she's a bit stand-offish because she's a soloist. I can make it look like I'm trying to include her in stuff. There's a barbeque tomorrow evening after the technical. I'll try to get her to come along.'

'Loosen her tongue with a glass of whatever Gavin's got lined up.'

'It probably won't be anything stronger than lemonade. He won't want them hungover at the dress rehearsal.'

'He can hardly ban them from the bar, though. I assume he's not closing that for the evening.'

Molly laughed. 'He'd have a riot on his hands if he did.'

23

The last two days of rehearsals ran smoothly, both on stage and off. On the Monday morning, a day of rest for the performers, Lucia took a late breakfast at Inverbank and Mickey took her on a tour of his glasshouses. Stamper had arranged for a hair stylist and beautician to visit her at the house in the afternoon and she returned to Inverbank for dinner and an early night.

Performances began on Tuesday and Ian and his security team would need to be on high alert, keeping an eye on the audience as they arrived and patrolling backstage. He was going to be on edge all week. He'd seen no more of either the red car or the flashing binoculars at Inverbank. Lucia was safe at night. Security was tight, with all doors locked after dark and one of the team on watch outside. The other guests staying in the hotel were all regulars and known to Mickey. It was a quiet area with no nightlife for miles, so everyone was safely tucked up in bed by midnight.

Daytime was different. Without a fixed schedule there was no way Ian could keep tabs on everyone at Dundas. The weather was lovely and most of the campers spent their days sleeping late and then lounging in the sun, waiting for the next performance. The problem had been what to do with Lucia during the day. After the dress rehearsal, Ian had called a meeting of the security team and included Stamper. 'We're still not sure what we're dealing with,' he admitted reluctantly. 'Lucia still feels that she could be in danger and from the research Molly and I have done, we have to agree with her. No obvious threat, but we can't afford not to take it seriously.' He pinned a chart to the wall. 'With Gavin's agreement, this is how I would like security to operate for the last few days.' Gavin nodded as Ian ran down the list he had made. 'Everyone involved in the opera now knows everyone else. Any strangers will stand out. We need to make sure that access to the site is patrolled.'

'What about people coming in to see the alpacas?' someone asked.

'Not really a problem,' said Ian. 'The only access from the public car park to the barns and campsite is through the entrance behind McLean's hut. It's also the only access for the audience once the performances get going. I've set up a rota for one of you to be with McLean during the day and two of you to be on the gate in the evenings. Anyone wanting to get through the tunnel to the house needs a keypad code, which Gavin's PA will change daily.'

'Is the campsite secure?'

Ian nodded. 'It's surrounded by a strong fence and the only entrance is through the gate behind the barn.'

Molly had run off copies of the schedule, which she handed around. 'I'm sending you all a link to an app. Download it now and read the instructions carefully. Depending on what type of phone you have, you will be able to set up a single key which you hold down to alert the rest of the team. Only use this in an emergency. Keep in touch by text message or just call one of us if you're worried about anything. I will be either in the office or the bistro.'

'What about Lucia?' Rob asked.

'You drive her down here as usual after breakfast,' said Ian. 'Gavin is letting her use the house during the day. If she wants to go out, Molly will contact one of you to go with her.'

It had all worked well. Lucia went out very little and spent her time enjoying the sun on one of Gavin's terraces, and the campers came and went without apparently noticing the heightened security. And now there was just one performance to go. Too soon to relax, of course, remembering what had happened last year, but Ian was beginning to feel a sense of relief. Just a few hours and it would all be over. Lucia had packed her bags and left Inverbank, her luggage safely stowed in the back of Tom and Rob's car. They would drive her to Edinburgh to catch a late-night flight to London as soon as the final curtain came down, and his job would be over.

Nigel and Joy arrived early and grabbed seats near the front. Molly greeted them, kissing her father and then turning to Joy and giving her a hug. She seemed to have accepted Joy in her father's life. It had done Molly a lot of good being at Dundas for the last two weeks. She'd offloaded her worries about her ex and was now seeing her father's love life in a more balanced way. She was right. However his relationship with Joy turned out, Nigel would never see Molly homeless.

Molly helped them settle in their seats and then joined Ian to watch from the ticket office in the foyer as the audience sauntered in, scrutinising them as they arrived. But none of them looked suspicious. They were friends of someone on stage, or locals with connections to the farm or the offices. As the theatre filled, Ian thought Mickey and Elsa must have decided not to come. He didn't blame them. They'd had an exhausting two weeks and had probably had enough of Lucia without having to watch her on stage as well. They were probably celebrating her departure with a leisurely drink. But as he and Molly were about to take their own seats, he spotted them. The best places had been taken but there were two seats near the back, on the end of a row. Ian edged his way through the audience to talk to them.

Elsa looked round at the packed auditorium. 'You can't join us?' she said. 'I hadn't realised it would be so full.'

'I'm still on duty,' said Ian. 'Molly and I are sitting on straw bales over there.' He pointed to the line of bales around the edge of the orchestra pit.

'It doesn't look very comfortable,' said Mickey.

'It's a bit prickly, but we can keep an eye on things. We've a good view of the stage, the wings, and the auditorium.'

'Will you be able to meet us for a drink at the end?' Elsa asked.

'If all goes well,' he said. 'I'll join you in the bar.'

'Lovely,' said Elsa. 'Good luck for this evening.'

The orchestra were still tuning their instruments as he slipped back to his seat next to Molly. The overture had started on the dot of seven o'clock every night so far. But not tonight. People were beginning to mutter and fidget. Ian was wondering if he should go backstage to see what was going on, when one of the smugglers appeared in the wings and tapped the stage manager on the shoulder. If he leaned back and peered around the edge of the curtain, Ian could see him and hear him but the audience could not. Which was just as well, as he was clad only in his underpants and a pair of boots. 'Someone's nicked my costume,' he hissed at the stage manager. Ian could see a lot of arm waving and shoulder shrugging between the smuggler, the stage manager and Mrs McFee, who as wardrobe mistress had been summoned to sort things out. She led the man away, and a light on the conductor's music desk flashed. Quentin raised his arms, the overture began, and the curtain went up. The smugglers didn't appear until act two and Ian supposed there would be time to kit the guy out during the first scene. Smugglers didn't exactly dress to impress, and Ian thought it would be easy enough to find him a pair of ragged trousers and a shirt.

The first scene went without a hitch. Molly smiled proudly as Ryan appeared with his drum, sang with the other children and raised a few laughs by mimicking the soldiers. Then he scurried off stage as the women appeared from the cigarette factory. Ian knew the children would be shepherded back to the open-air screen where Stamper had arranged yet more cartoons for them. It was good that they would be out of the way in case things turned nasty. *Relax,* he told himself. Everything was going to be fine. There'd been no more letters and the red Fiesta hadn't been seen for several days. What could possibly go wrong now? He ignored the small voice inside his head, reminding him that it was after the final night of last year's show that Andy Meade had died.

As the scene changed for act two, Ian was relieved to see the smuggler had now been kitted out with a pair of ripped jeans and a red bandana. Ripped jeans were perhaps a little ahead of their time, but the man looked convincingly ruthless. The boots helped.

Ian and Molly stayed where they were during the interval between acts two and three. The audience sauntered out for half an hour of fresh air and a drink at the bar. Tom and Rob were on duty backstage and pinged him a message to say Cara had been taken ill and was going home. An understudy was ready to take her place. Cara had been looking a bit peaky all week and Ian wasn't surprised she hadn't made it to the end, but he'd seen the understudy rehearse with George and he was pleased she was going to have a chance to perform, even if it was only for one act.

The orchestra were back and had just started playing the entr'acte when Ian looked up and spotted Caroline waving at him from the entrance. He waved back, surprised. She knew he was here, but they'd not arranged to meet since, well, he wasn't sure when he had last seen her. 'Won't be a mo,' said Ian to Molly, who smiled knowingly at him.

He left his prickly seat on the straw bale and walked to the back of the auditorium. 'This is a nice surprise,' he said, kissing her on the cheek. 'You should have let me know you were coming. I'd have reserved a ticket for you.'

'Thought I'd surprise you,' she said. 'Sorry I'm late. I got caught up in an accident outside Perth and then some maniac dressed like a pirate nearly crashed into me just outside the gates to the car park.'

'A pirate?'

'Well, he had a red neckerchief and an eye patch.'

The missing costume? he wondered. 'Are you sure it wasn't a smuggler?'

'Smuggler, pirate, I don't have a lot of experience of either. Does it matter? It was probably just some idiot going to a fancy-dress party.'

'What sort of car was it?'

'A Fiesta, I think. Red.'

'I don't suppose you made a note of the registration number?'

The Diva of Dundas Farm 203

'No, sorry. I was more concerned about not hitting it head on.'

What on earth was going on? The car had been seen twice near Inverbank, once by Ian himself and again a few days later by Rob. They knew it was a hire car and most likely it was being driven by an innocent tourist. There were plenty of small hotels and campsites in the area. But there were also two sightings of a similar car close to Dundas. The one he'd had to jump onto the verge to avoid and also the car that someone who looked like Cara had been pushed out of right here in the village. An event which Cara herself denied. It was a worrying coincidence. But as Molly had pointed out, red Fiestas were very common. They'd no reason to believe it was the same one, and if Caroline was right, it was leaving. Not arriving with some murderous plan. Had he driven there, stolen a costume and left? And if so, why? Did it have anything to do with Cara? Had she really been ill or was she just scared? Had whatever plan they'd had been thwarted? Tom and Rob had made a thorough search backstage during the interval and had not reported anything untoward. He and Molly had kept a close watch front of stage and again, there was nothing to worry about. Various thoughts ran through his head. Poison in the drinking water? Every singer had a bottle of water close at hand. Had Lucia left hers where it could be spiked? Was there some kind of booby trap? A trip wire, perhaps. But with the two security men backstage he couldn't see any way that could happen. The lead players had their own dressing rooms well away from everyone else and with a security guard at the foot of the stairs that led to them.

All the same, that Fiesta driver had been up to something. 'Look,' he said, squeezing Caroline's hand. 'There are no tickets left. Go and join Molly on that straw bale over there. It's a bit prickly but you get a good view.' He pointed to where Molly was sitting. 'I need to make a call, but I'll join you in a minute.'

The orchestra had finished the entr'acte and he watched as the curtain rose on the smugglers' cave. Definitely two of them, he noticed. So who was the one in the red Fiesta?

He pressed a number on his phone and called Duncan. 'Can you do something for me?' he asked.

'Ian, it's Saturday evening. I'm off duty and about to enjoy a nice meal in the garden with the love of my life.'

'This won't take a minute,' said Ian. 'It could be really urgent.'

'Could?'

'Please,' he said. 'I'll buy you a pint every night for the rest of your life if I'm wrong.'

'Okay,' Duncan sounded reluctant. 'What is it?'

'That red Fiesta you checked for me. The hire car. Can you find out who hired it?'

'Only if you have a very convincing reason. Hire companies don't like to give out that kind of information.'

'It's possible that it's on its way to back Edinburgh Airport. If it is, it'll be there in about an hour. Can you get them to delay the driver?'

'What's he done?'

'I'm not sure exactly, but it could be a matter of life or death.' Could it? Probably not, but best not to take any chances.

Duncan sighed audibly into the phone. 'Okay, I'll give them a call and get them to find something wrong with the car. Not sure how long they can hold him for, though.'

Ian did a quick calculation in his head. Acts two and three ran for just over an hour with a quick scene change. Lucia could be safely on her way in perhaps two hours. 'If anything's going to happen, it will be in the next two hours,' he said, wondering if the car hire people could hold him that long. Then he remembered that they would have details of his flight. 'They should be able to tell you which flight he's on.'

'Don't tell me. You want me to delay the plane.'

'Just stop him getting on it.'

'You're really going to owe me for this.'

'Thanks, you're a star. Got to get back.' He ended the call before Duncan could come up with any objections.

He sent a quick message to Tom and Rob, waited for their thumbs up and returned to his seat. Act three passed without incident, apart from the fact that Micaëla's role was taken by the understudy. A student, Ian thought, who'd obviously watched Cara very closely. In Cara's costume and the long, dark wig, it was hard to tell them apart.

Ian was beginning to worry that he might have made a huge mistake. Duncan would never speak to him again and he'd be hauled in front of Kezia Wallace for a reprimand, or worse. Although there was still act four to get through, and he started to pray that any incident would be enough to vindicate him without anyone actually dying. He looked at his watch. Only fifteen minutes or so until Carmen would draw her dying breath and Lucia could be safely dispatched back to London, where she could still be in danger, but not any danger that he was expected to get her out of.

They had reached the crucial moment. Carmen and José alone on stage. Carmen hurls her ring at José. And he in return stabs her. A bit of an overreaction, Ian thought, but this was opera and one had to allow for dramatic licence. They had reached the point that had caused so much trouble in rehearsal. Stamper, George and Lucia had spent hours on it. At the dress rehearsal it had run like clockwork. George had pulled the knife from his belt, stabbed Lucia, who clutched at her chest and released a pouch of red dye that had been concealed in the folds of her dress. At that point Stamper made his entrance – it was crucial that he did this at exactly the right moment – gathered the dying Lucia in his arms as George was arrested and the curtain fell. But that was the dress rehearsal, after which George had left the stage muttering that a good dress rehearsal was a bad omen and meant disaster on the opening night. He'd been wrong. The opening night also went like clockwork, as had the following three nights. So the dress rehearsal and four nights of performance had gone to plan. What could possibly go wrong tonight? The three of them would probably be able to do it in their sleep. All the same, Ian found himself holding his breath as the crucial moment approached.

In the background, the crowd were applauding Escamillo's triumph in the bullring. The toreador himself was about to appear to claim Carmen as his own. As Lucia threw the ring at his feet, George pulled the knife from his belt and raised it above his head, ready to plunge it into the folds of Lucia's dress. As he raised it, the blade of the knife glinted in the stage light. George looked up at it and for a split second Ian thought they were both thinking the same thing. *Plastic prop knife blades don't glint.* George, in what Ian was later to consider an act of genius, flung the knife down behind him and let it skitter across the stage into the wings. He'd slightly misjudged the distance, although who could blame him in the circumstances? The knife skidded on, to the left of the curtain and flipped off the edge of the stage, landing with a thud in the straw at Caroline's feet. In the meantime, George had lunged forward and grabbed Lucia round the neck as if to strangle her. He glanced up as Stamper appeared – *thank God he was on cue*, Ian thought. George flung Lucia towards Stamper as the soldiers rushed forward to arrest him and the curtain came down with Carmen dying, or on this occasion possibly not dying, in Escamillo's arms.

The curtain rose again to enthusiastic applause from the audience, who were apparently unaware of the sudden alteration to the traditional ending. The three soloists took their bows, appearing unfazed by the drama and the fact that they'd avoided a tragic ending both on and off stage. On their way home, perhaps some of the audience might wonder why a strangled woman would bleed profusely from a chest wound. Either Stamper or Lucia must have punctured the pouch of fake blood, as she was now taking her bow with a bright red stain on the white of her gypsy blouse.

A small girl presented Lucia with an enormous bouquet. A product of Mickey Rix's glasshouse, Ian suspected. The rows of performers on stage came forward to acknowledge the applause. After Stamper, George and Lucia came Cara's understudy, two gypsy girls and then two smugglers and an army captain. Then the group of children who had been brought back from their cartoons, and finally the chorus. The stage manager handed a second bouquet to Stamper, who stepped forward and presented it to the understudy for taking over at short notice. Ian doubted that anyone had noticed, but it was a thoughtful gesture. And where had Stamper managed to find a second bouquet at such short notice?

In the excitement of a dazzling last-night performance, no one seemed worried that a stage knife had been replaced with a real one. After all, no one had been hurt and George had been able to display his skill at improvising. Could he have set it all up himself as a way to show off his acting? Ian didn't think for a moment that George himself had replaced the knife so that he could upstage the others. He'd seen the expression on George's face when he saw what he was holding. And suddenly Ian realised what must have happened. He sprang into action. 'Molly,' he said. 'Call Duncan and tell him there's been an attempted murder and it's vital that he heads off the driver of the Fiesta.' He turned to Caroline. 'I need you to keep that knife safe and free from fingerprints while I go backstage. I'm afraid we might have a missing person.'

Caroline nodded. She leant forward and used her scarf to pick up the knife, which she then wrapped up and put into her handbag.

Ian pushed his way through the crowd that had gathered backstage and headed up the stairs to the dressing rooms. He found Lucia guarded by Tom and Rob. They were urging her to change as quickly as possible so they could get her to somewhere safe. Lucia was arguing that any danger was now over, and she was damned if she was going to miss a good party. Ian left them to it. He found George, who had changed into jeans and a t-shirt and was heading for the bar.

'You okay?' Ian asked. 'That was a quick bit of thinking on your part.'

'Yeah, guess I've just improved on the Bizet version. Need a drink, though.'

'Go ahead. Have you seen Cara?'

George shook his head. 'She went home, didn't she? It was a bit sudden. She was fine in act one. A sudden bout of food poisoning, perhaps. It can get you like that. One minute you're fine, the next, well… Lucky Joanne was wearing a suitably plain dress so we just had to grab Cara's wig from the dressing room and perk up her make-up a bit. She did well, don't you think? I'm glad she got the opportunity.'

'Is Cara usually unreliable like that?'

'I don't think so, but I suppose if she was suddenly sick…'

Ian checked the other two dressing rooms and then searched the marquee the chorus were using, where he also found Stamper congratulating everyone in sight. 'Did anyone actually see Cara leave?' he asked and was greeted with blank looks.

He made his way back to the orchestra pit, where Quentin was using an eraser to bad-temperedly rub out two weeks' worth of pencil marks made by the musicians. 'You'd think the players could do this themselves,' he muttered angrily. 'All in the bar by now, I suppose.'

'Have you seen Cara?' Ian asked.

'Why would I? I'm not her bloody guardian. Went home sick, didn't she?'

Ian left him to get on with it and returned to Caroline, trying to work out when Cara had left and who she had told. Had she slipped out during the interval? 'That car you saw,' he said. 'Could there have been two people in it?'

'Only if one of them was hiding on the back seat, or in the boot.'

Molly returned, putting her phone into her pocket. 'I called Duncan. The car's been returned to the hire place. They weren't in time to stop the driver, a guy called Kasra Mansour. He was booked onto a flight to Istanbul this evening. He checked in online but didn't turn up for the flight. Duncan's called in the Edinburgh police. I told him about the knife incident, and he's getting a squad to come here and look into it.'

'Kasra Mansour? That was the name of Lucia's ex-lover, wasn't it? Was he alone?'

'There was no record of anyone travelling with him.'

So where the hell was Cara? Was she safely at home in bed? Or had she hidden somewhere, or been forced into the boot of Kasra's car? 'I need to be here when the police arrive,' he said. 'But we're going to look pretty stupid if Cara is tucked up in bed at her gran's house.'

'Do you think she had something to do with the knife?' Molly asked. 'Shall I go and check with her grandmother?'

'I think you'd better.' Ian looked at his watch. A quarter to ten. Would Maudie still be up? Would she be terrified if people started knocking on her door at this time of night? There wasn't much he could do about it. They needed to know. 'Okay, but someone should go with you.'

'I'll go,' said Caroline.

He'd hoped she would offer. 'Thanks,' he said. 'It's not far and Molly knows the way.' He was about to warn them to take care along the road and then remembered Caroline's *reclaim the night* outings in Dundee a few years ago. She could take care of herself. They both could. 'Call me when you've spoken to her. If Cara's not there, we need to tell the police.'

The after-show party seemed to be going ahead as planned. Probably just as well. Ian didn't think anyone but the three soloists had noticed anything wrong. It was best not to panic the rest of the cast. Last year the party had been on stage, but *Carmen* was a far bigger production, so the rails of costumes had been packed into baskets and dragged away ready for collection. The marquee had been cleared and tables carried in, as well as plates of food. There was an impromptu dance floor made from pallets and some of the orchestra were playing jazz at the far end of the marquee. It looked set to carry on into the small hours, which was good. The police would want to interview people, and this would make it easy to find them. First up, Ian supposed, would be George, who had just arrived with a crate of beer bottles. 'No point in toing and froing to the bar all night,' he said. 'Oh, by the way, Ian, there were a couple of people asking about you in the bar.'

Damn. He'd forgotten all about Elsa and Mickey. 'Are they still there?' he asked.

'Doubt it,' said George. 'The woman looked a bit hacked off.'

He'd never have knowingly stood Elsa up. But events had taken over and it couldn't be helped. He'd drive up to Inverbank tomorrow with some flowers. No, not flowers, not when Mickey Rix was famous for his glasshouses. Chocolates, perhaps. Or a bottle of wine. Or an invitation to an expensive dinner.

24

Cara was not at her grandmother's house recovering from whatever it was that had forced her to abandon her role before the last act. Maudie returned with Molly and Caroline and demanded to know where her granddaughter was. Molly settled her down in Stamper's living room with a glass of brandy, while Caroline and Ian went to find out exactly when Cara had last been seen, and who had told the understudy she'd be needed for the second half of the opera.

They found Joanne with a group of friends, receiving congratulations on her performance. Ian took her to one side while Caroline questioned the friends.

'Who was it told you that Cara was ill?' Ian asked.

'Two of my friends saw her leaving. They said she looked really ill and I'd better get ready to take on the role.'

'When was this?'

'During the interval. We were getting ready for the mountain scene.'

'And did you check with anyone?'

'Yes, I asked the stage manager. He said he hadn't heard

anything but that I'd better get into costume and be ready to go on.'

'Micaëla comes on near the start of the scene?'

'That's right, just after the fortune tellers see Carmen's death in the cards. Cara wasn't waiting in the wings as she should have been, so I went on in her place.'

Stamper appeared with a glass of champagne and put an arm round her shoulder. 'You were brilliant, my dear,' he said. 'Don't you think so, Ian?'

'Definitely,' he said. He didn't know much about singing, but to him she'd sounded every bit as good as Cara. 'Gavin, when did *you* know that Cara was not going on?'

'The SM told me as I was waiting for my entrance.'

'That's just after Micaëla's exit.'

'That's right. Ready to be shot at by José.'

'And when did you last see Cara?'

'Must have been when she came off stage towards the end of act one. But that's not unusual. She's not on again until act three.'

'Where did she usually go when she wasn't on stage?'

'To her dressing room, I suppose.'

Ian had already checked the dressing rooms and there had been no sign of Cara. Caroline returned and told him that no one, apart from Joanne's two friends, had seen Cara since her duet with José in act one. She'd written down what they had said in a notebook, which she now opened and read to him. Cara had looked very pale, was wrapped in a grey blanket and was being supported by one of the chorus. One of the smugglers, they'd said. Although they didn't know his name.

'Did they tell you what he looked like?'

'Medium height and build, darkish complexion, nothing very helpful.'

That could be any of the smugglers. 'Hair colour?'

'He had a red scarf over his hair, but all the smugglers did so that didn't help very much.'

'Could it have been the driver of the Fiesta? The one you thought was a pirate?'

'Possibly. I only caught a quick glimpse of him.'

'Let's get back to Molly and compare what we know,' he said.

Molly had returned to the office. Maudie, she told them, was being looked after by Stamper's housekeeper.

'Did she tell you anything useful?' Ian asked. 'Had Cara been feeling ill earlier in the day?'

'Maudie said she was fine, but she'd been upset by a quarrel with her boyfriend a couple of weeks ago.'

'What did she tell you about the boyfriend?'

'That was interesting. She said Cara had known this guy, Kas, for a few years. Apparently, she'd been going out with him before she got together with Oliver. Then last year he'd appeared during *Pinafore*. Cara had been upset because Oliver had just broken off their engagement. Maudie liked him because he was very kind to Cara and thought he was taking her mind off the broken engagement.'

'Maudie met him?'

'He went to her house a couple of times, and a few months later she thought they were going out together. She wasn't sure because she didn't see much of Cara until she came here for this year's camp.'

'But they'd quarrelled?'

'That's what Maudie said. He came to visit Cara the week before camp. Cara was here for some voice sessions with Quentin before the serious rehearsals started. She said Kas dropped in and Cara told him to get lost.'

'Does she have any idea where Cara is now?'

'She keeps saying Cara's been kidnapped.'

'I'm beginning to think she might be right.' He picked up a pen and fixed a large sheet of white paper to the wall, hoping it wouldn't leave a mark and that if it did, Stamper wouldn't mind. Writing up what he thought had happened was the only way he could think it through. 'This is what I think,' he said to Molly and Caroline. 'Chip in if you've any ideas of your own.'

He wrote:

Kasra Mansour

Known to have a grudge against Lucia, who had been going to marry him so that he could claim UK citizenship, also a grudge against George if Kasra knew that he was the one who had reported him for a potential marriage of convenience.

Discovers that Lucia and George were both going to be at this year's opera camp.

Writes Lucia a threatening letter.

Sneaks in during the interval disguised in a stolen costume and replaces the knife that was left on the props table for George.

George would stab Lucia and be blamed for causing her death.

Molly tapped her pen on the desk and studied the list. 'There are a few gaps,' she said. 'How did he get the smuggler costume? If he'd been worried about being noticed swapping the knives, why risk being noticed stealing a costume first?'

'He could have got someone to steal it for him,' Caroline suggested. 'Perhaps he tricked one of the children. Told them it was a practical joke?'

'Possible,' said Ian. 'Or he might have got into the marquee after Friday's show, once everyone had left for the night. The security has been all about Lucia, so once she'd left for Inverbank it would have been easier to get in. He could have mingled with the audience as they left and hidden somewhere until it was all quiet.'

'How would he have got out again?' asked Caroline.

'The same way. The bar's open until late. He could have waited until the marquee was empty, snatched the costume and stuffed it into a bag, then slipped into the bar.'

Molly shook her head. 'Still not working,' she said. 'Why send the letter? Wouldn't it be better to take Lucia by surprise?'

'You're right,' said Ian. 'If it wasn't for the letter there would have been very little security. He could have just sauntered in during the interval and replaced the knife. If anyone challenged him, he could have said he was lost.'

'Suppose,' said Molly, 'that Kasra and Cara were in it together?'

'Why?' Ian asked. 'She doesn't have anything against Lucia, does she? We ruled her out once we knew she'd left London before Lucia was pushed down the stairs. And it still doesn't explain the letter. If she was in on the plan, why warn Lucia?'

'Perhaps she got cold feet and the only way for Kasra to keep her quiet was to kidnap her.'

'And where do you suppose she is now? Even if she'd been driven away from here in Kasra's car, she wasn't in it by the time he got to the airport.' A chilling thought. There were any number of places between here and Edinburgh where he could have offloaded a body. But he'd arrived at the airport and checked in his car sooner than they'd expected. He might have broken all speed limits on his way, but would that give him time to kill Cara and dump her body?

'All we know,' said Molly, 'is that Kasra was travelling alone from the airport. She could have been hidden in the car. She could still be there.'

'If she was hidden in the boot, could she have escaped?' Caroline asked.

'Maybe, but Kasra must have had some kind of plan. He couldn't just turn up to return his car with someone tied up in the boot. What's the check-in procedure for hire cars?'

'He probably just handed over the keys. They'll have his credit card details in case there's any damage to the car.'

'How long before they look in the boot?'

'I suppose it depends on how soon the car is booked out again,' said Caroline. 'I don't suppose there are many bookings this late, so possibly not until tomorrow morning.'

'Molly,' said Ian. 'You'd better call them. I can't believe Kasra would just leave her in the boot, but we'd better check.'

Molly picked up her phone and tapped in the number.

Before she'd finished the call, Ian and Caroline were alerted by the sound of sirens. They left Molly in the office and found a car with flashing blue lights in the car park, which was otherwise deserted. Two uniformed police officers climbed out of the car.

'Sergeant Waters,' said the taller of the two. 'From Perth. This is PC Jones. We've a report of an incident involving a knife?'

'Yes,' said Ian. 'Well, no, not exactly. It might be an abduction.'

'A child kidnapped at knifepoint?' The sergeant licked the tip of a pencil and wrote this down in a notebook.

Ian shook his head. 'No, a young woman is missing. The knife was a different incident.'

The sergeant sighed. 'What makes you think this woman

was abducted? Was force involved? Are there any witnesses?'

'Well, no, not exactly. We don't know.'

'And there was a knife, you say?'

'That was on stage.'

'Anyone hurt?'

'No, luckily.'

'And where is the knife now?'

'In my handbag,' said Caroline.

'You know, madam,' said the sergeant, scowling at her, 'that it is an offence to carry a weapon?'

This wasn't going well. 'We can explain that,' said Ian. 'You'd better come through to the office.' He led them through the tunnel to the office, where Molly was still on the phone.

'Thanks,' said Molly, ending the call and putting her phone down on the desk. 'There was no one in the boot,' she told Ian. 'But they found—'

'That will keep,' said Waters. He pulled up a chair and sat down at Ian's desk, indicating that the constable should do the same. 'Right,' he said. 'The knife.'

'It's here,' said Caroline, opening her bag.

'Not so fast.' Waters held up a warning hand. 'Pass the bag across the table and keep your hands where we can see them.'

Did they suspect Caroline of planning an attack? 'I hardly think...' Ian started, but Waters waved his hand to silence him.

Caroline smiled sweetly at them and slid her bag slowly across the desk.

'Constable,' Waters signalled for the PC to open the bag.

'Can't see it,' he said.

'It's wrapped in my scarf,' said Caroline. 'A blue one.'

The PC pulled it out and started to unwrap it.

'You should wear gloves,' said Caroline. 'You'll not want to leave your fingerprints on it.'

The PC looked embarrassed and pulled a pair of surgical gloves from his pocket.

'Why would you bring your knife to the opera?' Waters asked. 'It's illegal to carry—'

'I know,' said Caroline. 'You already told me that. And it's not mine. I picked it up as it fell off the stage and kept it as evidence.'

'And who had it before you so helpfully picked it up?' Waters smirked at her.

'José was about to stab Carmen with it. But he flung it onto the floor instead.'

'And where is this José now?'

'Probably at the party,' said Ian. 'Shall I get him for you?'

'Please,' said Waters.

'Would you like anything?' asked Molly. 'Tea, coffee?'

'Thank you,' said Waters. 'We'll have coffee.'

Molly left to make the coffee as Ian returned with George.

'Ah,' said Waters as George came in. 'Mr José, I assume.'

'George Strike,' said George, holding out his hand, which was ignored. 'José is the name of my character.'

'Your character?'

'In the opera,' said Ian. 'It's José that stabs Carmen.'

'So it's all play acting,' said Waters, looking irritated. 'Not a real stabbing incident.'

'It could have been a very nasty incident,' said Ian. 'If George hadn't noticed and taken some very quick action.'

Molly returned with a tray of coffee and biscuits, which she put down on the desk. She poured the coffee and handed round the biscuits. An act that considerably cheered up the constable, who helped himself to a handful of chocolate Hobnobs.

'You'd better tell me exactly what happened.' Waters looked at George in a way that suggested he had far better things to do on a Saturday evening than to spend it questioning a lot of hysterical opera singers. 'Constable, don't just sit there. Take notes.' The PC, who was biting into Hobnob number four, pulled out a notebook and pencil.

'Where do you want me to begin?' asked George, not looking a whole lot more cheerful than the sergeant.

'Can I suggest,' said Ian, who wasn't sure he should be sitting in on the interviews but had staked squatters' rights over his office, 'that you start by telling us about how the props are organised.'

The sergeant looked relieved. 'This is not yours, then?' he asked, eyeing the knife, which was now lying in front of him on Caroline's scarf.

George shook his head. 'They're provided by the hire company. You'd need to check with Gavin. He'll have paperwork.'

'You've had some problems with that scene, haven't you?' prompted Ian.

'We rehearsed it a lot with different knives. Some looked more authentic than others. I can't remember how many we tried out.'

'So,' said Ian again, the sergeant seeming to have lost interest. 'When you picked up the knife from the props table, you didn't think it was odd that it wasn't the usual one?'

'It was a quick costume change. I had to appear looking downtrodden. I changed my shirt for a more ragged, dirty one and strapped on the belt that had the knife in a sheath. Like I said, it was a quick change and I didn't have time to check the knife. I could only see the top part of the handle and that looked quite normal.'

'And it was part of the opera that you had to stab this lady, er... Ms Carmen in the chest?'

'Are you not familiar with the plot of *Carmen*?' George asked.

'I'm afraid not. Prefer a nice, cheerful musical myself. What was supposed to happen after you stabbed her? Isn't it dangerous to use a knife on stage?'

Ian sighed. 'The usual knife is a plastic one with a retracting blade. Not dangerous at all. But someone had replaced it with that one.' He pointed to the knife on the table.

'Mr Strike,' said the sergeant. 'Had you and Ms Carmen quarrelled?'

'Her real name is Lucia Pedro Morales. And we're always squabbling,' said George with an impatient sigh. 'But believe me, if I'd wanted her dead, I wouldn't have stabbed her in front of an audience.'

He's not helping, Ian thought. This sergeant was a dim-witted specimen. The kind that gave the police a bad name and made him less sorry that he no longer counted as one of their colleagues. But it was no use irritating him. He almost wished for Kezia Wallace, who was at least intelligent enough to get to the nub of a case quickly. 'Someone substituted the knife on the props table with that one,' he repeated. 'So someone obviously wanted her dead.'

'Were there any witnesses to this substitution?'

'It gets quite frantic backstage during a performance,' said George. 'The stage manager organises the table at the start of the show in a way that makes it easy for performers to find their props. There would have been people taking things and putting them back again all through the show.'

'I think it happened in the interval,' said Ian. 'A smuggler's costume went missing before the show, and someone saw a smuggler leaving in a car during the interval.'

'One of the cast?'

'No smugglers were missing from that scene. I assume someone dressed in the stolen costume replaced the knife and made a getaway in a car. We think it was a man called Kasra Mansour. He was booked onto a flight leaving Edinburgh Airport to Istanbul tonight, but failed to turn up. That's why you are here. Didn't your colleagues in Edinburgh brief you?'

At that moment the door burst open, and Maudie appeared followed by Stamper's housekeeper. 'Sorry,' said the housekeeper. 'I tried to stop her.'

'Ah,' said Maudie, noticing the sergeant and waving her handbag at him. 'I want to know where my granddaughter is.'

'A missing child?' asked the sergeant.

'No, she's not a child. She's been kidnapped.'

'We don't know that,' said Molly. 'But—'

'Is this lady involved in the knife incident?' the sergeant interrupted.

'What knife?' asked Maudie.

'Sit down,' said Molly kindly. 'Shall I get you a cup of tea? Once everyone has had time to change out of their costumes, we'll go and ask if anyone's seen her.'

'I don't want any more tea. I want to know where Cara is.'

'We all want to know that,' said Ian. 'Perhaps you could describe her for the sergeant.'

'I'm sure the constable and myself can manage here,' said Waters. 'I'd be grateful if you and the ladies could leave us.'

'Be happy to,' said Ian, leading them towards the door.

'But what about Cara?' wailed Maudie.

'You,' said Waters, pointing at Maudie, 'wait outside. We'll call you in when we're ready to question you.'

'I'll wait with her,' said the housekeeper. 'Don't you worry, now. She can't have gone far.'

'Any luck with the car hire people?' Ian asked Molly once they were out of earshot.

'That's what I was trying to tell the sergeant. There was no one tied up in the boot, but they did find this.' Molly clicked open a photo they had sent her. 'It's a scarf,' she added. 'I showed it to Maudie and she's fairly certain it's Cara's.'

One of Joanne's friends had told him that Cara was wrapped in a grey blanket. 'Did they mention a blanket?' he asked.

Molly shook her head.

'And did they find the scarf in the boot of the car or on one of the passenger seats?'

'In the boot.'

'So it's not likely that she left it in the car before this evening.'

'He could have gagged her with it,' said Molly. 'Or tied her wrists with it and bundled her into the car. She couldn't have struggled much if her wrists were tied.'

Ian had been wondering if they might find Cara somewhere close by. Perhaps Kasra had left her unconscious in a storeroom, or a cloakroom, or even an empty office. He'd get some of the backstage people to search, but if a scarf had been left in the car, this seemed less likely.

The office had been requisitioned by the police and they could hardly stand outside the door, where they were now, and work out what might have happened. 'Why don't you two go and order coffee and sandwiches in the bistro,' he said. 'I'll get Tom and Rob to start a search of the building and grounds, just to make sure Cara's not still here.'

By the time he joined Molly and Caroline, a search was underway. Tom and Rob had gathered a group of stage-hands and would report back to Ian once they had checked all the possible hiding places. Ian had asked Cara's friends if she remembered her wearing a scarf before she changed into her costume. One friend thought she had been, but added that it was a favourite of Cara's and she wore it most days. The missing blanket worried him. Could it have been used to wrap Cara's body?

On his way back to the bistro he noticed that Maudie was no longer sitting outside. He needed the laptop, so he tapped on the door and went in, interrupting what sounded like a fruitless and time-wasting interview in which Maudie was recounting her entire life history to the two policemen. He picked up the laptop and headed back to the bistro.

Caroline had ordered a large plate of sandwiches and, seeing them, Ian realised he hadn't eaten for several hours. He took a bite of one, started up the laptop and logged into Google Maps, highlighting the fastest route from Dundas to Edinburgh Airport.

'What are we looking for?' Molly asked.

'It depends on whether he dumped her or if she escaped. We'd better consider both.'

'If she escaped,' said Caroline, 'the car would have to have been stationary or driving very slowly.'

'Which rules out anywhere on the motorway except perhaps a service station,' said Ian, checking the number of services between Dundas and Edinburgh.

'And if he dumped her,' said Molly, 'it would have been somewhere quiet, so probably between here and Perth. After Perth it's motorway all the way to the airport.'

'If she'd escaped, wouldn't she have made contact with someone by now?' said Caroline. 'Do we know who her friends are?'

'We know she didn't call her grandmother or the two friends we spoke to. Could it have been someone in the chorus?'

'George or Quentin, perhaps,' Molly suggested.

Ian shook his head. 'The car was back at the airport before the opera finished. I can't see her hanging around a service station waiting. She'd have been scared.'

'She can't have called the police, or we'd have been told,' said Ian. 'Do we even know if she has her phone with her?'

'One way to find out,' said Molly, getting her own phone out and checking the numbers on Gavin's lists.

Why hadn't they thought of that earlier? It was so obvious. Someone's missing. You call them.

But Molly shook her head. 'No answer,' she said.

'No answer or turned off?' he asked. 'If the phone's turned on the police can trace where it is.'

'That lot in there?' Molly shook her head in the direction of the office. 'Those two are as useless as chocolate teapots. Anyway, the phone's turned off or out of battery.'

Ian's phone rang with a call from Gavin to say the police were now leaving and had arrested George. 'For God's sake,' Ian said. 'Why have they arrested him?'

'Possession of a knife for now, but they were muttering about attempted murder.'

'Where have they taken him?'

'Perth. They can keep him for twenty-four hours. Then they either have to charge him or let him go. But don't worry.

I've called my lawyer. A good bloke. He'll have George out within the hour.'

'What about Maudie? What did they say to her?'

'They just told her that a person can't be reported missing for twenty-four hours. She was a bit upset.'

Ian was not surprised. 'Where is she now?'

'She's here at the party, talking to some of Cara's friends and muttering threats about writing to the chief constable.'

Best place for her, probably. She'd be better there than back at her cottage worrying. And if Cara was found in one of the buildings, she'd be on hand to look after her.

25

They finished their sandwiches and Ian was wondering what they should do next when Tom and Rob appeared. 'We've done a thorough search,' said Rob. 'The other two are still searching the car park, but there are not many hiding places there, and there was no sign of her in any of the buildings.'

'Is Lucia still here?' Ian asked.

'Leaving in the next half-hour, we hope,' he said. 'Her Ladyship insisted on staying for a drink with the cast. Her flight doesn't leave until midnight, so we couldn't very well stop her. Anyway, it meant all four of us could look for Cara.'

'I suppose Lucia's not in any danger now,' said Ian. 'Except missing her flight.'

Dave appeared looking breathless. 'We found this,' he said, holding up a grey blanket.

Cara had been seen wrapped in a grey blanket when she left. 'Where?' he asked. Did that mean she was still here? Or had they dumped it as soon as they were in the car?

'It was stuffed into a litter bin in the car park, near the café.'

In a litter bin. So one of them would have to have got out of the car and that wasn't likely if they were in a hurry. 'No sign of Cara, I suppose?'

'We did a thorough search, but this is all we found.'

Ian drained his coffee cup, stood up and clipped on Lottie's lead. 'The bin outside the café? I'd better take a look.'

'I'll come with you,' said Rob. 'See if Dave missed anything.'

Dave shrugged. 'I did a thorough check and found nothing,' he said.

'Can't do any harm to take another look,' said Rob. 'I'll go with Ian. You stay here and get something to eat.'

Ian and Rob left the bistro and walked across the car park. The café was locked up for the night, with shutters padlocked across the windows and chairs and tables stacked up outside. Ian had never wondered about Lottie's skill as a bloodhound, but he let her sniff the blanket. Who knew what hidden talents she might have? Lottie obviously thought this was a game and tugged at the blanket with her teeth. Ian pulled it away from her. It had been a useless idea anyway. But then Lottie, with uncharacteristic bravery given the café's proximity to the alpaca fence, darted around behind it to where the bins were kept. Ian followed her. Was Cara hiding there? Rob pulled a torch from his jacket pocket, and they followed Lottie to the back of the building. There wasn't much there except a couple of large wheelie bins and a small shed. Rob lifted the bin lids and found only sandwich wrappers, stale bread rolls and plastic coffee cups.

The shed contained a few crates and a box of empty bottles. *Not surprising she wasn't here,* Ian thought. If Cara had managed to escape from the boot of the car, she wouldn't hang around any longer than she had to. She'd wait until the car had driven off and then make her escape. But where would she go? They'd already searched the theatre and bistro, even Gavin's house and there had been no sign of her. Could she be in one of the tents or hiding in someone else's car? And how long would it take to search all of them? If she'd been involved in the knife incident, even as an unwilling accomplice, she wouldn't want to hang around. And if she'd intended giving herself up to the police, she would have done it by now. She couldn't have missed their arrival with sirens and flashing blue lights. She didn't have a car of her own, so she couldn't have escaped that way. Where the hell was she?

'Not much point in hanging around here,' said Rob. 'She's obviously gone.'

He was right. Ian kicked one of the wheelie bins in frustration.

'What was that?' Rob asked, suddenly alert.

'What?' Ian asked.

'That noise.'

'Just me kicking the bin,' said Ian.

'The bins are plastic. It sounded like you hit something hard.'

'Probably just a stone,' said Ian, kneeling down and feeling behind the bin. He could feel grass and the sting of a nettle and then he felt something cold and smooth with the tips of his fingers. 'Help me move the bin,' he said to Rob.

They heaved it out of the way and Rob shone his torch along the ground.

'There,' said Ian, pointing at something lodged in a bunch of stinging nettles. He kicked them down with his foot and, not wanting to be stung again, edged a small rectangular object out onto the concrete path. A mobile phone. He bent to pick it up and tried to turn it on, but the battery was dead. 'We'd better take it back to the bistro and see if anyone has a charger,' he said. It was a smartphone but not the very latest model. With any luck it wouldn't be locked with a password.

'Any developments?' he asked, arriving back at the bistro.

Molly shook her head. 'Not a word from George. I can't believe they had enough to arrest him.'

'They seemed obsessed with carrying an illegal knife,' said Caroline. 'They nearly arrested me as well.'

'Poor old George,' said Ian. 'The knife will have his prints all over it. I hope they're not going to charge him for that.'

'Gav's got legal people lined up,' said Molly. 'They can't interview him until he has a solicitor with him.'

Ian supposed that was good. It might mean George was detained for longer, but having a solicitor with him could stop him from saying something stupid. George had a habit of opening his mouth and putting his foot in it. 'There might be prints on this as well,' said Ian, using a tissue to pull the phone out of his pocket. 'We found it behind the café. The battery's dead. Anyone got a charger? And some of those latex gloves?'

'They use gloves for serving food,' said Molly, running into the kitchen and returning with a box of them.

Caroline pulled a charger out of her handbag. It was a good match for the phone. *What were the chances of that?* But at least something was going well. He plugged it in and waited. After a few minutes the phone sprang to life and Ian grabbed it eagerly, but of course, he could only get as far as a screen that told him the date and time. It needed a passcode. Of course it did. No one left phones unlocked these days. 'It could be Cara's,' he said. 'She might have escaped from the car, made a call and then dropped it in the dark.'

'Can I have a look?' said Molly, pulling on a pair of gloves.

Ian handed it to her, wondering if there was much she could do. 'Do you think it might be Cara's?' he asked. She'd been trying to befriend Cara, but did women's friendships stretch to sharing phone codes? Molly was looking at it blankly, so presumably not. 'Is the lockscreen picture any help?' he asked.

'Do we know if she likes cats?' Caroline asked, as Molly held up the phone to show a picture of a black and white cat.

'No idea,' said Molly. 'She didn't like Lottie much.'

'So she's not a dog person,' said Caroline. 'Doesn't mean she's a cat one.'

They were wasting time. They should be out there trying to find Cara, not messing around with a phone.

'Shall I try calling her again? That would tell us if it's her phone,' said Molly, taking out her own phone. But before she could tap in the number, they all jumped. The phone was ringing, and a name flashed up on the screen. Quentin. Not Quentin Lyle, just Quentin. So the phone belonged to someone who knew him well. Ian clicked to answer it. He put it on speaker but didn't say anything.

'Olly?' Definitely Quentin's voice. He sounded more than usually bad-tempered. 'Olly, what the heck are you playing at?'

'This is Oliver's phone?' Ian asked.

'Who the hell are you? Where's my brother?'

'We don't know,' said Ian. 'We found this phone behind the café.'

'The café here at Dundas?'

'Yes, the one near the car park entrance.'

'He's here?'

'That's what we need to find out. Where were you expecting him to be when you called him?'

'He was supposed to be coming to help me clean up the scores and pack them away, ready to return to the hire people. He told me he'd be here during the interval. I was going to buy him a drink.'

'We don't know when he dropped his phone, or where he is now. You'd better come and meet us in the bistro.' Ian was aware of Quentin grumbling as he ended the call. But it couldn't be helped. The scores would have to wait. Right now, finding Cara was more important.

'Do you think Oliver has Cara?' Caroline asked.

'Why would he?' said Molly. 'They broke up a year ago.'

'Perhaps he's never forgiven Cara for breaking up with him,' Caroline suggested. 'Or perhaps he wants her back.'

'No,' said Molly. 'He was the one to break it off. Too ashamed about his involvement in the whisky scam.'

'It wasn't that,' said Quentin, arriving in time to catch the tail end of their conversation.

'What was it?' Ian asked, wondering if the ins and outs of Oliver's love life were relevant.

'I'd rather not say,' said Quentin. 'I'm more concerned about where my brother is now and why he left his phone behind the café.'

Ian went to the bar and bought him a pint. 'Have a seat,' he said. 'We're trying to unravel all of this.'

'All of what?'

Ian wondered how much Quentin knew. Did musical directors pay attention to the non-musical happenings on stage, or would he have been following his score and not looking up? 'You noticed they changed the action on stage at the end of the opera? Do you know why?'

'Bloody stars. They have a habit of changing stuff without telling anyone.' Quentin gulped down half of his pint and scowled at them.

'In this case it was a last-minute change that no one could predict,' said Ian. 'George noticed that the knife he was holding wasn't a prop one. It was a real knife. If he'd stabbed Lucia with it, he could have killed her.'

Quentin turned pale and put his glass down suddenly, spilling some beer onto the table. 'Someone substituted the prop knife with a real one? You don't think my brother did that, do you?'

Ian hadn't been thinking that. Perhaps he should have been. 'Is there any reason why he would? Does he have a grudge against Lucia, or George for that matter?'

'No. I don't think he's ever met Lucia and he definitely had nothing against George. They were good friends last year.'

Molly gave him a quick explanation of everything that had been going on since the delivery of the anonymous letter.

'My God,' said Quentin. 'And I thought this was just a quiet little opera company.'

'Did you know the guy who died here last year?' Ian asked. Probably not. As a voice coach he wouldn't see much of what went on backstage.

'I didn't know him well, but I know more about him than I'd like to.' He sighed. 'Look, I'd better tell you about last year.'

'Does it have anything to do with what happened tonight?' Or were they going off on another goose chase?

'It's possible, yes. I just wish Olly was here to tell his side of it, but…'

'I don't think it can wait until he turns up,' said Ian. He could be anywhere by now and they couldn't even phone him.

'He's ashamed of what he did,' said Quentin. 'He knew he'd been very stupid.'

'The business with the money?'

'That didn't help, but that's not why he ended it with Cara.'

'Why did he, then?' Molly asked.

'There was this bloke hanging around. A friend of Gavin's, I think, but he had a thing for Cara.'

'A thing?'

'He was always following her around. Cara wasn't interested. She was involved with my brother. But this bloke wouldn't let it go. He told Olly that Cara was having an affair with Andy Meade.'

'And was she?'

'No,' said Quentin. 'She wasn't.' He put his beer glass down on the table and stared into it.

There was more to it, Ian was sure. Quentin hadn't told them the full story. 'You're quite fond of Cara, aren't you?' he said.

Quentin nodded. 'I felt protective. Sorry for the poor girl. She told me Meade had attacked her and that Olly hadn't believed her. I was furious with him.'

So that's why he was so gentle with Cara; guilt that his brother had behaved so badly. He went to the bar and bought him a whisky, patting him on the shoulder as he put it down in front of him. 'Tell me more about the man who was pestering her,' he said gently. 'Was he part of the opera?'

Quentin downed the whisky in a single gulp. 'No. He hung about in the village. Didn't come up here very much. I don't think Gavin or George knew he was here. Foreign chap. Turkish, I think. He'd met Cara in London a couple of years ago and last year she and Gavin went to visit him in Edinburgh. Something to do with Fashion Week. That was a week or two before *Pinafore*. He turned up after rehearsals began and started to make a nuisance of himself.'

'Can you think of any reason he might have had it in for Lucia?'

'*Lucia?*' He looked at Ian in surprise. 'None at all. But I didn't know him well. Do you think he had something to do with the knife?'

'Either him or Cara,' said Ian. 'They're both involved somehow.'

'Cara would never do anything like that.'

'Not even as a final night prank?'

'Absolutely not.'

'She did change her duet with George.'

'That's quite different. She felt irritated with him – we've all felt like that at times – and thought it would make a good interpretation. But switching knives? No, never.'

He was probably right. Kasra had a far greater reason to hate Lucia and George. But why abduct Cara? Had she discovered what he planned? Had he intercepted her before she could draw attention to the knife? And where the hell were they both now? All three of them? 'Where does your brother live?' he asked.

'He's got one of those log cabins in Blair Woods. About five miles north of here.'

'Does he have a landline?'

'No, just his mobile. I should go and see if he's there.'

Was that where both of them were now? Had he rescued Cara and taken her there?

If Quentin was going, he should go as well. Who knew what might be going on with the two of them? After what had happened on stage, Cara's pulling out of her last act and a suspicious Turk on the loose, he doubted that they'd find a cosy couple making up after a lovers' tiff.

His phone rang. It was Duncan. 'Thought you should know,' he said, 'that a car was stolen from the long stay car park at the airport about an hour and a half ago. Unfortunately for the thief, the owner flew back in this evening and reported it missing. I'm calling you because it drove through a speed camera just outside Perth and looks like it's heading in your direction.'

'How up to date are you with what's been going on here?' Ian asked.

'I know the Perth police have arrested someone for possession of a dangerous weapon.'

'They've arrested the wrong man,' said Ian. 'George was actually something of a hero. He noticed the replacement knife just in time.'

'The wrong man?' Duncan asked. 'That suggests you think there's a right man.'

'I think the man who stole the car is Kasra Mansour. I also think he abducted one of the singers, who then escaped. Now he's on his way back here.'

'The singer is with you?'

'No, we don't know where she is, but if you want to find out who was responsible for setting up an attempted murder, you need to send a team back here to look out for the stolen car. Preferably not the two idiots you sent last time.'

'Edinburgh had to hand it over to the local team. It was out of my area. But I'll see if I can get a response unit out there to look out for the car.'

'What sort of car is it?'

'A bright green, eight-year-old Clio.' He read out the registration number.

'An odd choice,' said Ian.

'Probably the only one he could break into. Flashier cars have better security. And talking of security, have you got measures in place there?'

'I'll see to it,' said Ian, ending the call.

He clicked on Rob's number. 'You've not left with Lucia yet?' he asked.

'She's faffing around with her cases right now.'

'We need to keep her here for a bit longer. I'm sorry, it means extra work for you guys but I'm sure Gavin will make it up to you.'

'What's going on?'

'We think there might be a suspect on his way here in a stolen car. If he spotted your car on the road, you could all be in danger.'

'What do you want us to do with her?'

A good question. 'Ask Gavin if she can stay in the house. It's well protected. One of you stay with her, Cara's gran as well. And one of you needs to keep a lookout for the car. It's a bright green Clio. If you see it before the police arrive, be careful. He may be armed.'

What was one man going to do against an armed thug? Even a well-built, security-trained guy like Rob. He thought about the layout of the estate. The audience should have left by now. The cast were all at a party in the marquee behind the barn and the campsite was on the far side of that. The tunnel to the house had lockable double doors and there were gates between the barns and the car park that could be closed. He called Gavin and gave him a brief run-down of what was happening. Gavin promised to have all the gates locked and keep everyone in the marquee until it was safe to leave.

'Don't approach him,' he said to Rob. 'Call Molly if you see him. She's going to stay in the bistro and coordinate everyone's movements.'

'We've got some stingers,' said Rob. I could lay one near the gate. That would slow him down.'

'Okay, but don't use it unless you have to. You don't want to puncture the police tyres so don't use it unless you're sure it's him.'

'I'll keep watch from the ticket office. That way I'll see him as he turns into the car park.'

'Molly,' said Ian. 'Did you get that? You stay here and keep in contact with Gavin and the security guys. Quentin, can you stay with her? I'll leave Lottie with you. She'll bark if anyone's lurking around outside. Lock the doors after we've left.'

'Where are you going?' Molly asked.

'I'm going to pay a visit to Oliver's cabin.'

'You think that's where Cara and Olly went?' asked Quentin.

'I think it's quite likely. It's isolated and well away from the road. She'll probably expect Kasra to be on his way to Turkey by now. I don't know how much she's been involved with this, but there's something she's not been telling us, and she wants to lie low. I think she escaped from Kasra's car, hid behind the café and watched out for Oliver. Quentin, did she know he was coming to help you with the scores?'

'More than likely. I've been ranting on about them for days.'

'Can you and Molly text Duncan the coordinates for Oliver's cabin? If the green Clio's not been seen here, they'll want to get a unit up there as soon as they can.'

He and Caroline had been in a number of sticky situations together in the past. She had surprising self-defence skills and a clear head. She was also trained in first aid, although he hoped that wouldn't be necessary, and was exactly what he needed. He grinned at her. 'You up for it?' he asked.

'Absolutely,' she said. 'The old team back in action again.'

'It might be a complete waste of time,' he said. 'We could get there and find nothing.'

'But even if it's only Oliver and Cara, we need to talk to them, right?'

'Cara's got a hell of a lot of questions to answer. Oliver as well, I think.'

'Do you think it's all connected?' Molly asked. 'Andy Meade's death, his attack on Cara and the threat to Lucia and George?'

'It looks like it, doesn't it?'

Molly agreed. 'We were puzzled about the two cases, but it does seem as if Kasra is the link we were missing.'

'You don't think I should come with you?' asked Quentin. 'Olly is my brother. I feel a bit responsible.'

'I think you are more useful here.' Quentin had a vicious temper, but apart from that he was rather puny, and except when doing anything musical, he was uncoordinated, clumsy even. He'd be more of a liability.

Molly seemed to agree and winked at Ian. 'I'll need you

here,' she told Quentin. 'We're going to be busy keeping it all coordinated.'

'What if Kasra does turn up there?' Quentin asked. 'Won't you be in danger?'

'He won't be expecting us,' said Ian. 'We can surprise him. And hopefully the police won't be far behind us.'

26

Caroline keyed the location of Oliver's cabin into her phone. 'It's about twenty minutes,' she said. 'Through the village, then a few miles further on there's a turning to the forest. Looks like it's just a track.'

'We need a plan,' said Ian. 'And a plan B in case Kasra's already there.'

'So plan A is just to talk to Oliver and Cara? You think they'll want to talk?'

'We'll need to get them on our side. Be impressed by Cara's escape and work from there. Oliver sounds like a guilt-ridden type. He's probably longing to get it all off his chest.'

'*All* meaning?'

'That he may have been complicit in Andy Meade's death, that he might know who is behind the whisky scam.'

'Do you think he knows anything about the knife?'

Ian thought about that for a moment. 'Probably not, unless Cara's poured her heart out to him. It must be a couple of hours since they left Dundas. Plenty of time for a serious bit of talking.'

'Then we get them to spill the beans. What next?'

Ian wondered about that. 'Depends what the beans are, I suppose. We'll call Molly and find out if anything's happened at Dundas. Then play it by ear. If Kasra hasn't turned up there we'll need to keep a look out for him.'

'Or we can persuade them to come back to Dundas with us. What's plan B?'

'We'll need plan B if Kasra's already there when we arrive. We'll see his car, so we'll be expecting him, but he won't know about us.'

'You're planning to storm in and accuse him of... of what, exactly?'

'Attempted murder, abduction, murdering Andy Meade, that's enough for the moment.' Ian wished he felt as confident as he sounded. What if Kasra was armed? Well, it would be two against one. Possibly four against one if Cara and Oliver did their bit. And if he was right about Cara's abduction and it was not some elaborate plan that Cara was in on. But if that was the case, why had Kasra driven all the way to Edinburgh and then back here again in a stolen car? A man who blithely exchanged knives in order to cause a fatal stabbing was not likely to be conscientious about returning a hire car on time. No, Ian was sure he was right. Cara had thwarted his attempts to silence her.

Caroline was keeping an eye on her phone. They wouldn't want to miss the turning and waste precious time. 'We need a plan C as well,' she said.

Ian thought he'd got everything covered. 'Why?' he asked.

'Because Kasra might turn up while we are in the middle of our cosy chat with Oliver and Cara.'

A good point. He'd see Ian's car, so he'd know it was not just Oliver and Cara in the cabin. He and Caroline would lose the element of surprise, but it would still be four against one. If Kasra had a gun, would they be able to disarm him? He wasn't sure. 'Any suggestions?' he asked.

'One of us needs to keep a lookout for him. We'd probably hear his car or see the lights, so we could ambush him before he gets into the house.'

'He'd see my car when he arrived.'

'It's a forest,' said Caroline. 'We can park out of sight.'

They had arrived at the track into the forest. Ian slowed the car and turned off the road. 'How far from here?' he asked.

'About a mile.'

'Okay, a few minutes in and I'm going to turn my lights off. We want to surprise them whether Kasra is there or not, and there's enough light from the moon to see our way.'

He drove on slowly. As the track narrowed, the trees became denser. Ian wound his window down and stared out as he drove carefully through the forest. Mainly pine trees, he noticed, which was good. The ground was firm after the dry weather, but the floor of pine needles meant there was little noise from his tyres. That it was also less likely that they would hear another car approaching was something he tried to put out of his mind for the moment. As he manoeuvred the car round a bend in the track, he could see a dim light from one of the cabin windows about a hundred yards ahead. 'Someone's in,' he said. 'It hasn't been a wasted journey.'

'Unless it's just squatters,' said Caroline, with a nervous laugh.

'Or perhaps Oliver always leaves a light on.'

'Look,' said Caroline, grabbing his arm. 'A car.'

Ian pulled off the track and stopped his own car behind a cluster of ferns. *Not much cover,* he thought, but they were probably too far from the cabin to be noticed in the dark. He peered through the windscreen. They were too far away to see what kind of car it was. Probably Oliver's. If Kasra had arrived, wouldn't there be two cars? Unless this one was a green Clio and Oliver had parked somewhere else, it looked as if they had got there first. Which was good, but they should still be very careful. 'We'll walk from here,' he said. 'Keep to the edge of the track and hide behind a tree if you see anyone.'

As they drew closer to the car, Ian took out his phone and shone the flashlight at it. A green Clio. He lowered the light and shone it on the number plate. It was the stolen car. So where was Oliver's? Had they all got it wrong? Had Oliver just gone off on his own somewhere and left Cara to be recaptured by Kasra? And if so, what were they doing here? That didn't make any sense. If Kasra was holding Cara against her will, bringing her to the hideout of her ex-boyfriend was highly unlikely. In any case, however upset Oliver had been about his breakup with Cara, he didn't sound like the type to abandon her. And dropping his phone in the same spot as they had found the blanket was too much of a coincidence. He was sure they were together. But apparently, not here.

'Look,' Caroline whispered. 'The track bends round behind the cabin. Oliver's car might be at the back.'

She was right. 'Let's go and have a look,' Ian said.

They crept silently round to the back of the cabin and found a wooden shed. A door fastened with a metal pole slotted between two brackets. Unless the shed had another door, there was no one inside. Or if there was, they had been shut in there by someone else. An idea that sent a chill down his spine. He found a missing panel on the side of the shed. He placed his ear against the opening but could hear nothing. It was a small gap in the timber but large enough to shine his torch through. 'There's a car in there,' he said.

'Do you think they were trying to make it look like there was no one here?'

Ian looked at the cabin and could see a dim light moving inside. Another torch. Were Cara and Oliver hiding inside? Could he and Caroline break in and tackle Kasra before he found them? They crept up to the window and Ian peered inside. What he saw horrified him. He slid down the wall of the cabin and sat down in a heap of pine needles, dragging Caroline with him. He switched off the light on his phone and texted Molly. *Get the police here NOW.* Then he sat and waited for her reply, praying that she'd seen the message. Thankfully he didn't have to wait very long. *Police just arrived and now on their way to you.*

How long had it taken them to drive from Dundas? He looked at the time on his phone. About twenty minutes, and he'd taken that last stretch very slowly. 'We can't wait,' he said to Caroline. 'You need to see what's going on in there. Stand up very quietly and have a quick look.'

Caroline did as she was told and then sank back onto the ground. 'Oh God,' she said. 'What can we do?'

He knew the scene had imprinted itself on her brain just as it had on his. Oliver tied to a chair, blindfolded and with his back to the window they were looking through. A noose around his neck, the rope looped around a ceiling beam and trailing across the floor to Cara, who was standing on the other side of the room with her back to Oliver. The end of the rope was wound around her wrist. A man, Kasra he supposed, was standing behind her holding a knife to her throat. It was clear what the plan was. If her throat was cut, Cara would fall forwards. The rope round her wrist would pull Oliver and the chair up and away from the floor and he would hang, the noose strangling him. Kasra would remove the rope from Cara's wrists and tie it to the beam. He'd wipe the knife, put it into Oliver's hand to make sure that his fingerprints were on it and drop it near to Cara's body. He'd staged the perfect murder. It would look as if Oliver had killed Cara and then himself in a fit of remorse. Kasra would tidy up, leave in the stolen car and dump it somewhere. Ian suspected a convenient part of the Forth Estuary, where he could catch a bus into Edinburgh and escape by train or plane. Train, Ian thought, was most likely. It would be anonymous. He could be in London in four hours or so and then make his way to Dover and cross the channel as a foot passenger. He'd assume it would be hours, if not days, before the bodies were discovered and by then he'd be well away from the country. He'd be back in his Turkish home ready to claim he'd been there for days.

Ian glanced in through the window again. Cara looked as if she was keeping him talking, but the window was double-glazed against a Scottish winter, and he couldn't hear what she was saying. Considering the situation she was in, she looked calm. She was, of course, a trained actor. He just hoped she could keep it up for a bit longer. Until he and Caroline had worked out what to do.

Caroline was using a stick to scratch something into the pine needles that covered the ground around them. It was, he realised, a plan of the room. 'What are you thinking?' he whispered.

'We need to get the timing exactly right,' she said. 'And pray that they didn't lock the door.'

Ian peered at the door, which was on the other side of the room. It was a heavy-duty, modern door with a double cylinder deadbolt. Ian recognised it as similar to one Lainie had recently had fitted to her own house. She'd wanted a door that locked with a key from both sides, having locked herself out in the garden recently, unable to get in because she'd left the key inside the house. Oliver's cabin was the only building for miles and perhaps if he'd been a bit more careful about locking the door, they might not be in this position now. On the other hand, what were the chances that Kasra had thought of looking for a key? He'd have been too occupied. To start with, he'd have needed to disable one or both of them somehow. He couldn't have fixed up his elaborate concoction of rope with the two of them passively watching. On the right-hand side of the room he could see what he took to be a walk-in cupboard. *A larder,* he thought. The door was ajar, and he could see bottles and packets of food on shelves. He could also see a bolt. His guess was that he'd grabbed Cara and bundled her inside at knifepoint. They'd have been taken by surprise and Oliver was enough like his brother not to be the type to leap into action. Kasra was tall and muscular. It would have been easy to overpower a skinny, unfit type like Oliver and tie him up.

'This is perfect,' said Caroline, pulling the metal bar from the barn door.

'Perfect for what?' Ian asked, remembering Caroline's skill at improvising in sticky situations.

'For smashing the window,' she said.

'Okay, you're going to break the window. Then what?'

'No,' she said. 'You are. Give me a few minutes to get round to the door. I'll burst in and make a dive for the rope. From Oliver's side of the beam my weight will be a counterbalance. As soon as you see me, you smash the glass and climb in through the window. And while I'm hanging there, you disarm Kasra.'

'Well,' he said, seeing all the things that could go wrong.

'As long as I can break enough of the glass and get in fast, it could work.'

Caroline prodded at the window frame, which was only a foot or so from the ground. 'It may be double-glazed,' she said. 'But look how rotten the frame is. Distract them by smashing the glass, then give the frame a good kick, and you're in. Cara doesn't look the type to stand by and watch. She'll take any opportunity to get away from the knife. Anyway, having me on the rope will drag her away from Kasra. He'll take his eyes off her for a second and she'll have time to unwind the rope from her wrist and be able to... I don't know, run away or give him a good kick.'

'And while she's running away or kicking, I make a grab for the knife. Unarmed?'

'You'll still have the iron bar. You can whack him over the head with it.'

He looked through the window again. Cara was still talking, but Kasra was looking edgy. They didn't have long. 'Okay,' he said. 'I don't think we have a choice.'

Caroline nodded and disappeared round the other side of the cabin. Ian picked up the iron bar and waited. It felt like a long time. What could have happened to her? And what would he do if she failed to appear? Perhaps she had tripped and fallen. Or perhaps the door was locked. But then he saw it open. Just a crack at first as Caroline's head appeared and looked around the room. That was the moment for action. He raised the iron bar above his head and slammed it into the window. He'd expected more resistance from double glazing, but it offered far less than he thought it would. Not only had the window shattered but he felt himself plunging forwards and tumbling into the room. He'd have preferred a more dignified entrance, but it was quick and did have the desired effect. Kasra screeched and swung towards him, aiming the knife at his face. Caroline flung herself onto the rope and clung to it. Oliver was jerked onto the floor, smashing the back from his chair in the process. He writhed helplessly as both Caroline and the chair remained dangling in the air. Realising that Oliver was now safe, she let go of the rope and lunged towards Cara, who had been dragged forward by her tied wrist. She unwound the rope, freeing Cara and tried to help her to her feet. But Cara was too quick for her. She leapt up and hurled herself at Kasra, delivering a hefty kick between his legs. Kasra let out a howl of agony and dropped the knife, which Ian, still holding on to the iron bar, picked up and tucked into his belt, rather in the way George had tucked his weapon into his belt.

'Help me,' said Caroline, picking up one end of the rope and throwing it to Cara. The two of them managed to tie a still-howling Kasra by his wrists and ankles.

Realising that Kasra and Oliver were now attached to each other by the length of rope, Ian pulled the knife from his belt and cut the rope in half. And suddenly the room was lit up by the blue lights of police cars. There was much door-slamming and shouting and then not only Duncan but also Kezia Wallace appeared in the doorway. They both stood there speechless as they surveyed the scene in front of them. Caroline was bent over a still whimpering Oliver, trying to free him from the wreckage of the chair. Cara was standing over Kasra, kicking him viciously. And Ian was staring open-mouthed at the chaos in the room while holding not one, but two lethal weapons.

Cara stopped kicking and scowled at the two high-ranking police officers. 'What took you so long?' she asked, with what Ian considered an extreme lack of gratitude.

Duncan stepped towards Ian and held out his hands.

'You better let me have those,' he said. Ian handed over the knife and the iron bar with relief. Then he sank to his knees and started picking slivers of broken glass from his sleeves.

'Does anyone need medical attention?' asked Kezia. 'Or shall we just try to get to the bottom of whatever happened here?'

Oliver, his blindfold now removed, blinked in the bright light. Caroline helped him to his feet. 'I'm okay,' he muttered.

'Shall I go and make a pot of tea?' Caroline asked.

Kezia nodded and walked over to Kasra. 'Kasra Mansour,' she said. 'I'm arresting you on suspicion of smuggling illegal goods. You do not have to say anything, but it may harm your defence if you do not mention when questioned something which you later rely on in court. Anything you do say may be given in evidence.'

'What?' Cara shouted. 'He tried to bloody murder us.'

'Calm down, please, ma'am,' said Kezia. 'We'll get to that later. I suggest you sit down and have a nice cup of tea. Duncan,' she said. 'Could you call this in? Get a team to come and take Mr Mansour into custody. I suggest we all move to the kitchen. This room will need to be sealed as a crime scene.'

Duncan nodded and went outside with his phone.

'But you need to charge him with murder,' Cara was still shouting. 'If this lady hadn't burst in when she did, we'd both be dead by now. I'm sorry,' she said, smiling weakly at Caroline. 'I don't remember your name.'

'I'm Caroline Gillespie,' said Caroline, shaking her hand.

What about me? Ian thought. *It was a team effort.*

'I'm sure you need to thank Mr Skair as well,' said Kezia, rather to Ian's surprise.

'Oh, ah, yes, sorry,' said Cara, calming down. 'Thank you.'

'They're on their way,' said Duncan, coming back into the room. 'Should be here in about half an hour. They're coming from Dundee,' he told Ian. 'I had to a pull a few strings to get Kezia on the case and I'm not going to be popular in Perth, but frankly they seemed to be doing a rubbish job.'

'They arrested the wrong man,' Ian agreed. 'Have they let George go yet?'

'George?' said Cara. 'They arrested George?'

'I doubt that he'll be in custody for much longer,' said Duncan. 'I gather he's got top-notch legal help.'

'But he's innocent,' said Cara. 'He shouldn't need legal help. He's not done anything.'

'George wouldn't hurt a fly,' muttered Oliver, who was looking a lot less pale as he sipped the cup of sweet tea Caroline had given him.

'Perhaps we could get back to the matter in hand,' said Kezia. 'I suggest that once the SOCO team arrive, we all go back to Dundas Farm and get to the bottom of why the two of you were apparently about to be executed by a dangerous drug dealer?'

It was going to be a long night. Ian sipped his own tea gratefully. 'I'm guessing this goes right back to Andy Meade,' he said.

'Further than that,' said Cara.

'To Lucia's fall?' he asked.

'I can't be sure, but I think so.'

Kasra mumbled something and wriggled, trying to free his tied wrists.

'We'll get him sorted first,' said Kezia. 'And then you can tell me the whole story.'

27

Kasra was handcuffed and escorted to a police car. Kezia gave instructions to take him to Dundee and prepare him for an interview. 'Get him a solicitor, but no rush until the morning. We've got twenty-four hours to hold him and plenty of evidence to charge him with. Let Perth know we've got him and tell them they might be interested in adding to his charge sheet. Say I'll be in touch about it.'

'And tell them to let George Strike go if they haven't already,' said Duncan.

Ian called Molly and gave her a brief run-down of everything that had happened. 'We'll be there in about twenty minutes. Tell Gavin that it's all sorted, and he can carry on as normal.'

'What about Lucia?' Molly asked.

'She's free to go. You'd better get someone to sort her out another flight. What's she doing at the moment?'

'She's struck up a friendship with Maudie. Seems quite happy to stay where she is.'

A quite happy Lucia was not something he expected to

hear. Probably wouldn't last, though. Once she knew George was free and Kasra safely locked up, she'd return to her usual irascible self.

They left Oliver's car and the stolen Clio behind for forensics to inspect. Cara and Oliver were driven back to Dundas in Duncan's car, and Ian and Caroline followed in *his* car.

'That was all unexpected,' said Caroline, fastening her seatbelt. 'I thought I was just out for a nice evening at the opera. You should have kept me up to date with what you were doing.'

'I'm sorry,' he said. 'I know I should.' They'd always been able to talk over his cases. He felt bad that he'd not seen Caroline for weeks. A text now and then wouldn't have been too much to ask for, would it?

'Don't look like that,' she said. 'You've been on holiday and then up here. You don't have to account to me for every minute of your day. We don't have that kind of friendship.'

'I know, but I should have called you to let you know what was going on. The trouble is I got an earful from Jeanie for not taking you to France with me and I let it get to me.'

Caroline laughed. 'Jeanie doesn't mean it. She just likes to tease.'

'I should be used to it by now.'

'You should, but Jeanie needs to know we're not joined at the hip. Perhaps we should both be seen with other people now and then.'

'Do you have anyone in mind?'

'For me or for you?'

'For you,' he said, thinking that he might be blushing and glad that it was dark.

'Maybe,' she said evasively.

'Perhaps we should be seen on a double date.'

'Why? Do you have someone in mind for yourself?'
'Maybe.'

'I've put some extra chairs in the office and arranged hot drinks and sandwiches for all of you,' said Molly as the six of them arrived back at the bistro.

Bless her, Ian thought. *Nothing like tea and sandwiches to calm everyone down.* 'Brilliant,' he said. 'I can't speak for all of us, but I'm starving.'

'Are Cara and Oliver okay?' Molly asked. 'Or do I need to call the first aid people?'

'I think I'm the only one who was hurt,' he said, picking a few more slivers of glass out of his arm. 'But I don't need any medical attention. Cara thinks she was drugged. She threw up behind the café, but she seems fine now. Duncan's arranging for the area to be cordoned off. They'll need to collect a sample and find out what she was drugged with.'

'Rather them than me,' said Molly. 'I love being a detective, but I'd draw the line at collecting someone's stomach contents.'

'Can you update me on where everyone is now?' Ian asked.

'Still at the party. Gav says it will go on for most of the night. He's arranging a cooked breakfast at dawn. And after that everyone will go home.'

'Is Ryan at the party?'

'No, Dad took him home after the show. Ryan wasn't too pleased about that. I think he'd happily stay here forever, but Gav said he could take the radio-controlled buggy with him and that cheered him up.'

'What about Maudie and Lucia?'

'Once they knew Cara and Oliver were safe, they joined the party.'

'And Quentin?'

'I told him Oliver was okay and he'll be joining us here soon. He muttered something about having to see to everything himself. I guess he's gone back to his scores.'

'Any sign of George?'

'Still in police custody in Perth, I suppose.'

'Duncan called Perth and told them to release him, so he'll probably be back here soon.'

They sat around the desks in the office and tucked in. As they were both witnesses, Kezia told Caroline and Ian that they should stay. This was not a formal interview, just an account of events.

'Do I need a solicitor?' Cara picked at a ham sandwich and sipped her tea anxiously.

'Not right now,' said Kezia. 'Duncan and I were called out to arrest a suspect. The fact we found you in a dangerous situation caused by our suspect doesn't have any bearing on our case.'

'But he was trying to murder us,' said Cara. 'And you're saying he was arrested for something else.'

'As far as the attempted murder goes, Duncan and I were witnesses. We're already in a grey area by encroaching onto Perth's patch, but we can argue our way out of that by saying we needed to make an emergency arrest as the result of a tip-off, and that there was no time to liaise with the local squad.'

'So we have to call in the local squad?'

'I'll pass on what we saw, and they will need you to make

a statement, but for now treat us as family liaison and tell us, off the record, what happened.'

'I don't know where to start,' said Cara.

'Perhaps you could tell us about Kasra,' said Ian. 'How long have you known him?'

'Just over two years.'

'Did someone introduce you?'

'No, I was subbing for someone at a theatre in London.'

'*Aida,*' said Ian with a smile. 'Starring Lucia.'

'That's right. I was leaving the theatre one night and he asked me if I was in the cast. I told him I was, and he asked if I knew Lucia because he had met her once and wanted to catch up with her again. I told him he would need to go through her agent. We have to be careful letting people into the theatre.'

'And what did he say?' asked Caroline.

'Nothing, really. He asked me if I would like to go for a drink with him and we went to a bar in Highgate Hill. All very public and respectable. Then he called me a taxi and I went back to my hotel. He phoned me the next day and we went for a meal before the show. I didn't see him again until Gavin and I went to the fashion show in Edinburgh.'

'What did you talk about when you had this meal together?' Ian was beginning to form an idea of what could have happened.

'He asked a bit about the show, how I got on with the rest of the company, if Lucia was singing every night. Just chatting really.'

'And did you part company at the restaurant?'

'No, he walked back to the theatre with me and waited until I was inside. He said the backs of theatres were seedy places and he wanted to make sure I was safe.'

'Very gentlemanly,' said Kezia.

'He seemed very polite and caring,' said Cara.

'Tell us about the entry system at the theatre,' said Ian. 'Did you get buzzed in the by doorman?'

'No, there was a number pad. We were all given the code and had to sign a form saying we wouldn't tell anyone what it was.'

'Where was Kasra when you keyed in the numbers?'

'He was standing next to me, but I don't think he was close enough to read them.'

'Do you remember the code?'

'I don't remember the numbers, but it was a top left to right diagonal and back to the number in the middle. Why do you need to know that?'

'I was wondering the same thing,' said Duncan. 'He wouldn't need to see the numbers, just the pattern on the keypad.'

'Were you on stage the night Lucia had her fall?' asked Ian.

'No, I was only there for the first week. Then I came back to Scotland. I was going to stay a few days in London, but there was a lot of talk of lockdown, and I didn't want to get stranded there.'

'What did Kasra say when you told him you were returning to Scotland?' Caroline asked.

'I didn't see him again after we had that meal together. I didn't even call him to tell him. I didn't think we were that close.'

'And Lucia fell after the final performance at the end of the following week.'

'What are you thinking, Ian?' Duncan asked.

'That he made a note of the code and let himself in at the end of the performance. He did something to the time switch and tripped Lucia as she made her way downstairs in the dark.'

'Why would he do that?' asked Kezia. 'What makes you think he had anything against Lucia?'

Ian told them about Kasra hoping to take British citizenship by marrying Lucia and how George had prevented it.

'That would give him a motive,' said Duncan.

'And,' Ian added, 'a motive for the stabbing tonight. He gets revenge on both of them at the same time.'

'You're getting ahead,' said Cara. 'There's a lot more that happened last year.'

'Tell us about that,' said Kezia. 'I assume you picked up where you'd left off with Kasra.'

She nodded. 'Like I said, we met again at the Edinburgh fashion show. But then he became obsessed with me and started following me everywhere.'

'He turned up at Dundas during *Pinafore*?'

She nodded. 'I told him I was engaged to Oliver, but he still wouldn't leave me alone. I was quite scared of him, but it was really Andy Meade I needed to be afraid of.'

She started sobbing. 'Take your time,' said Caroline kindly.

'He cornered me in one of the dressing rooms and started groping me. Kasra found us there and took care of me. He was very kind and gentle and took me home to Gran's house. Then he kept leaving flowers and other things, perfume, and jewellery. And it all got a bit too much, so I told him I wasn't interested. That's when he told Oliver about me and Andy.'

'And Oliver broke off the engagement.'

'I'm sorry,' said Oliver in a whisper. 'That was unforgivable, but... well, I had so much to worry about then with the money I owed Andy.'

Ian patted his shoulder. The poor guy had repaid that debt multiple times tonight, he thought. 'Do you think he had anything to do with Andy's death?' he asked. 'Kasra, I mean, not Oliver.'

'I didn't give it much thought at the time. Everyone said it was natural causes and I suppose if attacking me gave him heart failure, then I wasn't all that sorry.'

'You said "at the time",' Kezia pointed out. 'You've thought about it since?'

'Not really. It all calmed down after the end of *Pinafore*. Kasra went back to Turkey. Oliver and I had split up. I just went back to Edinburgh and got on with work.'

'And this year?' Ian asked.

'I was thrilled when Gavin asked me to sing Micaëla. I don't know how Kasra got to hear about it, but he turned up at Gran's while I was at Dundas going through the role with Gavin. He was in her house when I got home. Just sat there drinking her tea and eating lemon drizzle cake. I didn't want to upset Gran, so I was polite and friendly. He said he'd take me out to dinner and Gran encouraged him. It seemed like it was easier to go and just tell him I wasn't interested in him any longer. He was charming at first but then he started to threaten me. He said he was here to get his own back on George and Lucia and if I didn't help him, he'd tell the police I'd killed Andy Meade. He'd say I'd taken some of Gran's heart pills and put them in his drinking water. I wasn't worried at first, because it was complete rubbish and he'd no evidence he could take to the police. But then I remembered that I did have a motive, but worse, that Gran had missed some of her pills around the time we were doing *Pinafore*. I thought she was just being absent-minded and didn't give it much thought. But when Kasra told me that, I was really scared, so I wrote a letter to Lucia to warn her.'

'You used one of your gran's knitting magazines and nail vanish?'

'Yes, but I didn't have her London address, so I was going to leave it with Gavin to send on to her. But Kasra had started turning up at the house, saying he wanted to make it up with me. I didn't want Gran to hear us arguing, so I went along with him for a while. But the morning I had the letter, I'd had enough. I told him we were finished and to let me out of the car. I told him I wasn't feeling well and wanted to go home. He more or less pushed me out onto the road and drove off. I was scared he'd come back, so I gave the letter to a woman who'd stopped to ask me if I was okay.'

'And what happened tonight?'

'He stopped me on my way out of the theatre last night and told me he'd leave me alone if I got him one of the smugglers' costumes. He put his hands round my neck and said he'd make sure I'd never sing again if I didn't. I'd no idea what he was going to do but I saw him near the props table during scene two this evening. I was going to tell Quentin in the interval. I knew he'd be easy to catch as he left the orchestra pit. I went back to my dressing room and waited. I drank some of my water and a few minutes later I started to feel ill. It's a bit fuzzy after that. I just remember someone wrapping me in a blanket and forcing me out to a car. The fresh air helped a bit and I realised I was shut in the boot.' She smiled at Caroline. 'I've seen you before,' she said. 'You won't remember me, but I went to a meeting you had in Dundee where you talked about how to fend off attacks.'

'I do them about once a year,' said Caroline.

'It was last September. I'd been scared by Andy Meade's attack and thought I should learn how to protect myself. Anyway, you showed us how to escape from car boots. There's always a safety catch, you said. The car slowed down at the car park entrance, and I pulled the lever, let myself out and made sure the lid didn't swing open. Then I ran behind the café and was very sick. I waited a bit then crept out. There was no sign of the car, but it could have come back any minute if Kasra discovered I wasn't there. I remembered that Olly was coming to help Quentin with the scores, so I called him and told him I was hiding from someone. I asked him to pick me up when he arrived.'

'And he drove you both to the cabin.'

'We thought we'd be safe there,' said Oliver. 'I'm sorry, I should have taken you somewhere else.'

'It's not your fault,' said Cara, reaching for his hand. 'You weren't to know he'd find us there.'

'How did he know you'd be there?' asked Kezia.

Ian was doing some calculations in his head. The hire car had been left at the airport quick check-in. It would have taken Kasra an hour to drive to the airport and another hour to drive back again, plus the time it took to break into another car. 'How long did you wait behind the café?' he asked. 'Could he have seen Oliver's car and followed you?'

She shook her head. 'We were at the cabin for quite a long time before he came. He knew I'd been there with Olly when we were together. I suppose he could have heard Quentin saying he was expecting Olly to come and help with the scores.'

'Had you locked the door?' Duncan asked.

'Yes, and when we heard the car I looked through the window. I was relieved because I knew it wasn't the same car Kasra had driven off in.'

'Did you go outside?'

'I opened the door thinking it might be someone wondering where Olly was. I thought it was safe, but Kasra was too quick. He grabbed me and dragged me back inside.

He locked me in a cupboard while he tied Olly up and rigged up that rope. I was trying to reason with him. I said if he let Olly go, I'd do anything he asked. I just kept talking, hoping he wouldn't go through with it. And then I saw Caroline edging through the door, and you burst in through the window. And, well, that's it really.'

'Right,' said Kezia, closing her notebook. 'Thank you for telling us all of that. The local police will be in touch, and I suggest you and Oliver get some rest.'

28

Breakfast had never been so delicious. The food was served from a trestle table at the edge of the campsite, where Ian's nostrils were experiencing a glorious mixture of early morning mist, alpaca and frying bacon. He tucked into a huge Scottish fry-up and watched the scene around him. People were packing up tents and piling luggage on top of cars. Molly had finished her breakfast and was inside packing up their office. Maudie had taken a protesting Cara home.

'I'm fine, Gran,' Cara had said. 'I need to sort out my dressing room and pack up my stuff.'

'You need your rest, young lady,' Maudie told her. 'You've a police interview tomorrow. You'll need to keep your wits about you for that.'

Quentin and Oliver had grabbed a quick breakfast and now, at Quentin's insistence, they were sorting out the orchestra pit. Picking up scores and dismantling music stands and lights. The two brothers amused Ian. So alike to look at they could almost be twins. But while Quentin was noisy and bad-tempered, Oliver was gentle and quiet.

Quentin should have been the one who got tangled up with Andy Meade. He'd have done a far better job of getting himself out of it.

Ian was intrigued by the idea that Andy Meade's death could have been the result of poisoning by Kasra. Had he really laced his drinking water with Maudie's heart medication? Or had he just been trying to control Cara? Ian didn't know a lot about it, but he assumed that medication to speed up a heart would have a devastating effect on someone with an aneurysm. But unless Kasra confessed, they'd probably never know, and from the little Ian had seen of him, he hadn't struck him as the confessing type. At least Cara was now free of him. Kezia's charge sheet was going to be a long one, and with attempted murder on top of that, Kasra was in for a long prison sentence, after which he'd be deported. So unless Cara fancied a visit to Turkey, she'd never have to see him again.

Stamper appeared with his own loaded plate of food. He sat down on the bench next to Ian and sighed happily. 'Another highly successful year,' he said.

Apart from poisoning and abduction, and a couple of attempted murders. 'Any plans for next year?' Ian asked.

'I'm thinking *Die Fledermaus*. Something lighthearted. What do you think?'

'Does anyone get murdered?' Ian asked.

'No, but there's a lot of mistaken identity and a wrongful imprisonment. Talking of which...' He looked up and grinned. 'George, old friend, did you escape?'

Ian turned to see George approaching with a laden tray. He deserved it after a night in jail. The food in Perth nick probably wasn't up to much. 'It's a relief to see you,' said Ian. 'We thought they'd let you go earlier.'

'A rough night in Perth, apparently. They were too busy arresting drunks to do my paperwork.'

'Come and join us,' said Gavin. 'Tell us all about it. We were just talking about *Fledermaus* for next year. Fancy the role of Alfred?'

'The wrongfully arrested singer? Well, I've got the experience.' He sat down between Ian and Gavin and tucked into a breakfast that would have served half the cast. 'Sorry to miss the party. Did Cara turn up?'

Ian gave him a quick summary of the night's events.

'So Kasra's in jail? Best place for him. Always knew he was a rotter. But I thought we'd seen the last of him years ago. Never expected him to sneak back here. I say, you don't think he had anything to do with that bloke's death, do you? What was his name?'

'Andy Meade? I don't think it can ever be proved one way or the other, although it's possible that the fraud charges he was arrested on might be connected to the scam Meade was involved in.'

George stared at Ian, a sausage poised on his fork. 'He wasn't arrested for his trick with the knife and abducting Cara?'

'Not last night. We were lucky. He was wanted by some ex-colleagues of mine for international fraud, drug dealing and bringing illegal goods into the country. It was a coincidence that they turned up just in time to rescue Cara and Oliver.'

'And he switched the knives to get revenge on Lucia and me?'

'I'm sure he did. The knife has gone to forensics, but I'm fairly certain they're going to find Kasra's prints on it.'

'Why did he want revenge on you and Lucia?' asked Gavin.

'I was the one who shopped him to the immigration people about his marriage to Lucia. It was the only way he was going to get UK citizenship.'

'But that was years ago,' said Gavin. 'It's a long time to hold a grudge.'

'I suppose ten or fifteen years is nothing if you're trying to manipulate global finance. He would have lost a lot, not being able to crony up to London bankers,' said Ian. 'I suppose it's easier to run financial fraud from London than Istanbul.'

'More coffee?' Gavin asked, waving to one of the students serving the breakfasts.

'Great,' said Ian, holding up his cup. Essential, actually. He'd been up all night and he needed to pack up everything here and get it back to Greyport, write up his report for Gavin and send him an invoice. He yawned and glanced down at Lottie, who was wide awake and alert, sitting at his feet, hoping that some sausage remains would come her way.

'We should do something for your friends up at Inverbank,' said Gavin. 'I paid for the room in advance, but they were great with Lucia. I'd like to show them how grateful I am. Any ideas?'

What do you give the hotel owner who has it all? And after standing them up last night, he needed to apologise. The usual peace-making gifts wouldn't do. Mickey had glasshouses as far as the eye could see, stuffed roof-high with exotic plants, so flowers wouldn't do. He had the best stocked wine cellar in Scotland and access to all the gourmet food he could want. There must be something lacking at Inverbank, but he couldn't think what it might be. He mopped up the last of his fried egg with a piece of toast and tossed it to Lottie. The gates at the bottom of the field had been thrown open for campers to drive away loaded with tents, gas stoves and sleeping bags. The recycling bins by the gates were overflowing with empty bottles and the field looked empty; only patches of flattened grass remaining as a memory of the last two weeks.

Not much to keep him here now. He piled his empty plate and mug onto a waiting trolley and made his way back to the office, ready to load up his car and drive home.

29

He left Molly in the office on Monday morning to tidy up the Dundas paperwork and to write up the case for the website and a new Facebook page she'd started. She'd be busy all day uploading photographs and writing up some carefully selected details. Gavin was keen to use the story of the diva and the way they'd changed the ending of *Carmen*, and no doubt the two of them would get together at some stage to work on it. They got on well and he wondered if there was any future in it for Molly. He was sure that if Gavin ever needed a PI, it would be Molly he'd go to rather than himself.

He drove to Inverbank with Lottie sniffing excitedly through the back window. She sensed a walk, and she might just be in luck. If Mickey could spare Elsa for half an hour or so, they could walk along the river and up into the hills. He was armed with gifts from Gavin, who had given him free range at the shop in order to choose a thank you present. A selection of alpaca products; a couple of rugs that Ian thought would look nice in his own living room until he discovered the eyewatering price. And he'd bought a gift of his own for Elsa. Alpaca wool was wonderfully soft to the touch, and he chose an ivory-coloured jumper that he thought would suit her red hair.

'What size is the lady?' Margot in the shop had asked.

He'd had no idea. The jumpers came in small, medium and large. Elsa was definitely not small. But would she be insulted if he bought a large one? Women could be touchy about things like that.

'Is she the same size as me?' asked Margot.

Ian looked at her. 'About the same height, maybe, but she's more...' He waved his arms around in front of his chest trying to find the right word.

'Curvy?' Margot suggested.

'Yes,' he said with some relief. All kinds of words had gone through his mind but most of them felt lewd and judgemental rather than descriptive. Curvy was good. No one would be upset by that, he was sure.

'They are quite generously sized,' said the woman. 'I'd go for a medium. We can always change it for you if it's not right.'

Ian handed over his credit card, hoping Stamper would pay up soon. He'd not paid that amount for a single of item of clothing, well, ever as far as he could remember. The woman wrapped it in tissue paper and put it in a box. 'Does she have a favourite colour?' she asked, showing him reels of ribbon.

Did she? Ian wondered. He pointed to an apricot ribbon, thinking he'd seen Elsa in a dress that colour once.

'An excellent choice,' said Margot, tying up the box and finishing it with an elegant bow.

. . .

As they turned into the hotel drive, Lottie jumped up excitedly and Ian suddenly felt nervous. What was he doing buying expensive presents for a woman who was only a friend? Although, admittedly, perhaps a little more than a friend since last week. He was out of his depth. Should he just take it back to the shop and get a refund?

Mickey met him as he arrived at the front door and handed over the rugs. 'A thank you from Gavin for all you did for Lucia,' said Ian.

'It was fun,' said Mickey. 'She's quite a character, isn't she?'

That was one way of putting it.

'Good for publicity as well,' added Mickey. 'Coming in for a coffee?'

'Is Elsa about?' Ian asked, looking around and hoping she'd appear.

'She's gone away for a few days.'

The sun had gone behind a cloud. 'Oh,' said Ian. 'She didn't say she was going away.'

'It was a bit sudden. She was looking rather peaky, so I packed her off for a bit of sea air with a friend of mine.'

What kind of friend? Ian wondered, feeling a sudden spike of jealousy. 'I wanted to explain what happened on Saturday evening.' Ian launched into an explanation of the near stabbing and the kidnapping, not to mention the arrest for fraud.

Mickey held up his hand and stopped him in mid-flow. 'She'd have understood all of that,' he said. 'What upset her was seeing you snuggled up in the straw with a not-unattractive woman.'

'Oh,' said Ian. 'That was Caroline.'

'I don't think it was the lady's name that bothered her so

much as seeing the two of you disappearing together at the end of the show.'

'Caroline and I have known each other for ages. She's helped on cases before. I could have explained all of that to Elsa if she'd been here. I've bought her something,' he said, reaching into the back of the car for his box. 'I could write her a note,' he added rather lamely.

'I'm sure she'll appreciate the gesture,' said Mickey coldly.

This was all going wrong. What was he supposed to do? He grabbed the box and climbed back into the car. 'I'd better be on my way then.'

'For God's sake,' said Mickey. 'You are such an idiot.'

'Yeah, I know.'

'Then do something about it.'

He drove away, Lottie slumping down onto her blanket, disappointed that she'd not had the expected walk.

Do something about it? What the hell did that mean?

∼

Want to find out?

Read **The Man in the Red Overcoat** Book 5 in the Ian Skair series

https://books2read.com/u/4DJRge

ACKNOWLEDGMENTS

I would like to thank you so much for reading **The Diva of Dundas Farm.** I do hope you enjoyed it.

If you have a few moments to spare a short review would be very much appreciated. Reviews really help me and will help other people who might consider reading my books.

I would also like to thank my editor, Sally Silvester-Wood at *Black Sheep Books*, and all my fellow writers at *Quite Write* who have patiently listened to extracts and offered suggestions.

ABOUT THE AUTHOR

Hilary Pugh has that elusive story telling talent that draws you in and makes you feel you are in the room with her characters.
   Michelle Vernal

UK based author Hilary Pugh has spent her whole life reading and making up stories. She is currently writing a series of crime mysteries set in Scotland and featuring Private Investigator Ian Skair and his dog, Lottie.

Hilary has worked as a professional oboist and piano teacher and more recently as a creative writing tutor for the Workers Educational Association.
   She loves cats and makes excellent meringues.

Visit my website: www.hilarypugh.com

ALSO BY HILARY PUGH

You can also meet Ian Skair in:

Finding Lottie

https://books2read.com/u/4NwDoY

The Laird of Drumlychtoun

https://books2read.com/u/3yaeQp

Postcards from Jamie

https://books2read.com/u/mYGLwd

Mystery at Murriemuir

https://books2read.com/u/mgj8Bx

Bagatelle - The Accompanist - free download included when you join my mailing list. Click the link below:

https://storyoriginapp.com/giveaways/470fd116-75b6-11e9-a014-fb6e89c4fba0

Visit my website for more information and to join my mailing list:

www.hilarypugh.com

Printed in Dunstable, United Kingdom